I've travelled the world twice over,
Met the famous: saints and sinners,
Poets and artists, kings and queens,
Old stars and hopeful beginners,
I've been where no-one's been before,
Learned secrets from writers and cooks
All with one library ticket
To the wonderful world of books.

© JANICE JAMES.

BRIDGE OF SAND

Ahmed Fosse, or so he called himself, had travelled a thousand miles through the Biblical ruins of the Middle East. He was not religious, and he certainly didn't believe in Jesus Christ, Allah or God. But he did believe that there was a man waiting in Galilee and that he would find him, and kill him.

FRANK GRUBER

◆

BRIDGE OF SAND

Complete and Unabridged

ULVERSCROFT
Leicester

First published in the
United States of America

First Large Print Edition
published February 1992

British Library CIP Data

Gruber, Frank
    Bridge of sand. — Large print ed. —
Ulverscroft large print series: adventure & suspense
I. Title
823.912 [F]

ISBN 0–7089–2588–X

Published by
F. A. Thorpe (Publishing) Ltd.
Anstey, Leicestershire
Set by Words & Graphics Ltd.
Anstey, Leicestershire
Printed and bound in Great Britain by
T. J. Press (Padstow) Ltd., Padstow, Cornwall

Israel – 1962

1

THE road was paved now, but the macadam had been laid during the span of a man's lifetime. It had been unpaved for four millenniums, perhaps five or six. The races of man had marched here. Chaldeans, Canaanites, Egyptians, Hittites, Babylonians. As conquerors, as slaves in chains, each in turn.

Jesus Christ had traveled this road from Nazareth, to his cross at Golgotha.

It had been a long road for Ahmed Fosse. It had led from the Aswan country of the Upper Nile, down the mighty river to the Valley of the Kings, to Cairo, and across the desert wastes of the Sinai. Past Gaza, Joppa, through Samaria, and now, inland, toward the Sea of Galilee.

A long road, a weary road.

That the Son of Man had probably used this highway occurred to the man who called himself Ahmed Fosse. But it

3

meant nothing to him. He was not a believer in Jesus Christ, in Yahweh, in Allah, or in God.

Ahmed Fosse believed in only one thing: that he would find a man in Galilee, that he would kill him.

He was an inch under six feet and weighed perhaps a hundred and seventy-five pounds. He was lean in build, but had powerful, flat muscles. The muscles were extremely hard. He was dark and but for his blue eyes could readily have passed for an Egyptian or a Semite. His passport said he was born of a French father and an Egyptian mother.

He wore paratrooper's boots, khaki trousers and shirt, and on his head an Egyptian fez. He carried a rucksack, swinging it in one hand by a strap.

It was very early in the morning, fifteen minutes past the dawn. He climbed the grade and stood for a moment, looking down the easy slope into a valley, studded with olive groves and here and there a whitewashed stone hut. A small flock of sheep grazed in a field on the left.

The jeep had run off the road, jolted

4

across a shallow ditch, caromed off an olive tree, and wound up against a low stone wall that had been there for a century or two. A wisp of steam was still coming from the radiator.

Ahmed left the road, trotted along the path taken by the jeep, and coming up to it, saw that the man bent over the wheel was still alive.

Alive, but not for long. Blood had soaked his tan shirt, his jacket. His eyes were open, but he did not raise his head as Ahmed came up.

Ahmed said, "That's a knife wound."

He reached into the jeep to pull out the wounded man. The man gasped and said, "No!" His mouth twisted in agony. Then: "Greatest discovery . . . ever made by man."

His right hand appeared, reached out to the jeep seat beside him, then suddenly went limp and dangled over the front of the seat. The eyes became glazed.

Ahmed Fosse took a crumpled package of Egyptian cigarettes from his shirt pocket, shook out a limp cigarette and stuck it in his mouth. He lit it, smoked a moment or so, then exhaled a heavy cloud

5

of smoke and reached into the jeep.

The man was dead and the body was quite limp. Ahmed stretched it out beside the jeep, then saw the cylinder on the floorboard. It was of copper, about four inches in diameter and perhaps a foot in length. It was old, very old, but gleamed as if it had recently been polished down. There was a lid to it, which Ahmed wrestled loose. He looked inside the cylinder, shook it. Nothing came out.

The cylinder was empty.

Ahmed put the lid back onto the cylinder and tossed the object to the ground beside the dead man. He searched the jeep. There was nothing of a personal nature in it, nothing that should not have been in a jeep.

A faint whining came over the quiet morning air. It was a truck toiling up the grade, out of sight. Soon it would appear, come down into view.

Quickly, Ahmed dropped to his knees and searched the dead man. He found a wallet, which he thrust into his own shirt, a couple of keys, an old worn envelope, a pocket comb . . . and a shiny .32-caliber automatic pistol. An American Colt.

The whining of the truck became a labored growl and Ahmed, bent low, ran for a clump of olive trees. As it turned out, the truck continued on down into the valley without stopping, but Ahmed had seen enough at the jeep and did not return.

The driver of the truck apparently did not see the jeep in the olive grove. The truck picked up speed as it came downhill.

Ahmed sat down on the ground and examined the things he had taken from the dead man at the jeep. The automatic pistol was a good one. He sniffed the muzzle. The gun had been fired recently. There were only three cartridges in the magazine.

Ahmed wiped the gun carefully so that it was free of his and anyone else's fingerprints and thrust the weapon into the ground. He heaped leaves over it.

The two keys were apparently keys for a door, but they were of no use to Ahmed. He dropped them.

The wallet.

It contained an American driver's

7

license, issued by the State of Illinois to Albert Doniphan Hill, 1846 Howe Street, Chicago, Illinois. The license, issued three years before, gave Hill's age as 44. It also said that he was five feet ten inches in height, a male Caucasian, and weighed, at the time the license was issued, 185 pounds.

The description was reasonably close, allowing for three years' lapse of time. Besides the driver's license, the wallet contained four American credit cards, membership cards for the Chicago Athletic Association, the University Club, the Hamilton Club, and the Archaeologists' Club. The late Albert Doniphan Hill had also been, according to additional cards, a member of the Adventurers' Club of New York, the Egyptian Club of Chicago, and the Authors' Club of Los Angeles.

There were eight hundred dollars in American money in the wallet and the equivalent of some four hundred dollars in Israeli cash. And an IOU, signed by one Miller Wood, for $450.00, dated two months ago.

That was all that was left of Albert Doniphan Hill of Chicago. A sheaf of club

8

membership cards, some twelve hundred dollars, and an IOU which might or might not be collectible.

None of it was worth anything to Ahmed Fosse. Not even the money. It might be good money, but in his situation he was not going to risk having any of it in his possession. It might be marked; it could be counterfeit. The numbers might be recorded by someone. He put everything back into the wallet, rubbed the leather against his trousers, and thrust it into the loose soil. He straightened, brushed his trousers, and continued on through the olive grove.

After a while he cut back to the highway. The morning was well advanced now, the sun above the eastern horizon, and there was a general feeling of another day begun. Ahmed passed a hut built near the road and was noted by an Arab youth, who was milking a goat beside the hut.

A wheezing Ford, driven by a Hebrew, came along. The car coughed once or twice as the driver took his foot off the gas pedal, apparently with a view to stopping, but then began growling regularly once more as the car sped on.

The country was too isolated as yet to pick up hitchhikers. Hitchhikers who wore fezzes.

Ahmed continued walking along the beaten road shoulder. Behind him, he heard the smooth humming of a power motor, heard it whine as the brakes were applied. The rubber did not squeal, however. The car braked to a stop a few feet ahead of Ahmed. There were two men in it. The car, Ahmed noted, was a Mercedes Benz.

Both of the men were wolves. Their sharp eyes examined Ahmed quickly, then lost interest in him. The car whipped away, disappeared over a rise in the ground.

Ahmed continued walking.

An Arab, riding a mule, came over the hill toward Ahmed. He rode past Ahmed, without even seeming to be aware of him. Ahmed Fosse gave him a quick glance, saw nothing of interest in him.

This was Arab country, almost as much as it was Hebrew.

The Mercedes Benz appeared on the crest of the hill, swooped down toward Ahmed. It went past him with brakes squealing, then made a screaming U-turn and came up behind Ahmed. It stopped beside him.

"Get in," said the man beside the driver.

Ahmed shook his head. "I need the exercise."

The man produced a stubby revolver. "I said, 'Get in.'"

Ahmed opened the rear door of the Mercedes Benz and climbed in. The man with the gun squirmed around so that he could keep Ahmed covered. The car leaped forward, zoomed toward the top of the crest. There the brakes were applied violently and the car bounced off the road, across the shoulder and into a rocky field.

A wheel jolted over a six-inch rock, sent a smaller one banging under the car. Then the car slewed around behind a low stone wall of hundreds of years' vintage and came to an abrupt halt. The driver killed the motor.

The man with the revolver gestured. "Out!"

Ahmed got out of the car. The man with the gun followed, then the driver.

"You been walking," said the man with the gun. "Couple, three miles back, there was a jeep off the road."

"Was there?" asked Ahmed.

The man with the gun bared teeth. They were very large, very white in his almond-colored face. "*You* don't ask the questions," he said. "I do."

Ahmed shrugged.

The smile became frozen on the gunman's lips. "And don't give us the inscrutable Far East business. You talked good English a sec ago and for all I know you're a European."

"French," said Ahmed. "French and Egyptian. I speak perfect English. Also French and Sicilian."

"Sicilian," said the man with the gun. "I'm a Sicilian."

"By way of America, probably," added Ahmed.

The man with the gun grinned at his companion, the driver of the Mercedes Benz. "We got us a smart one. Shall I make him holler uncle?"

"We haven't got time," said the driver, who was as almond-colored as the man with the gun, and whose hair was just as black and just as shiny from pomade.

"Okay." The man with the gun turned back to Ahmed. "You saw the jeep."

"I might have," said Ahmed. "I wasn't paying any attention."

The left hand of the gunman swept out, raked Ahmed's face with the back of the hand. "That's so you pay attention. You either see a jeep or you don't see one. *Did* you see it?"

"I saw it."

"You walked up close?"

"It was a hundred yards off the road."

"You went up close."

"You're saying that."

The knuckles raked Ahmed's face, harder this time. Ahmed said: "Don't do that again."

"I use the gun next time. You went up to the jeep."

Ahmed shook his head in impatience. The swarthy man lashed out with the snub-nosed revolver. It did not rake Ahmed's face, however. Ahmed ducked smartly and his fist buried itself in the gunman's stomach, folding him over and dropping him to the ground. It was a stunning, savage blow, delivered with

13

awesome power. Ahmed did not have to watch for the result. He whirled, sprang toward the driver. The second man, caught by the suddenness of Ahmed's act, was off-balance. Then his hand started to go for the gun in his shoulder holster. He never got it out.

Ahmed caught the gun hand in his fist, twisted . . . and the driver hit the ground with stunning force, on his back. He was slow to move, then, and Ahmed had to wait a moment. Then when the hand went for the gun and brought it out awkwardly, Ahmed kicked the wrist. The gun flew fifty feet away.

Ahmed turned, saw the first gunman on the ground, unconscious from the terrible stomach blow. His eyes skimmed the ground, saw the snub-nosed revolver a few feet away. He scooped it up and threw it away, a hundred feet or more.

He turned back. The driver was sitting up, his face twisted in agony as he gripped his right wrist with his left hand.

"You broke it," he moaned.

"I hope so."

Ahmed stepped to the car, got in

14

behind the wheel. He turned the ignition key.

The man with the injured wrist struggled to his feet. "Wait, you can't . . . "

"The hell I can't," said Ahmed.

He started the motor, shifted into gear, and whipped the car out of the field. He bounced it a bit but it reached the pavement intact and in a moment was purring smoothly toward Nazareth.

2

THE highway was a good one, stretching eastward, and the Mercedes Benz purred off the miles. The road left the Valley of Jezreel and climbed into the hills of Galilee. The road wound over a plateau which afforded an excellent view of the Jezreel Valley, containing two large, green kibbutzim, which did not interest Ahmed Fosse one whit. Passing a forest the road reached a small village, identified as Yafia, by a road sign.

Clearing the town, Ahmed noted a road sign: *Nazareth, 3 Kms. 2 Miles.*

The ancient city was already unfolded before Ahmed. It circled around a curved valley. The city itself barely reached the top of the mountain and sprawled out on the side, between the top and the floor of the valley.

There was a big police station on the right and Ahmed, slowing the Mercedes Benz, saw that there was activity in and around the station. He drove a hundred yards past the police station, pulled up beside the road, and got out of the big Mercedes. He wiped the steering wheel carelessly, smearing his fingerprints, then walked away from the car.

He entered Nazareth. It was a city of churches, missions, and monasteries. It contained the largest minority settlement in Israel, inhabited by Christians and a small group of Moslems. The Israelis lived chiefly in a suburb.

There were signs by the churches. They were in many languages. Ahmed could read some of them, but did not pause to do so.

He had made an early start that morning and was hungry.

He found a sidewalk café and, seating himself at a table, was handed a menu. It was printed in Hebrew, but there were penciled English translations beside the entrees. He put the menu aside. "Bring me something to eat."

The waiter was a shrewd-eyed young man, but he hesitated. "You are a Christian?"

"My stomach is neither Christian

nor Moslem," said Ahmed, "Bring me whatever's ready."

The waiter was not satisfied with that response, but he went away. In a little while he brought a bowl of cooked farina.

"Kasha," he said. "You name the country."

Ahmed poured cream over the cereal, added sugar, and ate. Before he was through with the cereal the waiter brought a platter of eggs. There was no ham or sausage with it, but there was a small plate with a side order of smoked salmon. That was playing it safe.

An Israeli policeman climbed down from a motorcycle at the curb, stood and looked over the outdoor café. His eyes rested on Ahmed and after a moment he came over.

"Your passport," he said in Arabic.

Ahmed handed it to the policeman. The man nodded. "You speak French?" he asked in English.

"In France," said Ahmed in Hebrew. "I speak whatever language is native for the country I am in." Ahmed looked up at the clean-cut young policeman. "I also speak Aramaic."

"Ah, a scholar! You're with an archaeological expedition?"

Ahmed shook his head. The young policeman examined his passport again, lingering over the entry stamp, which clearly gave the date of Ahmed Fosse's arrival in Israel. Three days before.

Something bothered him, but he did not know what he could do about it. He handed the passport back to Ahmed Fosse. "Where you headed for? Megiddo?"

"I thought I'd try Tiberias."

"Yes," said the policeman, "you might get on there."

"They're short of people?"

"I didn't say that."

"Megiddo's been worked for quite some years," said Ahmed. "They haven't been at Tiberias too long."

"You may be right, Mr. ah, Fosse, was it?"

"Fosse."

The Israeli policeman nodded and walked back to his motorcycle. But he did not mount it immediately, and when Fosse finished his breakfast and paid for it, the policeman was leaning against a light pole some fifty or sixty feet away.

Nazareth was an Arab city, yet Christian. Twenty-five thousand of its inhabitants were Christians, of Arabic nationalities, whose forebears had settled in the ancient city of Christ during its centuries-long Moslem rule. There were a bare seven thousand Jews in Nazareth.

It was a city of churches, monasteries, some ancient, some medieval or modern; the latter were usually built upon old ruins. It was a city rich in tradition.

None of which made any impression upon Ahmed Fosse. Nazareth was but a stopping point for him. His breakfast completed, he was soon striding along the narrow streets of the old city. The streets were a maze, beginning at points without reason, ending against stone walls. Only a few of the streets were wide enough for modern automobile transportation.

Ahmed Fosse kept to these and after a while found himself on the outskirts of Nazareth, headed eastward. A jeep came chugging along behind him. Ahmed, wary, moved to the road shoulder and stopped. The jeep contained a policeman. The policeman's eyes were on the road ahead, too carefully so.

A Volkswagen came along, then a small Italian car. One or two cars came from the east and zoomed past Ahmed, going to the holy city of the Christians.

A low whining came from the rear. Ahmed eased to the side, turned. This was an American car, a Cadillac convertible with the top down. The whining became a smooth purr and the car stopped beside Ahmed.

The driver of the car said, in English: "I can give you a ride to Tel Mas."

Ahmed's inclination was to shake his head, but Tel Mas was his destination. He could be there within a few minutes, grappling with his next problem.

The driver was an amazingly attractive woman, possibly twenty-eight or thirty. She wore a skirt and blouse of gaily colored material and a scarf over her head to keep her blonde hair from being wind-blown.

He said, "Thank you," and opening the car door, got in.

The car started off. Ahmed's eyes were on the pavement ahead. He was aware, however, that the driver gave him a sideward glance, but he was quite prepared to make the ten-mile drive without conversation. Indeed, they had gone a fifth of the distance without speaking, when she finally broke the silence.

"You're an Arab," she said, then, "yet I could be wrong."

"You're not." Then after a moment: "My mother was Egyptian, my father French."

"Ah yes," she said, in French, "the blue eyes."

He did not reply to that and she said, in Arabic, "You do not speak French?"

"I speak it," he replied, but added nothing else. She gave him a sharp look and released her pressure on the gas accelerator. The car began to slacken speed.

There was a dirt road, turning right from the pavement. A fairly fresh board sign said simply, in English, "*Tel Mas.*"

The car came to an abrupt halt. "I turn off here," the driver said.

Ahmed Fosse got out, bobbed his head briefly. "Thanks."

22

The car turned right in front of him, jolted up a rough road, made a sharp right turn, and disappeared into a dry wadi.

Ahmed Fosse could have spared himself a walk by telling the woman that he, too, was headed for Tel Mas, but the question had not been asked of him and he was not in the habit of volunteering information about himself.

He followed in the wake of the car, breathing the settling dust for the first hundred yards. He made the right turn into the rough dry wadi, went down between some outcropping rocks, then came into the clear. The road was straight and level now and headed directly for Tel Mas.

3

THE resettlement and recolonization of Israel by Jews is mostly a twentieth-century accomplishment, although it had its beginnings in the nineteenth century. The land occupied by the Jews was Arabic for a matter of thirteen centuries, with a brief interlude at the time of the Crusades when Christians conquered and occupied sections for comparatively brief periods.

The word "tel," used for so many modern Israeli sites, is an Arabic word. It means mound, a man-made mound of which the country has plenty. A tel is of little interest to an Arab, but to a Jew it means that here are the ruins — under many layers of earth sometimes — of an ancient town or city.

The Jews have a reverence for their past.

The land of Israel is dotted with tels. Many of them have been uncovered by archaeological expeditions, many are still in process of being excavated, and some have not even been touched.

One of the most important tels uncovered in recent years was that of the ancient city of Megiddo, just a few miles south of Nazareth. The country east of Nazareth, so rich in biblical tradition, had begun to receive archaeological attention only in recent years. A team was at work in and around the Herodian city of Tiberias.

The expedition at Tel Mas was a richly endowed one. Sponsored by the Lake Shore University of Evanston, Illinois, it was nominally headed by Dr. Will Sando, who had made a great name for himself and the university in Egypt, where he had, as a young archaeologist, assisted the great James Breasted, discoverer of the King Tutankhamen tomb.

The war had curtailed archaeology in the Near East, but Dr. Will Sando had used the time to cultivate Charles J. Holterman. Holterman, who did not use the prefix 'Dr.' before his name, although he could have done so, with a long string of letters after his name, had an advantage over his archaeological contemporaries. He did not have to seek endowments or assistance from universities. He possessed great wealth of his own and could therefore go where he pleased, dig where he wanted to dig.

It pleased him to excavate at Tel Mas. Nominally, the expedition was under the aegis of Lake Shore University and nominally, Dr. Will Sando was the head of the expedition . . . but the expedition would not now be in Israel if Holterman had not made a considerable grant to Lake Shore University, with the proviso that it be used for the Israel dig.

Dr. Sando gave the orders at Tel Mas, but the orders were usually suggested by Charles Holterman.

Sometimes the orders were given by Alice Holterman.

Tel Mas was roughly oval-shaped and consisted of approximately five acres. As a result of a nearby spring and a certain amount of shade the neighborhood had long been a favorite of Bedouin and Druse nomads who grazed sheep on the sparse vegetation. A few dung huts had been built, had disintegrated, and been restored. A half dozen houses of stone had also been established at some time in the past.

The native buildings were used by the Lake Shore University archaeological expedition. In addition, there were a number of Arabic tents.

There were perhaps fifty persons in the 'dig', a half dozen who belonged to the expedition proper and some forty-odd laborers who did the actual digging. These were under the command of a Druse sheik, who brazenly exploited his people.

Ahmed Fosse approached the camp. He noted that the tents were a short distance from the permanent structures, that the tents were apparently used by the Israeli natives, the Druse diggers.

In a canvas chair in front of one of the native tents lounged a hawk-nosed swarthy man, who wore dirty white linen trousers and a brilliant orange shirt. Since he was the only man in the camp who did not seem to be working, Ahmed Fosse turned toward him.

"Who is it here who employs the workers?" Ahmed asked in Arabic.

The hawk-nosed man regarded him dispassionately. He opened his mouth to speak, seemed to change his mind, then suddenly stabbed his index finger in the general direction of the stone huts.

"The American professor, the great Doctor Sando."

He sniffed, which might have been because he had to sniff or it might have been because it expressed his opinion of Dr. Sando.

Ahmed was indifferent.

He left the Druse sheik and walked toward the stone houses. There were little wooden plaques attached to the door of each. The plaques were painted black and on each black surface a name was lettered in white.

Hill, Wood, Dietrich, Caxton, Dr. Sando.

A woman came out of one of the houses. She wore a dirty tan smock, her hair was disheveled, but she had a fine golden complexion and very even features. She was blue-eyed.

The plaque on the door read *Dr. Sando.* Ahmed Fosse passed the young woman and went to the open door of Dr. Sando's house. He looked into a fairly large room that was littered with potsherds, repaired pottery, small statues, medium statues, large statues.

A man in drill shorts and khaki shirt, with gray hair, was standing behind a littered desk. He was bent over, scribbling on a pad. He looked up as Ahmed Fosse entered.

"Yes?"

"Dr. Sando? I've been told that you do the hiring here . . ."

"You're a native," snapped Dr. Sando. His eyes flicked to the fez on Ahmed's head. "A Turk. The sheik hires the natives."

"He sent me to you." Ahmed paused, then added. "Since I am *not* a native." Another pause. "I am a philologist."

"What?"

"My specialty is ancient Semitic languages. Hittite, Aramaic . . ."

Dr. Sando regarded him coldly. "What universities?"

"I worked with Dr. Heinrich Klausner in the Valley of the Kings."

"Dr. Klausner has done excellent work

in Egypt. What were your exact duties with him?"

Ahmed Fosse reached into his pocket, drew out his wallet and extracted a worn envelope. He handed it to Dr. Sando.

Dr. Sando read the inscription on the front of the envelope. '*To Whom It May Concern.*' He grunted and extracted a single sheet of paper on which was typed a recommendation for Ahmed Fosse.

He nodded abruptly and handed the letter and envelope back to Ahmed Fosse. "All very good, but the fact of the matter is we have no need for another philologist."

"One of your men may leave you," Ahmed suggested.

"That's hardly possible. Even if one does leave, we're overstaffed. Sorry, ah, Foss, is it?"

"Fosse."

"Ah, yes. Sorry I can't help you out."

Ahmed nodded, and walked out of the house. He was turning away from the house when a voice called from behind him.

"I say there!"

It was the woman who had given him

a ride to the Tel Mas turn-off.

"I didn't know you were headed here," she said, as she came toward him.

"You couldn't have known. I didn't tell you."

"I should have asked. Did you come here to see anyone special?"

"I've seen him," said Ahmed. "Dr. Sando."

"Oh." A look of annoyance flitted across her face. "I'm Alice Holterman. My husband is Charles Holterman, the archaeologist."

"Of course," said Ahmed Fosse. "This is his expedition."

"That's a rather direct way of putting it," said Alice Holterman. "But . . . " She shrugged suddenly. "Is there anything I can do for you?"

"I'm a philologist," said Ahmed Fosse. "I came here hoping to find work . . . "

"You read Hebrew?"

Ahmed nodded. "Also Aramaic and Hittite. And one or two other dead languages."

"I'll be damned," exclaimed Alice Holterman. Her eyes went suddenly to the door of Sando's house. "Will Sando cut you short? Because — " she grimaced a little — "the way you're dressed . . . the Egyptian fez."

"Dr. Sando thinks Turks wear fezzes," said Ahmed.

Alice Holterman shook her head and exhaled. "Come, let's interrupt Charles. He's worrying over the morning mail and the interruption will be good for him."

She turned, started away, then as he did not follow immediately, she stopped. "Coming?"

"That's going over Sando's head. He won't like it."

She made a moue with her mouth and went toward the largest of the old stone houses, the one beyond Dr. Sando's.

The inside was bigger, more messy, but cooler than Sando's.

The desk at which Charles Holterman sat was smaller than Sando's.

Holterman was forty-seven years of age and looked fifty-five. His hair was thick, almost snow-white. His face was tanned heavily, which was in odd contrast to his snowy thatch.

He was tall, heavy-set, and beginning to show a paunchiness. He wore a white sport shirt and tan slacks.

He looked up as his wife came in. His eyes went past her to the man who followed. His eyes remained on Ahmed Fosse until Fosse had come in all the way.

"Charles," said Alice Holterman, "this is . . ." She snapped her fingers. "I don't believe I know your name."

"Fosse, Ahmed Fosse."

Holterman did not offer to shake hands. He merely nodded shortly.

Ahmed said, "Mrs. Holterman was good enough to give me a ride from Nazareth. I'm a philologist."

The letter of recommedation was still in his hand. Ahmed moved forward, dropped it on the desk in front of Holterman. Holterman kept his eyes on Ahmed until the philologist had moved back a step. Then a faint exhalation came from his lips and he picked up the letter. He read it carefully, continued to look at it for a moment, then folded the letter and put it carefully back into the envelope.

"Dr. Klausner speaks well of you."

"Thank you."

"I'll have to talk to Dr. Sando."

"He's seen Will," said Alice Holterman.

Holterman looked inquiringly at Ahmed. The latter shook his head. "He asked me at what universities I studied."

"And?"

"None."

"Oh, come," exclaimed Holterman. "You didn't learn Aramaic by working for Dr. Klausner. I doubt if he knows the language himself. Egyptian, yes, Hittite, too, but Aramaic, no."

There was a step behind Fosse. Dr. Sando came in, walking heavily in his paratrooper boots. His eyes glinted, his mouth was set firmly.

"I was expecting something from the university, Charles," he said. "I thought it might be in the mail this morning."

"I don't believe so," replied Holterman. Then: "Oh, Will, Mrs. Holterman brought in this, ah, this man. He's worked with Dr. Klausner in Egypt. Rather a good recommendation from Klausner."

"Too many language men now," snapped Sando. "What we need are more diggers, less people in here."

"Yes, yes, you're probably right, Ah, Fosse, sorry."

"It's all right." Ahmed nodded to Holterman, ignored Sando completely, and gave Alice Holterman a low bow. "Mrs. Holterman," he murmured and went out.

As he left the house he thought he heard light footsteps follow him for part of the way. But then the footsteps died out.

He went out into the blazing sun.

He'd handled it badly and probably alienated both Holterman and Sando. There would be no chance later.

The sheik was still in the canvas chair, grinning, smirking. Ahmed stopped.

The sheik bared his teeth. "The great white lady couldn't help you?" he asked.

"Oxford," said Ahmed pointedly.

The eyes of the sheik became hard as basalt rock, but the whiteness of his teeth remained fully revealed. "Close. Cambridge. Who told you?"

"No one. Your act is a little too much, well, too much of an act."

"Bingo. Yes, I went the route. Cambridge, flat in the West End, box at the Derby, tea and crumpets. Unfortunately, my father went the same way and the money didn't hold out. It might have, if our Hebrew friends hadn't set up an independent state and nationalized this little part of Galilee. But they were very nice about it. They permit me to call myself Sheik and when they want some very cheap labor they let me provide it for them and they let me collect the wages and, ah, trust me to do right by my, shall we say, constituents. So I make both ends meet."

"You're a Druse."

"Anything against the Druse?"

"Half of me is your color."

"Which half, effendi?"

"The half that gets hungry, that needs a job."

"Ah! You braced Sando and Holterman both. They turned you down."

"They don't need another philologist. But in Egypt before I became a philologist, I was a *fellah*. I can dig as well as the next *fellah*. I can dig as well as a Druse."

"You can sleep with the Druse? Eat with them? Live on their pay?"

"Oh the pay *you* give me?"

The sheik's white teeth became partly covered by the full lips and his eyes became slits.

36

"Of course," said Ahmed Fosse, "I may cut your throat."

"Cut," said the sheik. "Any time." He leaned forward, pointed toward the tel. "Ask for Ali. Tell him I said to give you a shovel."

Ahmed nodded, started away. The sheik let him go about twenty feet, then called; "*Fellah!*"

Ahmed turned.

The sheik was smiling wolfishly. "Use a sharp knife when you cut my throat."

4

THE Lake Shore University Tel Mas Expedition was in its second year of operations at the Tel Mas site and a great deal of an ancient town was already exposed, but it would take another two years, possibly three, to completely uncover the town and then, if the results warranted, from five to ten years to dig deep, to lower levels of earlier civilizations.

A section of about an acre and a half of the old town was completely exposed, and while a number of workers were sifting the earth in this section, a gang of diggers was engaged in a new cut on the southerly side. The diggers and carriers of earth were chiefly Druse, and Ali, in charge of them, was a villainous-looking Bedouin with a beaked nose. He regarded Ahmed Fosse sourly.

"You have European blood," he said thinly. "You will not last in this heat."

"I have worked in Egypt," said Ahmed

calmly. "It gets warm there."

The Druse spat, missing Ahmed's foot by about an inch and a half. Then he pointed down into the cut.

Ahmed descended the steps into the cut. He stood aside while a Druse carried on his head a shallow close-woven basket. It was only half filled with earth and would not have caused a woman carrier any concern.

He passed two or three workers who were scraping at the sides of the cut, another pair who were filling — or partly filling — baskets. Then he was at the end of the cut.

Two desultory workmen stopped digging, exchanged a few words in their native Druse dialect. One of the men snorted and the other handed his shovel to Ahmed and retreated to pick up a basket and carry earth out of the cut.

Ahmed began to work. In less than a moment, the Druse at his side began to grumble and in another moment was exclaiming loudly.

"The man is mad, he works like one possessed," he declaimed. "The sheik is in his tent, Ali is not complaining, and he uses that shovel as if he were working for himself."

Ahmed said: "Did not the prophet say, give an honest day's work for an honest day's pay?"

"And who is getting an honest day's pay?" cried the digger beside Ahmed. "Does not Ali get a tenth share and the great sheik four times a tenth?" The Druse leaned on his shovel and sneered at Ahmed. "I get only half of the money that is paid out by the rich Americans, so I give but a half day's work. Only I must make it *look* like a day's work."

"You work your way, I shall work mine," said Ahmed.

"We shall see," cried the digger. He thrust his shovel deep in the earth and strode away from Ahmed.

Ahmed continued to dig at the face of the cut. He heard the slithering of footsteps behind him, then the voice of Ali said: "You are a good man, Egyptian. You do the work of two men."

Ahmed did not even stop in his work. Behind him the Druse straw boss chuckled. "Always, two men have worked here, but since you like it so well, you may work alone."

He went away. The digger who had protested to Ahmed did not return to work beside Ahmed.

Above ground, there was a breeze. Down in the cut there was not a breath of atmospheric movement. Ahmed's shirt was soaked, but he continued working. A Druse boy came by every fifteen minutes or so with a goatskin filled with tepid water and each time Ahmed drank. He would have been dehydrated had he not replaced the moisture he lost from perspiration.

Behind him the Druse workers performed their own tasks, doing as little as they could. The scrapers smoothed the sides of the cut. Those who filled the baskets took their time and those who carried them out of the cut walked slowly. They lingered over emptying the baskets and took their time about returning to the cut. Ten men did the work of five. In a more temperate climate and with the proper inducements two men could have done the work of the ten.

At twelve o'clock the foreman Ali

called to Ahmed, "You have done a good morning's work, Egyptian. Come now and eat. Eat, drink, and rest and then you may work again."

The native food was good and there was enough. Ahmed ate with the Druse workers under a tented canopy and afterward he joined the Druse for their rest. They accepted him as a worker, along with themselves, but he was an alien. He spoke their language, could understand their dialect well enough, but he was an Egyptian and they were natives of Palestine. Their way of life was different from his.

They ignored him completely.

The staff members of the expedition ate their meals under a large canopy which was set up some distance from the Druse eating place. Afterward, the staff members adjourned to their various quarters, for no work was done during the midday heat.

This rest was to be interrupted, however. A jeep pulled into the camp and was followed a moment later by a European sedan. The two vehicles disgorged several uniformed men and one official in a spotless white linen suit.

There was much going back and forth, but for a half hour the Druse workers were left alone. Then the sheik came with a uniformed policeman, who carried a riding crop.

"Up my cousins!" the sheik shouted. "A high official of the great State of Israel wishes to address you. You will please give him your full attention."

The policeman gave the sheik a sour look, then addressed the Druse workers. "A member of this expedition has been found dead some distance from here. It is my duty to ask questions."

"The man who has been found dead," the sheik amplified "is the great American, our friend and benefactor, Professor Hill."

His teeth were whiter and larger than ever. His words dripped with humility and Ahmed Fosse immediately suspected him of being somehow involved in the death of Professor Hill.

The policeman spoke in excellent Arabic. "Professor Hill was killed at approximately six o'clock this morning. Is there anyone here who was not here at that time?" The Druse looked at one another. Some shook their heads, a few shrugged.

"The question is an important one," continued the policeman, "because the professor was killed at some distance from here and it can be presumed that anyone who was here within a half hour of six o'clock could not possibly be involved."

"Speak," said the sheik, "speak now, or take the consequences later, if I find out you held your tongue when you should have spoken."

The Druse avoided the searching eyes of their sheik. The policeman waited while the seconds ticked away. A full thirty or more. Then he nodded and turned away.

Ali, the chief of the Druse workers, under the sheik, suddenly spoke.

"The Egyptian was not here at that time."

The policeman came deliberately among the Druse. He had already spotted Ahmed Fosse as the one alien of the group. He came now and stood, looking down at Ahmed, who sat on the ground.

"Where were you at six o'clock this morning?"

"In Nazareth," replied Ahmed Fosse.

"Indeed," said the policeman. "In Nazareth, or near it?"

"In."

The policeman tapped Ahmed with the riding crop. The tap was a sharp one. "On your feet."

Ahmed's feet were crossed in front of him. He rose, simply by propelling himself upward. The policeman flicked the riding crop at him, indicated with his head. "Come!"

He turned away, expecting that Ahmed Fosse would follow him. Ahmed let him go six or seven steps before he followed. His eyes went to the sardonic, grinning face of the sheik.

The sheik said: "I am sheik of the Druse only."

His teeth were bared as much as they could be bared. It was as wolfish a grin as the sheik could manage.

A half dozen members of the archaeological expedition were gathered under the canopy. Two policemen and the civilian official were with them.

The policeman, who was escorting Ahmed, saluted the official. "This man

45

was in the vicinity of Nazareth this morning."

The official sized up Ahmed. "Your name?"

"Ahmed Fosse."

"Your passport, please."

Ahmed Fosse extracted it. The official glanced at it quickly, but did not return it. "How did you enter Israel?"

"Bus," replied Ahmed Fosse. "To Tel-Aviv, then again to Haifa. I walked from Haifa."

"From what time?"

"I left there yesterday evening, shortly after seven. I walked until about eleven, then slept until dawn this morning."

"Dawn, ah, yes. And precisely what time did you reach Nazareth?"

"A few minutes before six."

"After how long a walk?"

"An hour and a half."

The official shook his head. "You walked twenty kilometers last night. I will concede that you walked very fast. Still, you went to sleep at eleven you said, and you started again this morning at five."

"Four-thirty."

"You walked fifteen kilometers in an hour and a half?"

"No, I got a ride into Nazareth."

"Indeed? And how long did you remain in Nazareth?" The policeman pronounced it "Natzrat."

"I left the city around eight o'clock, and was working here by nine."

The policeman smiled pleasantly. "All accounted for, eh? You made a rather fast trip from Nazareth to this place. Mmm, it's about eighteen kilometers."

"I gave him a lift from just outside Nazareth," volunteered Alice Holterman.

The official turned to Mrs. Holterman. "Ah, yes." He hesitated, then turned back to Ahmed Fosse. "I think that will be all. For now."

Ahmed Fosse did not move. The police official said sharply: "I said that was all."

Ahmed Fosse walked off.

Dr. Sando said, "Who put that man to work?"

"The sheik," said Alice tartly. "Natives are under his jurisdiction."

"Yes, but I thought I made it clear that I did not want him here," persisted Sando.

47

Alice Holterman walked away from him. She passed her husband nearby, and went into the house that was occupied by them. Charles Holterman nodded thoughtfully, then moved toward the police official.

"Dr. Hill's death is an unfortunate occurrence," he said, "but none of us here at Tel Mas had anything to do with it. I am certain of that."

"Are you, Mr. Holterman?" asked the official evenly.

"Yes."

The official nodded. "I will probably return later to get statements."

He walked to the European automobile, where he held a brief inaudible conversation with one of the uniformed men. Then he drove off. All of the policemen climbed into the jeep.

5

IT was time for the Druse to get back to work. The sheik, who had remained with his people, reminded them of that sad fact. "The Europeans kill each other, but that has nothing to do with us, my cousins. We are workers. We work for the Europeans and the Americans, so let us do that for which we have been engaged."

He led the way by returning to his ordinary employment, stretching out under the canopy. The other Druse followed Ali back to the tel. As they neared the scene of the dig, Ali, the straw boss, fell in beside Ahmed Fosse.

"You may carry dirt this afternoon."

Ahmed nodded, made no reply. The Druse cleared his throat noisily. "It is easier than digging and not as hot."

Ahmed gave him a quick look. The Druse straw boss was looking straight ahead.

Ahmed carried dirt out of the cut for

49

about an hour, then as he came out of the cut, he was accosted by the sheik, who had left the camp.

"This morning, *fellah*," the sheik said cheerfully, "you came to this tel unwelcome, unwanted. You were rebuffed by the great ones from the rich land of the Americans. Who was it, then, who listened to you? Who was it who took you in when the Americans cast you out?"

"All right," said Ahmed, "it was the great sheik, Yussuf ben Adhem."

"You will remember that?"

"Every payday, when I get my pay from you, minus your commission."

"Every payday, even if *others* pay you?"

Ahmed shrugged. "You'll get your share."

"Remember it, *fellah*. And now for the good word. Your work, *fellah*," the sheik said, "has attracted the attention of the Americans. You have worked hard, and in my English public school I was taught that hard work was always rewarded. The American sheik requests that you report to him."

"Charles Holterman?"

"Ah, no, the great Dr. Sando. He passes

out the rewards. He also deals out the punishments."

"Which am I going to get?"

The sheik smiled expansively. "Have I not been talking to you about rewards . . . and benefactors? Would it be punishment if I talked about remembering me?" He moved aside. "Go, with Allah's blessing."

Sando was waiting for him in his office, but his face was not the face of a man who was about to dole out rewards. It was long and sour-visaged and seemed to become even longer when Ahmed Fosse entered.

He indicated a vase before him. "Read that."

There was a band about the vase. Before the ancient potter had fired the clay he had painted on the band in a crude, yet firm hand.

"'May the great Yahweh live always in the house of Jacob, son of Enoch, son of Jacob,'" read Ahmed aloud.

The scowl grew deeper on Dr. Sando's face. "Date it."

Ahmed examined the restored vase and grudgingly admitted to himself that the restorer who had put the pieces together was a skillful artisan. He fingered a rough edge, where a tiny fragment was missing. "Late first century, B.C.," he said finally.

Dr. Sando exclaimed. "Dr. Hill put it late first century, A.D."

Ahmed re-examined the ancient inscription. "The pot could be as late as that," he said, "but not the writing. It is Hebrew, but the formation of the letters indicates that the author was familiar with the Edomite language. Herod the Great was an Edomine. Under him Edom scribes flourished, although not usually this far north. Certainly not after his death. Herod Antipas, who succeeded him as tetrarch of this area, curried favor with the Romans, as well as the Hebrews. His predecessor never favored the Hebrews. The Romans, yes, but not the Jews, whom he ruled. I still say late first century, B.C."

Dr. Sando got to his feet. He poked a finger at a scrap of parchment, moving it across the desk. There were only a few words on the yellowed, decaying fragment. "This?"

"Aramaic," said Ahmed. "The words are mere fragments. One could be a name." He hesitated. "A Greek name, Petros . . . Peter Archimedes, perhaps."

"All right," Sando said. "Hill's death leaves us one man short. I'm not happy over your training, your lack of any degrees, but I'll give you a chance. You're on trial. Do the work and you stay on. Fluff it and — " Sando snapped his fingers. "You can make a reputation with this expedition, Foss — "

"Fosse."

"Foss-say," snapped Sando. "Charles Holterman is a man with a reputation and I've had my share of publicity. We're on the threshold of some important discoveries and every member of the expedition has a chance to become famous. You, too Foss — Fosse!"

Ahmed nodded.

"Well?" snapped Sando. "What're you waiting for? You'll share quarters with Miller Wood. I hope you can augment his knowledge. Or he, yours."

Miller Wood was in his late thirties, a spare, graying man with short, graying hair. He was a chain cigarette smoker and he smoked the cigarettes very short.

"Maybe," he said to Ahmed Fosse, "maybe Sando's softening. I would have bet against it last year, last week, even this morning, but . . . " He shook his head. "You *told* him you were Egyptian?"

"And French."

"That's worse, to a man like Sando."

"And to a man like you?"

Wood regarded Fosse imperturbably. "Oh, you've got a sharp tongue, hey? Uh-uh, not me. I'm German, a long way back. Guess the name was Holtz originally. That means wood. But whether I'm German, English, or American, my people were barbarians — same as the French — when your mother's people had passed their great civilization. When your ancestors were building the pyramids, mine were painting their faces blue and wearing skins, with the hair inside. I'm an archaeologist, Fosse. I've got respect for the ancient races, white, black, brown."

6

THERE were at dinner five members of the Lake Shore University Archaeological Expedition. Dr. Sando sat at the head of the table, aloof, absent-minded. He read a lengthy printed paper while eating. To his right was a woman with coal black bangs and a physique that would have been the pride of a Pennsylvania coal miner. This was Jacqueline Dietrich, who could look at a fragment of a potsherd and give a description of the potter. She was right more often than wrong.

Across from Jacqueline was Carolyn Caxton, who had lost her name in a Nazi concentration camp, who had wandered across most of Europe as a child and had finally found a name and a reason for living. Both had been given to her by an English Jew and his wife in Cyprus.

With them, she had come to Israel, and in the new country, that was so young and yet so old, Carolyn had turned to the old ways. She had studied archaeology at the Hebrew University in Jerusalem and was here at Tel Mas as the official representative of the University.

Carolyn Caxton was thirty-one, give or take a year. She could not have told you for a certainty any more than she knew her birthday or her real name.

She was a natural blonde and wore her hair in a tight bun that did nothing to conceal its gloss, its fine texture. As it did nothing to conceal the smoothness of her skin, the fineness of her features.

Miller Wood said to Ahmed Fosse, across the table: "It's no good pretending you're not aware, Fosse."

Jacqueline Dietrich said: "Pass the sugar, Wood, and shut that big trap of yours."

Miller Wood picked up the sugar bowl and moved it about six inches closer to Jacqueline Dietrich. "I'm off for the fleshpots of Nazareth. If anybody cares to join me, I have transportation and a few dollars left from my paycheck, which I am willing to squander on a person who does not mind enjoying frivolous things forbidden by the great prophet."

"You're not my type, Wood," said Dietrich crisply.

He turned to her and smiled humorlessly. "For which accept my thanks," he waited a moment, his eyes on Carolyn Caxton.

"Miss Caxton," said Miller Wood patiently, "the invitation is open to you."

"Thank you, no."

"No, what? You're not going out this evening? Or, no, you don't want to go with *me*?"

Carolyn Caxton said clearly, "The answer is no to both parts of your question."

"That," said Wood heavily, "is what is wrong with the twentieth century. If we were back in the good old days of the good old Tel Mas, you would not refuse my invitation. In fact, I would not extend it. I would merely grab your beautiful hair and drag you to my lair."

"In two hundred B.C.," snapped Jacqueline Dietrich, "you would not have dragged *me*."

Miller Wood regarded her owlishly. "No," he said, "not even then." He pretended to duck a thrown object and scrambled away from the table.

At the door he caught Ahmed Fosse's eye and winked. He went out.

"Sex maniac," mumbled Jacqueline Dietrich. She pushed away from the table, got up to her full height, which was considerable. Her eyes flicked to Ahmed Fosse, went on to Carolyn Caxton. "Carolyn, my dear, we could do with a bit of exercise. Shall we take a little stroll in the desert?"

Carolyn Caxton shook her head. "I've got some work to do and besides — " she frowned — "I've got a headache."

The big woman's eyes returned to Ahmed Fosse. "Mr. Fosse, does the Egyptian half of you indulge in an occasional sip of alcohol? Not that we'd find much in Nazareth, but ... " She shrugged.

"I, too, must work," said Ahmed. "I am new here and there are many things to learn."

Jacqueline nodded and started for the door. Before she reached it, she turned. "Like me to stay and give you a briefing?"

He shook his head quickly.

When she went out, Ahmed said to Carolyn Caxton, "That leaves us."

"It doesn't," she replied, "because I really do have a headache."

He nodded briefly.

A jeep almost collided with Ahmed Fosse as he came out of the communal dining room. Miller Wood yelled at him, but he was shifting gears at the time and the grinding noise drowned out his words.

Ahmed started toward his quarters and headlights, suddenly switched on, almost blinded him. The car glided toward him. It was the big Cadillac convertible.

"Get in," Alice Holterman said.

"I was going to work," Ahmed replied.

She leaned across and opened the car door.

He climbed in beside her and the car moved away.

"It's eight miles to Nazareth," said Alice Holterman, "twelve to Tiberias."

"And?"

"If you want to pray, Nazareth is the place. But if it's a drink you want — "

"Tiberias," said Ahmed Fosse.

Alice Holterman nodded. She gunned

the motor and it leaped along the rutted road. She was a careless driver, whipping the car off the dirt onto the pavement with tires screeching, heedless of headlights coming from the east. She righted the car in time, however, and sent it zooming along the pavement.

"You got the job you wanted," she said then. "With a slight assist."

"From the person or persons who killed Dr. Hill."

Alice grimaced. "From them . . . and a little from me. I had a talk with Charles. It's his money that brought this expedition here, that's kept it going for two years, without finding anything worth smuggling out of the country."

"What does the expedition expect to find?"

"What does any digger expect to find? Gold, trinkets, mummies."

"Mummies? In Israel?"

She shook her head. "My husband's the archaeologist, not me. I wouldn't know a — what is it they're always talking about? — a potsherd. I wouldn't know a potsherd from a Dead Sea scroll."

"Then why come to Israel? I imagine

there are more interesting things to do in Chicago."

"I've done them. This is the first time I've gone with Charles on an expedition. I thought it might be interesting — for a change. It isn't."

She lasped into silence. Ahmed Fosse, shooting a sideward glance at her, saw the muscle ripple in the jaw that was turned to him.

She concentrated on her driving. There was considerable traffic on the road in both directions. Most of the cars were small American-made or European cars. They passed two Opels, four Fords, and an Italian Fiat.

Lights shimmered ahead, when Alice spoke again. "Sando doesn't like you," she said. "You haven't got any college degrees."

"Is that why he doesn't like me?" asked Ahmed. "I thought it might be because I've got brown skin."

"Rot," she snapped. "A brown-skinned man's more attractive than a pasty-skinned one."

Red taillights were ahead and headlights were approaching on the left side of the road. Alice pressed heavily on the car horn, swung the car to the left, and beat the approaching headlights, with not to many yards to spare.

Street lights appeared. She slackened the speed of the Cadillac, made a sharp right turn, then a left. The car bounced over rutted dirt and broken pavement, then hit smooth macadam. Alice Holterman applied the brakes and pulled up before a squat, sprawling building made of stone and concrete and what seemed to be dried mud.

A large neon sign in bilingual red and blue tubing read: *Salome and the Seven Veils.*

7

A DOORMAN, wearing a burnoose, opened the door of the café. Oriental music assailed their ears as they entered and were greeted by a waiter, also wearing Arabic costume. He bowed and looking at Ahmed, said in Arabic: "You will want wine?"

"I am half French," replied Ahmed, "and that part of me drinks alcohol."

"Then you shall have wine," replied the waiter, "and perhaps the prophet will not know of it."

Alice interrupted. "We'll talk English tonight. I don't understand the native jabber and I don't like people saying things I don't understand."

The waiter said, in accented English: "I will wait on you myself, Madam, hand I speak pairfect Henglish."

"Talk it, then," snapped Alice shrewishly.

The waiter led them to a small table on which was a candelabra, containing three fat candles. There were electric lights at strategic places about the interior, but they were dimmed and some were blue and green. The lighting in the center of the room, which was cleared of tables, was poor.

An Oriental orchestra of five men played at the far end of the room.

The table at which they were seated was small, with two rattan chairs and a skin-covered couch on one side. Ahmed tried to take one of the chairs, but Alice signaled for him to sit beside her on the couch.

"A bottle of wine?" asked the waiter in English.

"You have imported wine?" asked Alice.

"It is expensive," was the reply. "Hi would like to recommend a bottle of hour domestic — "

"Italian," snapped Alice. "Chilled."

"Cheeled?"

"Cold!"

The waiter went off. Alice shook her head. "The trouble with these countries," she said, "is that there are too many foreigners in them."

"Who is the foreigner?" asked Ahmed. "The waiter who just left, or you?"

"Him," said Alice. "He's no more Arab than I am. He's a Greek or a Turk."

"I am an Egyptian," Ahmed reminded.

"You're also French." She looked at him. "From your name, I take it your father was French, your mother Egyptian. Where were you born, Egypt or France?"

"Egypt. I never knew my father. As a matter of fact, my mother hardly knew him. He went back to France before I was born." He paused. "Before he and my mother were married. But she gave me his name."

"Ah," Alice exclaimed, "that explains it."

"Explains what?"

"The lines in your face. They've been there a long time. So has the harshness — the hardness — in your voice. You hate your white father, all white people. Because of what your father did to your mother." She leaned back and studied his face. "You'd kill him, wouldn't you? You'd kill him if you ever met him."

"My father has been dead for twenty years."

"But your hatred for him is still alive?"

Ahmed saw the waiter coming toward

the table and was spared replying. The waiter was still pouring wine into the glasses when the orchestra's tempo suddenly increased. The ceiling lights went out and a spotlight appeared on the center of the floor.

"Ah, the lady with the veils," exclaimed Alice.

The music became muted. The dancer appeared on the edges of the spotlight, slithering here and there in the semi-light, now and then moving a few inches into the light, then retreating again.

"Is beautiful," said the waiter. He moved aside, but remained a few feet from the table.

Alice picked up her glass. "To your bitterness," she said. She clinked her glass against Ahmed's, drank a mouthful of wine, and added, "And mine."

She drank the rest of the wine and refilled the glass herself. She reached over to Ahmed's glass. "Down the hatch, Buster. You're not getting me drunk and staying sober yourself."

She refilled his half-empty glass. "Down," she said, "then we start together, glass for glass."

"I'm not a drinking man," protested Ahmed.

"You're going to be tonight," snapped Alice. "I'm going to get good and drunk and tomorrow to be sick as a dog, but he'll be out of my system. Gone, dead and gone."

Ahmed put down his wineglass. "Hill?"

"Albert Doniphan Hill. You got his job. It's better than shoveling dirt, isn't it?"

Alice's left hand caught his wrist. Her nails dug into the skin, then relaxed. She stared at him fixedly for a moment, then suddenly she exhaled.

"Watch your Salome!"

Ahmed's eyes went to the dancer on the floor. She was in the center of the spotlight now. She was a lithe, somewhat overweight girl, but she performed smoothly. The veils seemed to float with her, and when she shed one of them, to the applause of some of the audience around the edges of the room, the veil floated about her for a moment or two.

She began to loosen a second veil and the tempo of the music rose. She got rid of the veil, a third, then a fourth, and now the music was wailing and there was stamping of feet and clapping of hands. Cymbals began to clang and bang. The dancer moved out of the brightness of the light, discarding the fifth veil, and kept to the semi-light most of the time, only now and then slithering into bright light for a second or two. The sixth veil floated out into the spotlight and the dancer swirled madly at the edges of the light. Calls in Arabic, in Greek, and even in English came from the audience.

A very American voice cried out: "Take it off!"

The twentieth-century Salome took her time about it. She darted into the light, leaped back into the dark. Then at last the seventh and final veil was wafted out. The girl appeared for a split second at the edge of the spotlight, then was gone.

The applause was heavy and she came back — wearing a dressing gown.

"Take it off!" yelled the American voice.

She didn't, however.

"And now," said Alice Holterman, "John the Baptist's head."

The lights came on, revealing a very fat, perspiring man standing by their table.

"I am Hercules Petrakis," he announced, "the proprietor. You are enjoying the performance?"

"Your dancer was excellent," said Alice Holterman. "She would have received even greater applause on Halsted Street."

"Halsted Street?" beamed the proprietor. "But that is in Chicago! My cousin, Aristide Petrakis, he has a res — restaurant on Halsted Street."

"I'll look him up when I get back to Chicago," said Alice coolly.

"Is permitted?" asked Hercules Petrakis, pulling out one of the rattan chairs. He seated himself, pulled up the chair, and rested both arms on the little table. He leaned forward.

"Chicago, it is a very rich city. So writes my cousin. When he was a boy in our village in Thessaly, he was poor, just like me. Then his father die and Aristide, he sell his poor farm and go to Chicago. Now he is rich."

"You're not doing so badly yourself," said Alice, somewhat tartly. "You own this night club."

"Ah, business is very poor. Israel is a poor country. Sometimes I think I make

69

the big mistake coming to this country. The Jews are such a serious people. They do not patronize night clubs. Their Allah does not permit the Arabs to drink." His eyes went to Ahmed's face. "I am begging your pardon. You — you are not an Arab?"

"I'm an Egyptian."

"A thousand pardons, Effendi, ten thousand pardons."

"Mr. Fosse is pulling your leg," said Alice Holterman. "He is only part Egyptian. Part French."

Hercules Petrakis beamed again. "Ah, that is better. Mr. Foss — Fossay, did you say? I wonder if you would indulge me for a moment or two. There is something in my office I would like to show you. Madam will excuse?"

"No," said Alice, "I will not excuse. If you have anything to show us, bring it here."

"This is, forgive me, Madam, this is intended for men only. I will send to you a bottle of my best wine. From my beloved hills in Thessaly. The finest vintage . . . "

"No," said Ahmed abruptly.

"Is nothing," exclaimed the Greek. "There will be no charge for the wine. It is my gift to you for — for my stupid blunder. Come, Mesheer, come to my office for just a moment . . . "

"You heard the man," snapped Alice Holterman. "He's not going to your office and any wine we drink we'll pay for."

The flabbiness of the fat man's jowels quivered. His eyes became piggish as they slitted. "I insist. I have tried to be polite, but you force me to speak bluntly. Mesheer Fossay, it is a personal matter I wish to speak to you about and I advise you to come with me. It will be only for a moment and I am sure you will regret not coming with me."

"Oh-oh," said Alice, "the man's getting nasty."

"I'll listen to him," said Ahmed, sliding away from Alice.

She reached out, then stopped. "Don't be long."

Ahmed got to his feet, signaled to Petrakis to lead the way. The fat Greek ambled across the floor, heading for a door beside the orchestra. He opened the door, went into a cluttered

71

office. Ahmed, followed, pushed the door violently, sending it against the wall before he entered.

There was no one behind the door, no one besides the Greek proprietor and himself in the office. The Greek, Petrakis, however, would not speak until he had closed the door.

"Mr. Fossay," he said then, "this morning you were seen some miles south of Nazareth. It was very early in the morning and . . ."

"Chicago," said Ahmed. "I got the drift when you mentioned your cousin in Chicago. He's got some Italian friends . . ."

"You stole their automobile," chided Petrakis. "That is a crime in this country. And you were not very nice to them."

"I'll be nicer the next time I see them."

"Please," said Petrakis, "this is important. You took something from — from an automobile that had run off the road."

"What," asked Ahmed, "what did I take?"

"It is not necessary to fence, Mesheer. You know the object I am referring to. I

72

am willing to buy it from you. I will pay you cash and no hard feelings."

"How much cash?"

"The object we are talking about has a certain value. It is not genuine, but all such things have a — a certain value. In Jerusalem they have established a price. So much per square inch . . . "

"You're talking about the Dead Sea scrolls." said Ahmed. "They pay the Bedouins who bring in the scraps something like four dollars a square inch. That's what you're offering me?"

"Perhaps I could better the price a little."

"Five dollars? Five dollars an inch for parchment scraps?"

"Scraps?" The fat Greek winced. "I am not talking about scraps." Then he suddenly reached out and grabbed Ahmed's arm. "It is *not* scraps! Please! It hasn't been . . . " His words died out.

"Take your hand off my arm," said Ahmed quietly.

Petrakis paid no attention to Ahmed's command. His piggish eyes were glaring at Ahmed. "The manuscript has not been damaged?" he cried. "You wouldn't dare . . . "

Ahmed reached across with his left hand, caught hold of Petrakis' arm, and twisted it so savagely that Petrakis was hurled to the floor. The man landed heavily, was stunned for an instant, then on his knees scrambled toward his desk. A drawer was partly open and it was obvious that he was headed for it. Ahmed took a quick step, kicked the drawer shut.

Petrakis caught himself, then. Painfully he climbed to his feet. "They did not exaggerate. You are a savage, Fossay."

"Don't grab my arm again," Ahmed said. "I don't like to be touched."

Petrakis' jowls were quivering again. "I will forget this for the moment. You have not answered me about the manuscript."

"I haven't got a manuscript," snapped Ahmed. "I took nothing from Hill's car . . . "

"Hill!" cried Petrakis. "I did not mention his name. But you knew it."

"I'm working at the North Shore Tel Mas diggings," said Ahmed. "Hill was a member of the expedition. The police have been all over the place. I would have been deaf, dumb, and blind not to have heard about Hill. As a matter of fact, it's no secret that I've replaced him. But I don't know a damn thing about him . . . or about this manuscript you're babbling about."

The door of the office was opened. Alice Holterman stood in the doorway. "You said a minute. I want to go now."

"Please," cried Petrakis, "a moment more."

"No," said Ahmed, "We're through."

"If you'll give us the check," said Alice wickedly, "I'll see that you get a good tip."

Petrakis pawed the air. "There — there is no check." He swallowed hard. "We will talk again, Mesheer Fossay."

"Don't count on it," said Ahmed and walked past Alice Holterman into the night club. She followed, remaining quiet until they were outside, getting into the car.

"It's too early to go home," she said then.

"Not for me. I've got work to do."

She backed the car, shifted into forward,

and made a sharp U-turn, tires screeching. She drove a block, turned left.

"You missed the turn," Ahmed observed then.

"A shortcut." She laughed shortly. "I know my way around these ruins."

8

THE car was going downhill and Ahmed could smell sea air. The car left pavement, bounced over rough road, and went into a street barely wide enough for an automobile. Alice drove swiftly, heedless of cross-street traffic and street corners. Fortunately, there was little traffic and she reached level ground without mishap.

The city here was decrepit. Houses were old, many unoccupied and crumbling. From his readings, Ahmed knew that they were in the old part of the city, the new one having been built on higher ground, up toward the slopes of the mountain that led down to the Sea of Galilee.

The car was suddenly in the open then and Ahmed saw ahead the shimmering of the moon upon a placid body of water.

The Sea of Galilee, or Kinneret as the Hebrews preferred to call it. There were buildings, dark, ghostly-looking to the left. Ruins.

Alice stopped the car twenty feet from the water's edge.

"When I was a child," she said, "a Sunday School teacher told me that Jesus Christ walked on this water." She added, with a trace of hardness in her tone, "And He didn't even get His feet wet!"

"If He was the Son of God," said Ahmed, "He could do it."

"Do *you* believe it?"

"Mohammed believed that Christ was a prophet, the greatest . . . after Mohammed himself." He looked at her. "That was your way of asking if I was a Christian or a Mohammedan."

"Well?"

"What a man believes is his business. You're a woman who asks a lot of questions. You're going to get some answers, but not many."

She nodded thoughtfully and looked out over the Sea of Galilee. Ahmed Fosse sat beside her, looking where she was looking, but not seeing anything.

She said: "I'd like a cigarette."

"I don't have any. I'm not much of a smoker."

"You don't drink — much, you don't

smoke. What else don't you do?"

"I don't make love to married women."

A gasp was torn from her throat. Her left arm came up, her hand open to strike at him. But she restrained herself.

The moonlight caught her eyes for an instant and he saw that they were blazing, the eyes of a savage . . . or a frustrated woman.

Ahmed said, "I've still got to work tomorrow."

"I got you the job," she retorted. "I can take it away from you."

"But you won't. Not yet."

"Give me one good reason why I shouldn't have you fired."

"Because you haven't broken me yet."

"No," she said, "I haven't."

She opened the glove compartment, took out a package of cigarettes and a lighter. She lit a cigarette, put the package and lighter back into the compartment. She inhaled deeply and blew out a stream of smoke.

"What's between you and the Greek?" she asked suddenly.

"A couple of his friends gave me a lift this morning. South of Nazareth, before you picked me up. I took their car and drove into Nazareth with it. Petrakis says that's against the law."

She turned, stared at him. "Two men, dark. Pin-stripe suits. Look like Chicago gangsters?"

"You know them?"

"I saw them yesterday. At Tel Mas. They were talking with Donny Hill."

Her teeth worried her lower lip. "He was afraid of them." She flicked her cigarette out of the car. "You said you took their car from them. They didn't impress me as the kind of men you could take anything away from."

"They got careless."

She shook her head. "There's something about you I can't put my finger on. You're hard — that I saw the first time I looked at you. It's what attracted me to you. I'm not exactly a creampuff myself. After my hus — "

"Your husband," Ahmed said quietly.

"What about him?"

"Nothing. You started to mention your husband, that's all."

"It isn't all. You want to remind me that I have a husband. Yes, I have a

80

husband. In name. Rather, I've got his name. And that's all I've got of him. He's Charles D. Holterman. Put that in capital letters. Ahmed, my friend, have you ever tried to sleep with a man whose name is printed in capital letters?"

"Even in Egypt women divorce their husbands."

"Not capital-letter men. Sometimes, when it suits them, men like that divorce their wives. It doesn't suit Charles D. Holterman to divorce me."

"He'd rather you slept with men like A. D. Hill?"

"That tongue of yours has got a sting, *fellah*," said Alice Holterman. "I think it's time to call it a night."

She started the car, backed away, and making a U-turn, started the climb up the hill. A few minutes later they passed the *Salome and the Seven Veils.*

She made the twelve miles to the Tel Mas turn-off in ten minutes, in spite of a winding road and darkness. She spoke not a single word until she had turned off the pavement. Then she braked the car.

"Sorry, Buster," she said then, "but you walk from here. It's too conspicuous driving up together."

He got out and she gunned the car away. Ahmed began walking. He passed through the twin bluffs, turned right into the dry wadi. A figure appeared out of the shadows.

"You walk in the night, Effendi," said the voice of Sheik Yussuf.

"So do you."

"The night is the friend of the people of the desert. We are shepherd people, Effendi."

"What's this effendi business?"

The sheik bowed and Ahmed knew that he was smirking to himself. "You have moved in with the white people. You work with the white people, you associate with them, so you must now be treated as one — Effendi."

"All right, Sheik, play the game, if it gives you pleasure. Laugh up your sleeve."

"Laugh, Effendi? I do not laugh. I mind my business. What I see remains with me."

"I suppose that's referring to Mrs. Holterman dropping me here and driving on alone."

"Mrs Holterman? The wife of the great white father, who owns the great American city of Chicago. Effendi, I am a poor Druse Arab. What have I to do with the wife of such a great one? I would not even dare to speak her name."

"This person whose name you would not dare to speak . . . she went out with other men now and then?"

"I have just told you, Effendi, I see nothing, I hear nothing. The night has a thousand eyes, but I have just two. They do not see into the night."

9

AHMED had been assigned the former quarters of A. D. Hill, deceased. It was a room that was shared with Miller. Ahmed had moved in before dinner, deposited his rucksack containing his few belongings on an unmade bed.

When he entered now, he found that the bed had been freshly made up with sheets, new blankets, smelling faintly of mothballs. His personal things had been refolded neatly and placed on a chair beside the bed.

Miller Wood was still out.

Ahmed undressed, stripping to shorts. He examined his spare khaki shirt, found one in need of mending, and put it on in lieu of pajamas.

The diggings were equipped with electricity from a portable electric plant and Ahmed pulled out the lamp cord near his bed and slipped in between the sheets.

Ahmed had assumed an iron control over his conscious and self-conscious many years ago. He could will himself to sleep in moments, could awaken at a precise, predetermined time.

He decided now to remain awake awhile and assembled certain things in his mind, things that had happened that day . . . and during the evening.

He had slept in a field the night before, had awakened at the crack of dawn and started walking toward Nazareth. In a short while he had come upon a man dying from a knife wound in his back. He had found an ancient copper cylinder in the man's car, a cylinder that could at one time have contained a parchment or scroll of papyrus. The cylinder was similar to ones he had seen in pictures as having been found in the caves of the Dead Sea area.

The Chicago men had been cruising the highway. They had found Hill dead. They had probably been the ones who had knifed him, but he had eluded them somehow and they had pursued. They had found him too late. The contents of the copper cylinder were gone.

Ahmed was in the vicinity. He had certainly passed the car containing the dead or dying man. He had quite probably investigated, and if so, he might have found the contents of the copper cylinder.

So they had reasoned and so they had acted. But Ahmed had proved to be a tartar. He had eluded them.

In Tiberias a man had identified Ahmed as the one who had encountered the killers south of Nazareth. How had he recognized Ahmed, how had he known what had taken place in the olive grove?

The killers knew that Ahmed had joined the Tel Mas expedition.

Ahmed sat up in his bed. The room he was to share with Miller was some fourteen by twenty feet. One bed was on each side of the room, but there was a window between the two beds. The window was only three feet from Ahmed's bed. Admed got up, moved the bed against the wall. It was now seven feet from the window. Only an edge of the bed could be seen by a man standing just outside the window. Only a sleeper's feet could be seen, not his body or head.

Ahmed got back into bed.

Alice Holterman.

She had been friendly with A. D. Hill, more than friendly. But not in love with him. She had known Hill better than anyone in the expedition.

Had she known that Hill possessed a copper cylinder, which quite possibly had contained an ancient scroll?

Had she known that Hill was having traffic with Sicilian-Chicagoans?

Charles Holterman.

Ahmed closed his eyes and willed himself to sleep.

He was awakened by the lights going on in the room. He lay still, watching Miller Wood stumbling about as he sat down on the bed. Early that evening Alice Holterman had said to Ahmed Nazareth was for praying, Tiberias for drinking. Miller had gone to Nazareth, but it was apparent that he had not gone there to pray.

He had been drinking heavily and was mumbling to himself.

"Billion dollars," he said reasonably audible. "Hun'erd million, two hun'erd, billion."

"In Egypt," said Ahmed, "we count sheep when we want to sleep."

Wood lifted his head, regarded Ahmed owlishly. "Who're you?"

"I'm the new language man," Ahmed said, "replacement for the late A. D. Hill."

"Hill, Hill, yeah," muttered Wood. "Told him he was playin' with fire, but he wouldn't listen. Million dollars, he said, ten million, maybe a billion."

"I just said we count sheep in Egypt. Evidently you American's count money. Millions of dollars."

Wood had removed his shirt and one shoe. He got to his feet.

"What the hell you talkin' about? You're nothin' but a goddamn Egyptian. Hill was my friend." He came across the room, stood over Ahmed drunkenly.

"Can't talk to me about my friends. Get up and I'll knock your head off."

"Go to sleep, Wood."

"I don't sleep with natives. Who the hell told you you could come in here and sleep same room with white men?"

Ahmed threw back the sheets and swung his feet to the floor. The drunken Wood took a wild swing at him, which

Ahmed ducked easily. He straightened then, gave Wood a judo cut across the throat, and as Wood fell forward, gasping, hit him on the side of the head with his fist. It was a restrained blow, but it did the job neatly.

Wood fell to the floor on his face. He was out cold. Ahmed picked him up, carried him across the room to his bed. He deposited him on it, straightening out the unconscious man.

Then he switched off the light and returned to his bed.

He remained awake until he heard loud, even snoring. Then he went to sleep himself.

10

AHMED was up with the dawn. Miller Wood, across the room, was lying on his side sleeping heavily. He was good for several more hours. Ahmed dressed, washed, and went outside.

The only sign of life was at the quarters of the Druse. Ahmed turned away, walking swiftly to the tel. He stood near it for a few minutes, sizing it up. The Lake Shore expedition had been here for two years but the tel was only partly exposed. A half dozen years and considerably more men would be required to complete the task of evaluating the findings.

All of the excavation was on the eastern side of the tel, although a trench or two had been dug on the northern side also. Ahmed made a complete circuit of the tel. He estimated that the circumference was less than a mile, which meant that the original village that was buried here had been a fair-sized one for its time, but small in comparison to modern villages or cities. It had probably in its heyday contained a population of a thousand to fifteen hundred persons, possibly two to three hundred houses. Why had Charles Holterman chosen this tel for his expedition?

Megiddo, to the south and west, was a famed Biblical city. Tiberias to the east was also a well-known spot. Nothing in ancient history or in the Bible had referred to a village ten miles east of Nazareth as being of importance.

That did not necessarily mean much. Nineveh had been lost for two hundred years. Ur had been unknown until modern times, yet it might have been one of the earliest cities of antiquity.

Charles Holterman, according to his biographies, which Ahmed had read, had come to the Holy Land early in 1940. The war had not yet touched Palestine, but the time was not good for archaeological expeditions and he had remained only a few months. He had served with the American Intelligence in the Far East, but whether he had spent any wartime years in Palestine, the biographers had not said.

His war service was glossed over with the brief statement, Army Intelligence, O.S.S. Hush-hush stuff.

His biography became more detailed in 1946. He had served a year with the British archaeological team at Jericho and then had branched out on his own. He had tried the Sinai country for a year or two, then had moved gradually northward. Megiddo was already being exploited. He had leapfrogged into Syria, into Iraq. He had escaped the Israel War of Independence but by 1952, with peace restored and Israel a nation, he had returned to the Biblical country. He had discovered Tel Shelmen, unearthing the Biblical city of Beth-Barma. He had spent six years there, had written two books about it and delivered two-score lectures in America and Europe. He had prepared himself for Tel Mas and had come here two years ago.

Had he found something in Beth-Barma that had pointed to Tel Mas? The Lake Shore University knew little of his progress here. Either very little had been found or learned, or it had not been reported to the University.

A. D. Hill had found something.

On the south side of the mound, more than a thousand feet from the eastern workings, Ahmed found the beginnings of a trench. It had stopped at the rubble of a wall. That much was known then — that ancient Tel Mas had been a walled town. No attempt had been made to penetrate the wall.

Ahmed turned away.

There were rocks to the south, not too far away. Had a man flitted from one rock to another as Ahmed turned? Was he being watched?

Ahmed returned to the buildings housing the members of the expedition.

The Druse were astir. Not Yussuf the sheik, but his chief janissary, Ali.

The Druse came toward Ahmed. He was smiling fawningly and bowed to Ahmed.

"The effendi is to be congratulated and your humble servant wishes to inform the effendi that the Druse will give him their support and help, since they feel that he has been one of them and understand them better than the Americans."

"Those are *your* words, Ali, or the

words of the great sheik?"

"The words are mine, the thoughts are my noble cousin's. He expressed them to me last night, when we discussed your promotion."

Ahmed nodded. "Tell me, Ali, you have the eyes and ears of all your people. Have any of them reported Americans hereabouts other than those connected with the expedition?"

The Druse hesitated, then shook his head. "No, Effendi. No Americans have been here. They would not be permitted."

"Would not be permitted by whom?"

"The American doctor, Effendi."

"Not the Israeli police?"

Ali spat. "The Israeli police! They run over this country that is rightly ours. They are our masters, but they do not know their country, they do not know ours. They are foreigners, as much as . . . " Ali winced.

"As much as I."

Ali shrugged. "You, at least, are part Arab. You speak our tongue. My cousin Yussuf says that you have lived in the desert."

"Your cousin and you have apparently

94

discussed me at length."

"What is there to talk about here, Effendi? The work we do, the sweat we wipe from our brows? The miserable pay?"

"I should think you would have had something to talk about yesterday. The murder of the American, Effendi Hill."

"As you said, Effendi, the American! We are not interested in Americans. If they wish to kill each other, that is not our affair. As long as they do not involve us . . . " Ali shrugged again.

Ahmed's back was turned to the houses of the upper echelon of the expedition, but Ali was facing them. Ahmed saw the Druse's eyes narrow. Ahmed looked over his shoulder.

Charles Holterman had come out of his quarters and was standing some fifty or sixty feet away, watching Ahmed. Ahmed started toward his own building, which would take him at a right angle. Holterman started forward diagonally and it was apparent that he intended to block Ahmed's path.

Ahmed turned toward him.

"Good morning, Mr. Fosse," Holterman

95

said cheerfully. "You're out early."

"I'm an early riser."

"So am I. My wife suffers from insomnia and is up most of the night. Then toward morning she sleeps. I try to avoid awakening her . . . " Holterman pursed up his lips. "Dr. Sando tells me that you're taking hold very well. It's hard to believe that you have no university degrees."

"I have worked in the field and I have studied evenings."

"That is good. You also have a keen interest in the subject and that, I believe, is most important. I regret to say this, but Dr. Hill leaned more toward the commercial end of archaeology. He was an excellent speaker and took full advantage of it. His reputation stemmed chiefly from his lecture tours. He was lacking in wide field experience. While I regret the manner of his demise, I am certain that your substitution in his position will enhance the work of this expedition." He hesitated, then nodded abruptly. "As a matter of fact, I was already in touch with the university in Chicago, asking them to send a replacement. That will now be unnecessary."

Holterman cleared his throat. "I don't believe I have asked you, Mr. Fosse; are you a Christian?"

"My father was."

"But your mother was not." Holterman nodded. "I gather from the way you answered that *you* profess the Moslem faith."

"I didn't say that."

Holterman frowned. "You're not suggesting that you are an unbeliever? An agnostic or . . . an atheist?"

Ahmed said evenly, "I know the Christian doctrines. It is not necessary to believe that Jesus Christ was divine, the son of God. His own people did not believe in Him. They drove Him out of Nazareth."

"That is true, alas. As He said: 'A prophet is without honor in his own country.'" Holterman shook his head. "Do you believe that Jesus Christ *lived*, Mr. Fosse?"

"I have found no reason to disbelieve it. The contemporary records are still lacking, but Josephus wrote of Him only forty or fifty years after His death and the apostles and disciples wrote of Him within the span of their own lives. They could not all have invented the same fictitious character."

Holterman brightened. "We are in the same, ah, vineyard, so to speak. This is the land of Jesus. He lived here, He was familiar with these hills and valleys, the villages. He knew Nazareth, Tiberias, Capernaum. You say you've studied the New Testament? Have you taken the trouble to add up the number of days that are actually documented by the apostles and disciples?"

"Very few. Approximately thirty."

"Twenty-nine! Twenty-nine days of a life of thirty-three years. Yet based upon those twenty-nine days is all Christianity, a faith that has endured for almost two thousand years, that has instilled untold billions of people with the will to live, the courage to endure and the most frightful persecutions, death, destruction . . . "

"Pagans died for their gods," said Ahmed Fosse.

Anger caused Holterman's features to twitch. "I am a Christian. I have studied the New Testament, not as an atheist, but as a Christian. I have devoted a great deal of time to pursuing the careers of each of the original twelve apostles. Everyone knows the fate of Judas, the betrayer. The deaths of Peter and Paul are also known. But there were nine other apostles in the original group. All died deaths of violence — crucifixion, stoning to death. Only one of the original twelve died a normal death. John. John, the youngest of the twelve disciples, and the gentlest.

"He was dearly beloved by Jesus and perhaps He saw to it that John lived to the fullness of age and died a gentle death. John lived to be one hundred and two years of age. His final years of residence are generally believed to have been in Ephesus, in what is now Syria. I found evidence at Tel Shelmen that causes me to believe the John lived out his last years and died at a village known in the first century, Anno Domini, as Beth-el-Arkam. This mound we are excavating is Beth-el-Arkam. At least, I think so. The geography fits the ancient descriptions."

Ahmed nodded thoughtfully. "And you expect to find John's tomb?"

"That would be asking a great deal. I

hope to find *some* record of him, some mention, some evidence that he not only lived here, but that he *lived*."

"For that you financed this expedition?"

Holterman exclaimed. He started to gesticulate, then caught himself. He said coldly: "I am beginning to wonder, Fosse, if I have not made a mistake about you. Professor Klausner wrote an excellent recommendation for you. You professed also to be devoted to archaeology . . ."

"I know my work, Mr. Holterman."

"Perhaps you do. A. D. Hill also knew it. I've told you my opinion of him. I trust that you do not turn out to be like him." Holterman started to go off, then turned back.

"You will have your chance. Sando employed you, Fosse. He thought you could do the work and I'm not going to interfere with his judgement or decision, but I think in all fairness that you should know that Dr. Sando expects the best. You will have to meet his standard. Good morning!"

He went off. Ahmed watched him walk back into his repaired stone house, where his wife was still sleeping.

11

THE camp came to life. Miller Wood did not appear for breakfast, but Jacqueline Dietrich and Carolyn Caxton were already at the table when Fosse sat down.

The breakfast, served by a Druse, was a plain one. Coffee, condensed canned milk, a wheaten gruel, and scrambled eggs, apparently made from powdered eggs.

"If that Druse devil could read," Jacqueline complained, "I'd give him a cookbook and show him that there are other things that can be eaten. We've had this mush and ersatz eggs eight mornings in a row. You'll get awfully tired of the same food morning after morning, Mr. Fosse, especially after a rough night in the fleshpots of Tiberias." She smirked at him.

"Did you enjoy the dancing?"

"I don't dance."

"Who said anything about *you* dancing? I was referring to the little lady with the veils. Let's see, Herod Antipas' descendant by marriage, Salome with the Veils. Without them, too."

Ahmed gave her a quick glance and spooned scrambled eggs onto his plate.

Carolyn Caxton said, "Why don't you shut up, Jacqueline?"

"Whoa-whoa!" cried Jacqueline. "Look who's diving into the pool. Our little Hebrew friend. Well, well and well well! Perhaps there is hope of peace and coexistence between the Arab and the Jew, after all."

Carolyn pushed back her chair and sprang to her feet. Her mouth opened to retort to Jacqueline, but then she thought better of it and rushed out of the room.

The Amazon, Jacqueline, chuckled masculinely. "She likes you, Ahmed!"

Ahmed said: "What was it she said? Why don't you shut up?"

Jacqueline slapped a huge palm on the table and stared at him. "Oh, this is a happy little group! It wasn't bad enough before with Donny Hill romancing all the skirts in the expedition and a few on the outside. Now we've got a new one. I saw you come in last night, Mr.

Fosse. About five minutes after the great effendi's missus roared in with her dusty Cadillac. That's the way it used to be with our dead Donny-boy. She'd come in, then five minutes later he'd sneak up. Nobody knew what was going on. Nobody, if you mean Mr. Holterman. Everybody else knew, but not him."

Ahmed drank his coffee in two huge gulps, set down the cup, and got up from the table. Jacqueline stopped talking and he went out.

The workroom of the language experts contained a table some fifteen feet long. On it were vases, statuettes, scraps of parchment and papyrus. There were two smaller tables in the room, one for Miller Wood and another for A. D. Hill, which was now to be Ahmed Fosse's.

Miller Wood had still not made his appearance when Ahmed entered the workroom. He poked among the specimens at the long table. There was a broken, flat chunk of black basalt, which had apparently been a stele.

It was covered with carvings, Hebrew consonants, as was all ancient Hebrew writing. The vowels had to be guessed at since ancient Hebraic writing was supposedly used merely to refresh the priests' and scholars' memories.

The writing was merely an admonition to priests to observe the proprieties and ritual of the old Mosaic laws. It belonged to the pre-Christian era. Ahmed dated it mentally around 350 B.C. He examined some of the vases, many of which had painted inscriptions.

These inscriptions seemed to be divided almost equally into Hebrew and Aramaic lettering and were somewhat later than the stele. The table contained some thousand of broken sherds, which had not yet been sorted. Ahmed scrutinized some of the sherds and saw fragments of writing on them. From this he gathered that all sherds containing writing were brought first to the 'readers'.

If all of these pieces had to be read and evaluated by Miller Wood and Ahmed, the work was woefully behind. The sherds alone would take months of time. The assembling of the parchment and papyrus fragments was work enough for a half dozen persons for a year.

Ahmed spent a half hour making rough

calculations of the worth of the items in the room and came to the conclusion that the expedition had assembled during its period of excavations little if anything of real value. There might be, among the inscriptions and fragments, some knowledge that had never been learned by other archaeological expeditions, but Ahmed doubted it. Before being dumped on the table, Miller Wood and A. D. Hill had certainly given each piece and chunk a quick appraisal. If anything unusual had been noted, the camp would have been aware of it.

Yet A. D. Hill had been murdered. In his car Ahmed had seen an empty copper cylinder, an ancient one. And the things that had happened to Ahmed seemed to indicate that Hill had found something and that knowledge of it had leaked out.

Petrakis, the Greek of Tiberias. The two Sicilian-Chicago gangsters. The drunken mumblings of Miller Wood, the hints from Alice Holterman.

All referred to a 'treasure', all pointed toward the late A. D. Hill.

Ahmed was at one of the tables when Miller Wood came in. He was unshaven, his eyes were bloodshot, and he was suffering from a bad hangover.

"That's my desk," he snapped.

Ahmed shrugged and went to the other table. He pulled out a chair and seated himself. Miller Wood watched him.

"You think I was drunk last night," he said challengingly.

"Weren't you?"

"Not drunk enough not to know what I was doing. You took a crack at me. You think you could do that when I'm cold sober?"

"Yes."

Miller Wood's face distorted. He took a step toward Ahmed's desk, but stopped. "I told you last night that I didn't like you and I'll repeat it now."

"Do I have to like *you*?"

"I don't give a goddam what you think," snarled Wood. "You wormed your way in here, but you're on your own. You'll get no help from me. I'll do my work and no more and you do yours."

"That sounds like a fair proposition."

"There's an American expression, Fosse, or whatever your name is. You wouldn't know about it, but I'll give it to you just

106

the same. It's — keep your nose clean, that's all."

He stalked to his desk, seated himself, and began shoving things around. A large sherd fell to the floor and broke into smaller pieces. Wood cursed articulately.

Ahmed was still sorting out the articles on his table when a Druse padded into the room. He bowed to Ahmed and said, in Arabic, "The effendi doctor wants you."

Wood snarled at the Druse, "Next time you come in here, talk English. I'll stand for no Arabic chatter around me, not when I know damn well that you can talk English. You tell your sheik that, too!"

The Druse scurried out of the room. Ahmed got up, glanced at the glowering Wood, and went out.

He found Doctor Sando seated at his desk, his hands together in a praying attitude. He was not thinking holy thoughts however. "You want this job, Egyptian?" he snapped.

"I want it very much."

"Then keep out of people's way and keep your mouth shut."

"Mr. Holterman's complained about me?"

"He doesn't complain. He merely said he'd had a talk with you and wasn't entirely pleased with your attitude. About religion, for one thing. You're not a Christian. Neither is Miss Caxton, but she has a belief and the Jewish and Christian faiths are not at war basically. We both believe in the Old Testament."

"So do I," said Ahmed. "I believe it is history. Archaeology has done much to vindicate the Old Testament — from a historical viewpoint. I'm familiar with Kathleen Kenyon's work at Jericho. I accept her proof that the walls of Jericho did fall at the approximate time of the Jewish conquest. Where the archaeologist differs from the theological viewpoint is in the cause. I believe an earthquake destroyed the walls. I do not believe they fell because Joshua blew his horn."

"And what causes an earthquake?" snapped Dr. Sando. "Yes, I know what scientists say. Fissures and faults below the surface of the earth. But who made those fissures and faults? And could not a divine providence move them at will?

Could not God have caused the earthquake at the time that Joshua blew his blast upon the trumpet?"

Ahmed remained silent, which was not what Sando wanted, apparently.

"Speak, if you've got any answers."

"I have none," said Ahmed calmly.

"That's better, at least. Talk when you have to talk, keep quiet when it's necessary. Charles Holterman is my friend, my benefactor, you might even say. He could have this expedition called back to Chicago, if he felt like it. I don't intend to have that happen. Understand?"

Ahmed nodded.

"Then keep out of his way."

"Anything else, Doctor?"

Sando's eyes glinted. "One final caution. No, I'll put it bluntly, so there'll be no mistaking it. Keep away from Mrs. Holterman."

Ahmed's nod was low enough to be considered a bow. He waited, bent forward, and when Sando did not speak again, he turned and walked out of the room.

Outside the sky was azure. There wasn't a speck of a cloud and the sun beat down upon the desert. The temperature, although it was still early in the morning, was close to a hundred degrees.

Carolyn Caxton, wearing a sun helmet, came out of a building. She nodded to Ahmed.

He fell in beside her.

"The effendi doctor has just explained a few camp rules to me," he said. "Number one is don't talk to the effendi Big Boss."

"Mr. Holterman?" exclaimed Carolyn. "But he's wonderful. He talks to everyone, even the Druse. No one's ever seen him angry; he's never raised his voice."

"That's Mr. Charles Holterman?"

"Of course. There's no one else here by that name. Except his wife, Mrs. Holterman."

"And she?"

"What do you mean?"

"What you said about effendi Holterman. Does that apply to Mrs. Holterman? Is she wonderful?"

Carolyn Caxton showed agitation.

"Is she wonderful to everyone?" prodded Ahmed.

"Please, I don't discuss her . . . or

anyone. It's — it's not right."

Ahmed came to an abrupt halt. Carolyn, striding past him, stopped and turned.

"I'm sorry," she apologized. "I didn't mean to be abrupt."

"I've got to get to work."

They had gone some fifty yards from the camp, in full view of the excavation work at the tel. She said: "Mr. Wood and — and you — are not forbidden to spend time at the tel. In fact, you're expected to observe the work. The Druse are careless, at best. They don't have the interest we do. Which is only natural."

Ahmed drew a deep breath and moved forward. She fell in beside him.

"I'll keep off the subject of personalities," Ahmed said. "Tell me, have any really worthwhile things been uncovered as yet?"

Her agitation, instead of going away, seemed to increase. "That depends on what you mean by worthwhile. If we've found any gold, jewels, or — or treasures, the answer is no. The discoveries have been very rewarding, however."

"For the expedition on the whole?"

"Of course." Then she shot him a

111

sharp, sideward glance.

He said: "Everything goes into the pot. Everyone who discovers anything turns it in?"

She stopped again. Her agitation was so great now that her breasts rose and fell, tightening against the khaki shirt she wore, then releasing it into folds.

"There's nothing to those rumors. No member of this expedition has found anything . . . anything valuable that was not revealed to the others."

"But A. D. Hill was murdered yesterday morning."

"Not here! What Mr. Hill did on his own time is no concern of mine. Or anyone in this camp." Her voice became sharp. "I am an Israeli, Mr. Fosse. I am exceedingly proud of my homeland, even if it is an adopted one. I love Israel and everything in it. I love its people, its way of life. But I am not so naïve as to believe that every country is perfect, that all people are perfect. We have crime in Israel; there are criminals. We are a new country, a new people. Our country was born in misery and blood. There are dissident elements in it, enemies without. We have made mistakes, but so have others. Mr. Hill was murdered. Israeli police have verified that. They have not said, however, that his murder was committed by anyone in this expedition. They have not said that the cause of the murder came from here — from one of us." She exhaled heavily, trying to stem her agitation. "He might have been killed by robbers."

"Of course," agreed Ahmed. He added thinly: "You are a very patriotic citizen of Israel, Miss Caxton."

"What's wrong with that?" she asked angrily. "Just because you ... " She caught herself and winced. "I'm sorry. We Jews who've suffered so much are too quick to offend, perhaps because we've been offended against so much and so long. I was going to throw your mixed parentage in your face. Believe me, Mr. Fosse, I apologize most humbly."

"It doesn't bother me, Miss Carolyn."

"It does — I know it does."

He shook his head. "I like it. Gives me an out. I can hate Frenchmen when I want to, because I'm an Egyptian. When I get angry at Egyptians and Arabs, I take refuge in the fact that I'm a Frenchman. It's convenient."

She regarded him sceptically, but he nodded and turned toward the tel.

The glint of sunlight upon glass flicked across his eyes. Ahmed turned to the left, toward the rising slope of rocks.

Carolyn exclaimed, "There's someone over there with a pair of field glasses."

"I think I'll take a look!"

"No! Please . . . "

She was so earnest that Ahmed's eyes narrowed. "It could be one of our own people."

"The Druse have no glasses and everyone else is in the camp."

"It could be the police."

"They wouldn't spy."

"Then the Israeli police are very different. A French policeman would not only spy, he would lay traps and bait them. So would American police . . . I am told. So would Egyptian police." He hesitated. "When in Israel, do as the Israelis do."

She half smiled, although it was forced. "You paraphrased that very neatly. It should be Rome — "

"And the Romans. Thank you, Miss

Caxton. I'll get to my sherds and parchment now."

He left her and headed back for the camp.

He was turning toward the building containing his workroom when he glanced toward the area of the Druse. Sheik Yussuf was taking it easy in his canvas folding chair.

Ahmed went toward him.

"Allah is merciful," exclaimed the sheik as Ahmed came up. "The effendi is well today?"

"I'm well. Look, Yussuf, I want a gun."

"Mohammed be damned," exclaimed the sheik in Arabic, then caught himself. "A gun, Effendi? There are no guns here, none within miles that I know of."

"I'll bet there are," said Ahmed harshly. "That is, if Mohammed allows you to bet. I'll bet a hundred there's at least one revolver in this camp and I'll bet another hundred dollars you know where to put your hands on it."

The sheik squinted at Ahmed. "You're talking about two hundred American dollars as if you had them."

"I have."

"You have them *on* you?"

Ahmed reached into his pocket and brought out a thin sheaf of three bills. Each one was a hundred. He skimmed off one of the bills.

"No, no," said Sheik Yussuf. "Do not put it away. We will talk. But not of wagering, Effendi. We will discuss business, the business of buying and selling merchandise. Suppose I did have — or know of — a gun. Would you be willing to pay those three hundred dollars for it?"

"Two hundred."

"Three . . . and no questions asked."

Ahmed dropped the bills in the sheik's hands. Sheik Yussuf straightened them out, examined each bill on both sides. "They seem genuine, although how would a poor Druse know, who has never seen American hundred-dollar bills?"

"You've seen them," snapped Ahmed. "That poor Druse routine's for your people."

Sheik Yussuf chuckled. "I do it well, do I not?"

"No."

Yussuf sighed. "Every thespian faces critics. It has come to a sorry pass, however, when a man who was a *fellah* only yesterday has three hundred-dollar bills. The lady pays?"

"I didn't get that money from her."

"It is too bad. You are a handsome man, and you seem to possess a vitality that is lacking in some men I know . . . "

"The gun, Sheik."

"Ah yes, our business transaction is uncompleted. Return to me in an hour and perhaps I will have the, ah, the merchandise you seek."

"I want it now."

"You are a strong one, Ahmed. Such vitality . . . "

"The gun!"

The sheik reached into his burnoose and produced a flat .32 automatic. He sent a quick look around, leaned forward. Ahmed took the automatic from him and thrust it into his pocket.

"It is loaded, too," murmured the sheik, "although we did not bargain for the cartridges . . . "

"Enough's enough."

"Quite. I will not haggle. But tell me

117

something, Effendi. You — you have mates of these fine American specimens of engraving?"

"Why?"

"I am a businessman. Things can be bought, things can be sold. Things that are not in the village bazaars, perhaps."

"Such as?"

"How should I know? I am a merchant. I sell. You are the customer — the buyer. If you require any merchandise — and you have the cash to pay for it — perhaps we can do business."

"I'll keep it in mind."

"Intangibles are bought and sold also. Information is an intangible . . . "

"I've had it in mind. I want no information. Yes, I do. Who's up there in the hills?"

The sheik smiled blandly. "I should charge you for that, but you would probably be angry then. I'll throw it in with the — the sale I have just made. It's probably why you bought the gun, anyway. And you were quite right to buy it, Effendi. Because the men up there have guns of their own and I have an idea that they would not hesitate to shoot you."

"Men?"

"There are two. Although sometimes there is only one and now and then there have been even three. For short periods. The third one is a Greek and he is rather fat. He does not like the sun too much. For an agreed price, I will furnish the names of the men. Alas, I do not have them yet, for my Druse are somewhat chary of them, since those aliens do have firearms and my poor people are forbidden by law to carry them."

"You wouldn't, of course, break the laws of Israel?"

"Not the laws of Israel, Effendi. But consider, my father was a ruler of this land, as was his father and his father's father to the forty-second generation. My father and his fathers before him made laws for this land. The Jews have been here but a speck of time."

"They were here before your people."

"Ah, were they? You are referring to the time of David and Solomon. But who was here before there was a Jewish people? Before Abraham roamed south from Ur, who lived in this land of Canaan? Arabs, Effendi, my people and your mother's. Arabs were here from the dawn of civilization. The Hebrews came and they went. So did the Egyptians, the Hittites, the Chaldeans. Before they were here, there were Arabs. It is the history of my people. There were Druse here when man lived in caves, in holes in the ground. It was my ancestors who domesticated the animals, who chipped knives from the native rock, who learned how to reap the wild grain and plant it again. Be proud of your mother's blood, Effendi."

"The Greeks had a wonderful civilization twenty-five hundred years ago," said Ahmed. "They fell before a stronger people. For one reason, Sheik Yussuf. Too much education. It got to the point where every farmer spouted philosophy. When people get that smart they stop fighting and people who're willing to fight lick them . . ."

Sheik Yussuf chuckled. "Well put, Effendi. I gave up civilization myself. I gave up education and the so-called finer things of life and I don't believe I was any happier then than I am now. I lead the simple life and I like it."

Ahmed nodded and walked off.

He turned east out of the camp. A half mile and he entered a wadi that ran roughly north and south. The camp was out of sight from the bottom of the wadi and he walked along swiftly. After a while the wadi turned west, but it became shallower and he walked bent over. Soon he had to stop.

On his hands and knees he crawled to the lip of the wadi.

The tel was almost a half mile to the north, slightly to the east. On the left, the ground began to rise no more than a hundred feet from where the wadi rose and became a mass of rubble and rocks that blended into the rough, rising hillside, which in turn became a ridge of high and rugged crags.

Ahmed studied the rough terrain. As nearly as he could determine the general area from where the flash of light had come was a quarter mile to the west and slightly north of where he now crouched.

There was plenty of shelter between him and the hidden watchers. The trouble was that the shelter was also excellent for the men with the field glasses — men who were armed and quite willing to kill.

Ahmed, however, had started on a mission and the thought never occurred to him to turn back. If there had been a dozen men on the hillside he would still have persisted, having once started his campaign.

He rose to his knees, then bent over, came to his feet. He ran swiftly out of the remains of the wadi, for the shelter of a clump of boulders. He paused behind the boulders for a moment, picked out a patch of salt bushes, sped to them and from them to an outcropping of basalt rock. He paused there only long enough to survey the roughening terrain, then went on.

In five minutes he was in the general area from which the flash of light had come. He crouched behind an outcropping. At his back the hillside rose sharply. It would take an experienced mountaineer to negotiate the terrain at any speed. An amateur might climb it slowly and painfully and at considerable risk.

Ahmed doubted if his quarry were

experienced mountaineers. They had impressed him as city men. Their retreat therefore would have to be to the west, where the terrain as it encircled the tel was gentler.

Yes!

He saw them, then — two men, keeping close to the rough ground, slinking along to the west. They were fully a quarter of a mile from where Ahmed had taken shelter. They were at the edge of the flat desert with easy access to it.

They probably had a car parked in the area and could reach the paved road a mile or so to the north without too much difficulty.

They were moving quickly and Ahmed knew that if he came out in the open and they saw him that they could outdistance him. Or stand in the open and shoot him down as he approached them.

Had they seen him come out of the wadi?

Ahmed wondered. He searched for the wadi from his present position and saw that it was impossible to locate it from here. If the Italians had been looking in that direction they might have seen him flit from cover to cover. But if they had seen him coming in that manner, would they have fled? They were two to one. They were not cowards, in spite of their defeat by him the day before.

No, they had left of their own volition. They had completed their spying for the day.

Stretching his back muscles, cramped from much crouching, Ahmed looked around. He walked erect for a few minutes, knowing that he would not be seen from the tel, or if he were seen, would not be recognized.

Suddenly he saw something on the ground and scooped it up. It was a half-smoked cigarette butt that had been flipped away. By a recent smoker. He searched the ground quickly and saw footprints in a patch of sand, then found the observation post recently vacated by the spies.

It was a boulder some three feet tall. Sand surrounded it and the boulder was a convenient height on which to rest elbows and watch with field glasses. Other cigarette butts were scattered about — nine altogether — as were empty beer bottles. The men had made no attempt to hide their presence.

From the vantage point, Ahmed studied the tel. With the naked eye he could see the workers going into the trenches, coming out. The distance was too far to identify anyone, but you could tell pretty well what the workers were doing. Even as he looked he saw a woman with a helmet come out of a trench. Carolyn Caxton, although he could not recognize her features.

Ahmed turned after a while and began studying the rocky terrain that sloped into rugged cliffs to the summit of the ridge some five or six hundred feet from the floor of the valley. It was not an especially high mountain or an impressive one, except for the rockiness of it.

He had never been at the Dead Sea cliffs, but he had read — and studied — every book that had been published in recent years on the Qumran Dead Sea scrolls and it struck him that this country was not too dissimilar. There was no body of water nearby, but the wadi had apparently been a stream of some size at one time. The water had perhaps come from a mountainside spring, had gushed down the hill and formed the wadi. At some indeterminate time the spring had dried up and the wadi had become dry sand, instead of a river or stream.

Within the time of civilized man, unless there was another source of water below, the spring here had possibly made possible the village below. When the water had dried up, the village had been evacuated. Sand and time had formed the tel.

There was another possibility regarding the water supply. In his brief survey of the tel early that morning he had noted the section of wall. In ancient times the village had been walled. An attacker or besieger could have concluded that the spring that formed the stream supported the walled town. By diverting the stream, or choking up the source of it, the walled town would be waterless. The besieged inhabitants would die of thirst or be forced to surrender.

Pompey's invasion of this land in 67 B.C. had been an easy one. He had fought few battles, the might of his legions having overawed the populace. In the early imperial days, Vespasian, then his son Titus, had almost destroyed the entire Jewish population, as a result of the revolt that ended in the siege of Jerusalem, in which a million Jews had lost their lives.

Yet the Jews had sprung up again, and again in 132 A.D. they had risen to revolt. Bar Kochba, the last of the Messiahs, had fought a three-year war against the Roman masters. His defeat had resulted in the final dispersion of the Jews.

Jerusalem had been rebuilt by Hadrian, but as a Roman city. The country remained to the Romans and the Arabs, and after the rise of Mohammedanism in the seventh century, the Jews only rarely filtered back into the land, and then as unwanted residents of a land that was no longer Jewish.

That condition had prevailed until the nineteenth century when a weakening Turkey could no longer hold its provinces. Awakening Zionism had brought Jews back to the land that had once been theirs. World War I had brought them relief from the Turks, but only increased their desire for a homeland. The British mandate had not encouraged them in their ambitions, but Jews streamed into the country. And then World War II and after it the bloody War of Independence, from which the lost people had finally wrested a country, a country much cut up and only partially theirs, but still their country.

A nation rich in history and tradition. A monotheistic land, to which the One God had first brought his chosen people. The country in which Jesus had been born, where He had lived and died.

Only a few miles from where Ahmed Fosse, the Unbeliever, now stood.

The man who called himself Ahmed Fosse had no university degrees, but he had educated himself in history and archaeology. He had studied the books, and he had evaluated them. He had made his own decisions without benefit of teachers. His field experience was limited, but in his years of study he had given his chosen profession much, much thought.

What happens when an army is defeated, routed on the field of battle? The defeated soldiers invariably panic, throw away their weapons, and run blindly. Pursurers catch them, kill them.

But always in a rout and panic, there are survivors.

In modern warfare, when a town or city was bombed to extinction, there were always a few survivors. In ancient times, when a city was stormed and sacked, the entire population was frequently exterminated. Yet even then there were survivors. There was never total extinction. Josephus himself had written of his experiences during the seven-month siege of Jetapata.

Joseph, as the leader of the Jewish army, had made a valiant defense against the attacking Romans. Day by day, he had seen his people die from hurled missiles, from wounds received on the walls, eventually from starvation. He had still not capitulated. Finally, when the storming of the city was accomplished, Joseph, with forty-one followers, had taken refuge in a room constructed off and at the bottom of a city well. For days he and the survivors had hidden in this room, while above them the Romans depopulated the city. Finally, the survivors had come to a decision. They would kill each other in turn, the last man to die by his own sword.

One by one the survivors had died until there remained only Josephus and one soldier. The soldier chose death, but Josephus had come to a decision. Death ended everything. He did not believe that he had been born to die by his own hand. He came out of the well, surrendered to the Romans, and was brought before the legate Vespasian. The Roman general treated him well and Josephus made an astonishing prediciton, that Vespasian would one day — not too far off — become emperor of Rome.

Within a year the prediction was fact. Josephus, still with the Romans, was prized by the emperor's son, Titus, and went with him to the siege of Jerusalem.

The Jews condemned him as a traitor, but Josephus was cherished by Titus and after the campaigns went to live with the Romans of the Tiber. He was the friend and confidant of three emperors, Vespasian, Titus, and the latter's brother, Domitian. He lived to a ripe old age and wrote the great epic of his people. He died in the fullness of his years and to him the ancient as well as the modern world is indebted for the history of the Jews, the wars of the Jews against the Romans, and the first historical reference to Jesus Christ.

Ahmed Fosse thought of the writings of Josephus as he regarded the rising mountain ahead of him. In the great Josephus tome that he had studied for some weeks, there had been many illustrations of Jews living in caves in cliffs, of their capture by Romans, who climbed from below, who were lowered by ropes from above. There were many caves in this land.

The scrolls in the Dead Sea area had been found in caves near the Qumran communal dwellings of the Essene sects. Archaeologists deduced that the scrolls had been hidden when the community was threatened by approaching Roman armies. They had themselves died or been dispersed and the scrolls had remained in the caves for upward of nineteen hundred years.

The ancient tel on the valley below had once been the Jewish town of Beth-el-Arkam. So Holterman believed, at least. It had been a walled town and could have been destroyed during the Roman campaigns of Vespasian or Titus or possibly during the later campaigns of Hadrian.

Nothing much had been uncovered by the North Shore University archaeological team in almost two years of excavations. That much Ahmed had already learned.

Yet A. D. Hill had gasped out with his last breath: "greatest discovery . . . ever made by man." Hints and rumors picked up during his short stay had impressed Ahmed with a similar feeling. And last night the drunken Miller Wood had mouthed a verification. Wood had been perhaps closest to A. D. Hill, having shared sleeping and working quarters with him. He had perhaps even spied on him.

If A. D. Hill had unearthed any treasure, Wood was possibly the man best able to know of it.

Had Hill found his treasure in the diggings below . . . or up here somewhere on the rugged face of the mountain?

A man fleeing the doomed village below could well hide his prize up here

— especially if he had lived long in this country and knew every rock and cranny.

One miserable human being would not be sought too long by conquerors.

12

AHMED had already faced the wrath of Dr. Sando, the nominal head of the North Shore University Expedition. It was time he made himself seen and busied himself with his work. It was time he began earning his salary and keep.

It was nearing noon when he entered the workroom, which he shared with Miller Wood.

Wood glowered at him, but made no comment. He sat at his desk, smoking a cigarette. Whether he had done any work, Ahmed did not know. He looked rocky, even this late in the morning.

Ahmed sat down at his desk and began sorting out pieces of parchment. After a half hour's work, a Druse appeared.

"Lunch is ready," he announced in English.

Wood grimaced. The thought of food was apparently repugnant to him. Ahmed, however, rose and went to the building

134

where the members of the expedition ate their meals.

Jacqueline Dietrich was already at the table.

"And where have *you* been all morning? I stopped in at your place and Wood said you were out making like an archaeologist."

"So?"

"You weren't at the digs, buddy-boy. I looked for you there, too."

"I was probably sneaking a smoke behind a fence," replied Ahmed, "or perhaps I was behind a rock, doing my daily duty."

"There's no reason to get vulgar," snapped the big woman. "I was merely trying to caution you that the big, ah . . . " She suddenly smiled brightly as Dr. Sando entered. "Well, Doctor, I trust your appetite's good?"

"There's nothing wrong with it," retorted Sando. He shot a quick glance at Ahmed, then nodded. "Making headway, Fosshay?"

"I'm trying to," replied Ahmed carefully. "I think I'm beginning to pick up a few of Hill's threads."

"Good. The department's been behind for weeks and you and Wood have got to work a little harder — and longer — to catch up."

Ahmed nodded.

Carolyn Caxton entered and sat down opposite Ahmed. Wood remained absent, however.

"You look peaked, Doll," observed Jacqueline. "You've been out in the sun all morning. It's me for the shade when that sun gets hot enough to curl your eyebrows."

"It isn't hot today," remarked Dr. Sando. "It doesn't get really hot in Israel." His eyes flicked to Ahmed. "The Valley of the Kings, that's where you get real heat. Eh, Mr. Fosshay?"

"Being a native of Egypt, I'm acclimated to heat."

Alice Holterman entered the dining room. "Mind if I join you?" she asked of the table at large. "Charles has a headache and is taking a nap."

Dr. Sando leaped to this feet. He started to pull out a chair beside his own place, but Alice was already moving to a place opposite Ahmed.

"What are you having for lunch?" she asked.

Jacqueline snorted. "Mutton, what else? Sometimes it's lamb, but *I* never can tell the difference. Their lambs get old very early, it seems to me. You know, back in Chicago, I never eat mutton."

"Neither do I," retorted Alice Holterman. "This is a disagreeable country. I dislike the heat, I don't like the food, I don't care for the people." She smiled sweetly at Carolyn Caxton. "No offense, my dear. You're not a native."

"I'm a Jew," said Carolyn warmly. "I love my country."

"Is it really your country, my dear? I understood that you were brought here by your foster parents when you were quite young."

"That is right, but I still feel — "

"Not only that," persisted Alice Holterman, "but the story, as it was told to me, was that you are not even sure if you are Jewish."

"I am," said Carolyn fiercely. "I know it. I — I *feel* it."

"Oh, come now! How can one feel Jewish any more than one can feel

English, German or . . . or Egyptian?"

She turned abruptly to Ahmed Fosse. "Are they keeping you busy, Mr. Fosse?" she asked brightly.

He shrugged. "I'm feeling my way."

"That's good. We're a small family group here. We have no secrets from one another. What one person does affects everyone else. Ugh! Where's that waiter? This meat tastes like an Arab's boiled slipper . . . "

"Abu!" yelled Dr. Sando.

A Druse came quickly through the door.

Alice Holterman picked up her plate. "Take this away. It smells."

"Madam not like?" asked the waiter anxiously.

"You eat it," snapped Alice Holterman. "Open a can for me. American can, understand?"

"Understand, sure. Beans?"

"You fool," exclaimed Dr. Sando. "There are things besides beans in cans. There's chicken, crabmeat, ham — all sorts of things."

"Like chicken, Madam?"

"If it's from a can, yes. I don't want

any of your Arab chicken. It's stringy and tastes . . . Where are you going, Mr. Fosse?"

Ahmed had pushed back his chair and risen to his feet. "I'm through eating. Excuse me, please."

"You disapprove, Mr. Fosse?"

"Of course not. As you reminded me before, it's my first day on the job and I've got a lot of work to catch up on." He bowed to her, turned and nodded to Dr. Sando.

He went out.

It was the custom, he knew, from the day before, for the camp to indulge in a two-hour rest at noon. The Druse required it, would not work without it, in fact, and the members of the expedition themselves like it.

No one would expect him to be at work during the noon period, so he went to the quarters he shared with Miller Wood.

He found Wood sitting on his cot. The archaeologist got to his feet and came toward him. He extended his hand. "I've got to quit the booze, Fosse," he said. "I'm a bastard when I'm drunk and worse the morning after. I apologize."

Ahmed took the hand.

"All right?" asked Wood.

Ahmed nodded.

"I wasn't up to lunch, but the whiskey's wearing off and I'll probably be back to normal after I sleep for a couple of hours. I feel better now that there's no hard feelings between us."

"I think I'll work," said Ahmed, "and now that we're talking, I want to ask you about the work. What's expected of me?"

Wood grimaced. "That's a good question. Wish I could answer it. Sando's looking for gold mummies, statues, ornaments like they found in King Tut's tomb." Wood chuckled. "You knew he was with Breasted, didn't you?"

"I've read his history."

"The one he wrote himself? Hell, he gave himself all the best of it. Confidentially, I've heard that he was an office boy, or ran errands for Breasted. But he outlived the King Tut man, which was only natural, since he was less than half his age and he's made the most of his association."

"What's your opinion of Holterman?"

"My opinion?" Wood shook his head. "I thought we'd made up."

"We have."

"Then don't put me on a spot, asking about everybody in the expedition. You know the score. You've read Sando's books and I'm sure you've read Holterman's."

"I have. But he hasn't published one since 1959. That was before he decided on the Tel Mas expedition. What do you think Holterman's after here?"

"He hasn't confided in me. That's one difference between him and Sando. Sando wants gold, jewels, things worth money. Holterman's got money. Mmm, I'd say he's after glory. Yeah, fame. He hasn't quite found it, in spite of the money. Breasted discovered King Tut's tomb and his fame exploded around the world. Holterman knew Breasted, since they're both from Chicago and I think he'd like what Breasted had." Wood shook his head. "He won't find it here." A sudden cloud flitted across his features. "At least, I don't think so."

He crossed to his cot and sat down.

Ahmed said: "You and A. D. Hill were close friends, were you not?"

Wood looked up. "What made you ask that question?"

"No particular reason. I've stepped into his shoes and I'm trying to get a picture of him in my mind. Might help me in my work."

"You and A. D. Hill are about as different as any two men could be in all this world." Wood smiled reminiscently. "Hill was a woman's club man. He liked to give lectures before groups of five hundred and a thousand women and he could spot the prettiest one from the platform and he wined and dined them. He was a great man on a couch. As far as I knew, he'd never been married. He lived at a fancy club in Chicago. He made good money on the platform, but he had to do a certain amount of work in the field, or he couldn't get lecture bookings. What he knew about languages or archaeology you could stick in your ear. But he could talk, man, he could talk! The women on his circuit didn't know if he found King Tut's tomb, or if he was Lawrence of Arabia. He could tell them either one and they'd believe him, too."

He chuckled. "Only similarity between

you and him, Fosse, is that Alice Holterman went for him, too. Little Jacqueline took it upon herself to tell me this morning that you'd been with the Missy last night."

"Apparently the only one who doesn't know that yet is her husband," Ahmed said harshly.

Wood held up a cautioning index finger. "Don't be sure that he doesn't know. Holterman doesn't miss much around here. He may give you the impression that his mind's on lofty things all the time, but uh-uh. I've caught him looking at the little Jewish girl." He made a raucous sound with his lips.

"She's a shicksa, Little Carolyn. I've tried to give her a tumble, but she's seen the way Mr. Money looks at her. She likes it." He threw himself backward on his cot and, staring at the ceiling, went on.

"Little Carolyn, Big Jacqueline. There's a pair for you. Jackie girl can't even get the Druse to give her a rumble and Little Carolyn, that any of the men'd give their life savings for, won't even say hello unless you twist her arm. S'tough, Fosse. That's why I drink." He groaned.

"Why'd I have to mention that? Let me get some sleep, Fosse. We'll talk tonight, all you want."

Ahmed went to the workroom. He came to a decision and began removing everything he had inherited from A. D. Hill. He piled the sherds on the floor; the scraps of papyrus and vellum he deposited against the wall.

The desk cleared finally, he found cleaning rags and wiped the desk free of dust and dirt. Then he went to Wood's table and studied the litter on it.

There was a fairly clear spot in the center and here Wood had been matching together pieces of parchment. He had put together a rough rectangle some three by seven inches in area, including perhaps twenty separate pieces. They seemed to match reasonably well, although Ahmed thought he was taking a chance on a couple of pieces.

The writing on the parchment was faded, but reasonably legible, especially with a magnifying glass. The glass was on the table and Ahmed examined the patchwork of pieces.

The writing was Aramaic and seemed

to be a bill of sale for a farm and its livestock. Fourteen sheep, three with lambs, a bullock, an ass, and three birds. What kind of fowl the parchment did not indicate.

Ahmed shook his head. Thirty thousand baked clay tablets had been discovered in the Hittite at Nineveh. Twenty-nine thousand of them recorded household transactions of an ancient court and contained nothing that would add to the knowledge of the ancient world or the modern. If the Lake Shore expedition could find no more than ancient bills of sale or priestly rituals, the money for the expedition could have served a more useful purpose — even in Chicago, where the money had been earned in the first place.

He left Wood's desk and went to the long table. His eyes skimmed over the litter and picked out the basalt stele. He carried it to his table and, propping it up, studied it with a magnifying glass. It was difficult to read, for the rock had been worn through the ages. Pieces had been chipped from it and there were holes and gaps in the carvings.

That it was an official edict, Ahmed was aware. But the precise message was difficult to decipher. As was the issuer of the edict. The fragment of a word suddenly became focused under Ahmed's eye ... A chip was missing immediately afterward. It was large enough to have contained the letters s-h Iskander.

That was a Greek proper name. Alexander had divided his conquered realms on his deathbed. His generals and companions (one of whom may have poisoned him) had been given kingdoms. The one who had been given Judea had ruled it for years and he had issued edicts and laws. The stele had been carved to his orders and placed in one of the towns.

That proved one thing. That Beth-el-Arkam had been a town of some consequence as far back as Alexander's time, or the time of Alexander's successor.

The Greeks had held a firm grip on their holdings. The Greek Ptolemy dynasty in Egypt had lasted until Caesar's time and Greeks had ruled almost continuously in Judah and Israel until the Romans came under Pompey. There had been one gap of a few years, when the

Maccabeans had driven the Greeks out of the Holy Land. But the Maccabeans had gone the way of other Hebrew rebels. The Greeks returned and imposed a harsher rule upon the Jews.

By comparison, Roman rule had been benevolent, until the final days of the doomed people, when they had been destroyed. Even then, they had brought it upon themselves.

The Jews had been a turbulent people in ancient times. That character trait had never died out, Ahmed mused.

Carolyn Caxton had shown it, during the lunch period that day.

Miller Wood came in and saw Ahmed studying the basalt stele.

"That's a jigsaw puzzle," he observed. "I had a crack at it and so did Don Hill. It's no Rosetta stone, that's for sure. Greek, the Jews wouldn't have been able to read it. They never did take to the language." He came over and looked down at the stele. "You're wasting your time with it."

Ahmed shrugged. "I need the practice."

"I'll give you something better to practice on." Wood went to his table, stooped, and took out an enameled steel box from underneath. He brought it to Ahmed's desk and set it down.

The box was unlocked and he raised the lid. Reaching in with both hands he brought out a small scroll. He set it down gingerly before Ahmed and helped him smooth it out, placing weights on the corners.

The scroll was of parchment, and although there were three missing corners and a hole in the center almost an inch in diameter, the parchment was surprisingly clear and the ancient writing black and bold.

"I wouldn't admit this to Holterman, or even Sando, but my Aramaic leaves a lot to the imagination. I don't know the language. I've had to fake with the big boys. Hill read it, but he wasn't sure of some of the words and he was a lot better with Aramaic than I am. Hebrew, yes, even third-century B.C. Hebrew, *that* I can read. But Aramaic, uh-uh. I know it like you know pig-Latin, of which I'm sure you've never heard."

Ahmed scanned the parchment.

Wood stood beside him, waiting for

Ahmed's comments.

Ahmed finally shook his head. "Perhaps it isn't your Aramaic that's at fault. I think the fault was with this writer. He couldn't write Aramaic very well, probably didn't understand the language too well. About two-thirds of it is Aramaic, the rest Hebrew. And the Aramaic's bad Aramaic. Words are mispelled, misused."

"Show me."

Ahmed picked out a line. " . . . 'The caravan will bring you fourteen bales of straw.' . . . But 'straw' can't be the word. Nobody would send straw by a caravan. Mmm, I wonder if he meant to write 'straw cloth'. No, that couldn't be." He frowned. He skimmed through a few sentences, then nodded quickly.

"The merchandise was coming from Persia, to which it had been brought from the East. China, possibly. Silken cloth. The word that reads 'straw' is unfamiliar to a scribe who could write neither Aramaic or Hebrew very well. Silk was not a common article during the period in which this was written and it may have had a vernacular word among merchants and traders that was close to the Aramaic straw."

"Then the letter was from one merchant to another?"

Ahmed shrugged. "A merchant in Persia, possibly a transplanted Jew to a Jew living here at Beth-el-Arkam. This was on the old caravan route from the East. Although I imagine it was more a stopping place than a destination for the caravans. They would have been traveling to the coastal cities, or even Jerusalem."

"Not Jerusalem. There was no Jerusalem at that time."

Ahmed looked up at Miller Wood. "You've dated the parchment?"

"Old Holterman gave it the Carbon-14 treatment. Went to Jerusalem himself with it. Came back, said 110 A.D. give or take twenty years."

"During which there was no Jerusalem," observed Ahmed. "Holterman's seen this, then?"

"Of course. Don't confuse me with Donny Hill." Miller Wood exclaimed at the slip of the tongue. "Sorry, old man. That temper's going to get me yet." He cleared his throat, forced a smile. "Holterman gives me my salary

— indirectly, yes — but I'm working for him. I live on my pay. I don't make my living lecturing, or . . . or otherwise."

He stabbed down at the parchment. "That's the best piece we've found to date. It's not worth much, but we've just scraped the edges of the tel. The new trench is promising. It's gone through a heavy stone wall that seems to have been a temple or house of an official. We ought to be finding a few things in the next day or two . . . if the Druse don't slip them out under our noses. Thieves, the lot of them. They take your pay, steal everything they can get away with, and smuggle it to Haifa, or as far away as Jerusalem. The Bedouins are their kissing-cousins and those boys know the markets for artifacts."

"You think the sheik is selling things?"

Wood grimaced. "Don't let that boy fool you. He's as slippery as they come. By the way, did you know he's a Cambridge man? Yeah, educated, but he likes to act the poor, downtrodden native Druse. He whined to me once how he longed to get a few sheep and roam these hills with them. Hell, the Druse would be more at

151

home in a London West End club than with a flock of sheep."

He removed the weights from the scroll, permitted it to spring back into its natural roll, and putting it back into the enameled box, carried it off.

13

MILLER WOOD was sober at the dinner table. He ate sparingly, cautiously, and refused to be goaded by Jacqueline Dietrich. There was no stopping the irrepressible Amazon.

"The fleshpots of Nazareth, Mr. Wood?" she asked with hoarse sweetness. "Or is it Tiberias tonight?" She turned her attention to Ahmed. "Have you told him about the Seven Veils girl, Mr. Fosse? Mmm, what's her name? The one who chopped off John the Baptist's head? Salami, isn't it?"

Dr. Sando, late as usual, came in and Jacqueline desisted. The nominal head of the expedition looked around the table.

"Missed you at lunch, Wood," he said crisply. "Too much sun?"

"Or something," put in Jacqueline.

"Dr. Sando," Carolyn said suddenly, "would it be all right if I borrowed one of the jeeps this evening? I find there are some things I need and I thought I would run into Nazareth."

"Alone?"

"I'm not afraid. It's only ten miles."

"I'll go with you, Doll," Jacqueline offered. "Maybe you and I can find us a couple of boy friends."

"No," cried Carolyn. "I — I want to go alone."

"I'd rather you didn't," said Sando. His eyes went to Wood, then continued on to Ahmed. "Feel up to it, Fossay?"

"I offered," said Jacqueline, tartly.

"I think a man should take her," replied Sando firmly. "I'd take you myself, Miss Caxton, but Mr. Holterman has asked me to visit with him this evening."

"I'll take her," said Ahmed quietly.

His eyes went across the table to Jacqueline and he blinked at the venom he saw there.

"You don't mind, Mr. Fosse?" asked Carolyn quietly. "I won't be long. I — I'm ready as soon as you are."

"That's now." Ahmed pushed back his chair.

"Have fun," said Jacqueline. "Perhaps Mr. Wood can tell you where he was last night. The liquor there is excellent, and — "

"Miss Dietrich!" snapped Dr. Sando. "You go too far at times."

"Well!" said Jacqueline. "Excuse *me*."

Carolyn went swiftly through the door. Ahmed followed. Outside, it was still twilight. A jeep stood nearby.

"Can you drive?" asked Carolyn.

"I guess I can manage, although I've never tried a jeep." Ahmed climbed into the vehicle, studied the dashboard, and switched on the ignition. Carolyn had gotten in beside him.

He shifted into gear and the jeep sprang forward. The motor was well tuned and there was great power in the little vehicle. The wheel handled as easily as a toy in Ahmed's strong hands.

Carolyn did not speak until Ahmed had turned left onto the Tiberias-Nazareth paved road. "I shouldn't say it," she said then, "but Jacqueline gives me the creeps. She's always putting those big hands on me."

"She's a Lesbian," said Ahmed easily. "If not, she's halfway there. If she could find a man, she'd probably be all right, but she's not exactly a beauty and the man that takes her is going to have to be blind or look worse than she does."

"That's unkind," shuddered Carolyn, "but I — I think you're right. I mean about her being unattractive. My foster mother was not really a beautiful woman, but she had a wonderfully kind personality and at times her face was so filled with — with kindness that I thought she was beautiful."

"I don't know Nazareth," said Ahmed. "You'll have to direct me when we get there."

"I have to buy some — some personal things. I haven't been into the city in more than a month." She looked suddenly at Ahmed. "That's not really true. I mean about not having been in the city in a month. That part of it's true. It's ... needing things badly. I don't need anything. I just wanted to get away from camp for a while."

"Alone?"

Her eyes averted themselves quickly. Ahmed glanced at her. Her face was turned down.

"No," she said. "I thought you might

offer to take me. Dr. Sando stepped in, though." She hesitated. "Were you going to offer to take me?"

"No," replied Ahmed.

She winced under that. "Would you rather go back?"

"We've started for Nazareth, we'll go to Nazareth."

"You don't mind . . . too much?"

Ahmed looked suddenly into the rear-vision mirror. A car was a hundred yards behind the jeep. It had not been there when he had turned onto the pavement.

The car was keeping down to the speed of the jeep. It was a Mercedes Benz.

"Damn," he said.

Carolyn gasped.

"Not you," he said quickly, "the car behind. It's following us."

She looked quickly, turned, and stared at the road behind. "How do you know it's following us?"

"Take my word for it."

"It's a Mercedes Benz," she said. "No one in the expedition has a Mercedes."

"Those are a couple of friends of the late A. D. Donny-boy, Hill."

She turned around and stared at him. "I don't understand."

"We got on the subject this morning," Ahmed said. "You clammed up."

"Clammed up?"

"I picked that up from Miller Wood. He talks Chicagoese. You didn't want to talk about Hill."

"I didn't think it was proper. So soon after his — his death." A little shudder ran through her. "I didn't care very much for him. He was always trying to make, I guess you'd say passes, he was always making passes at me. He caught me once outside and . . . it wasn't pleasant." Then she added hastily, "He kissed me, that's all. But I wasn't in a kissing mood." She looked into the mirror. "They're dropping back."

"They'll catch up when we get to the city. They can outrun this jeep."

"There's a police station in Nazareth, but it's on the other side of the city."

"I saw it yesterday. That's where I left the Mercedes Benz." An ironic twinge twisted the right corner of his mouth. It wasn't a smile, for Ahmed Fosse had not smiled in many years. But it was close to

158

it. He said: "I borrowed the car for a few minutes."

"Borrowed? You mean . . . ?"

"All right, I stole it from them. They gave me a lift, then they got a little rough. So I took their car and let them walk a few miles."

She was silent until the jeep went around a turn and up a low rise. From the top of the rise the lights of Nazareth shimmered in the falling dusk."

"It gets dark earlier in Nazareth," she said then. "The hills on the western side cut off the sun."

"Hold on," said Ahmed. "I'm going to run for it."

He jammed his foot down on the accelerator and the little car zoomed ahead. He took a curve at a speed that threatened to overturn the jeep and then came suddenly upon a slowly driven vehicle ahead. He shot out, endangering a coming car and themselves, then, ahead of the other vehicle, whipped past a few houses and a store or two.

They were in Nazareth then and the narrowness of the streets forced him to cut down his speed. He didn't mind now, since the Mercedes Benz, even if it caught up to them, could not pass them and block their passage.

"Where to?" he asked.

"It's all right now?"

"As long as we keep moving."

She caught his arm. "There's a policeman!"

"I see him."

"Aren't you going to stop?"

He shook his head and the jeep rolled past the Israeli policeman. Carolyn stared at Ahmed.

"You're a strange man. You're not afraid of the men back there, are you?"

He did not reply.

The street they were on seemed to come to a dead end, but as the jeep reached the end, Ahmed saw a narrow lane turning at right angles. He negotiated a turn and could have touched the buildings on his side by reaching out with his hand. The Mercedes Benz, a bigger car, would almost scrape the houses.

The street was rough, cobbled, and the jeep bounced along.

"Oh, I almost forgot," exclaimed Carolyn. "Turn left at the next corner."

He made the turn into a wider street. It was lined with stores.

"This is where I had meant to stop, but if you don't think we should . . . "

He swerved the car to the right and braked it quickly. The Mercedes Benz came around the corner and the driver apparently saw the jeep. The Mercedes shot past the jeep.

The two swarthy men were in the front seat, but Ahmed, searching, was certain that he saw a huddled figure in the rear, someone who did not want to be seen.

Beside him, Carolyn inhaled sharply. "I've seen those men. At Tel Mas. They were talking with . . . " She broke off.

"A. D. Hill?"

"No," she said, "with . . . Mrs. Holterman. It was . . . " She turned away from Ahmed. A sob seemed to be racking her body. Then she stiffened and climbed out of the jeep.

Ahmed rose, took a quick step, made a light spring, and was on the street beside her. She had forced herself under control. For a moment she was stiff, then she said: "Do you mind if I go inside here — for just a moment or two?"

He looked at the building before which they stood. A plaque identified the building in two languages. "This is a Christian church."

"The God of the Christians is also my God," she said simply.

There was a scarf about her throat. She unfastened it, raised the scarf, and draped it over her head. "You . . . you're coming with me?"

Ahmed stared at her. This slip of a girl had caught him unawares. She said: "I don't know if you call him Allah or God. It doesn't matter. I call him Yahweh, but He's the same." She touched his arm lightly.

"It's twenty-five years since I've been in a church," Ahmed said evenly.

"You're not . . . afraid?"

"Afraid?"

He caught her arm in a hard grip, led her to the doors. Near the entrance door, he stopped and read the sign. She read with him, but silently.

"The Church of Joseph, built upon the site of his carpenter shop. It's very old . . . "

"Not that old."

"There was a synagogue here before this was built."

He had released her arm and now stepped ahead of her. He pulled open one of the heavy doors and held it as she entered. He followed her.

It was early evening and there were no services, but in the dim light of the interior Ahmed could see figures scattered about the pews. More than fifty persons were in the church. Many of them were tourists, but there were just as many who were swarthy, with Semitic features. Four or five, from their garb, were obviously Arabs.

Carolyn gave him a quick glance and turned into a pew. She knelt and then focused her attention upon him. She made no sign of the cross, but she bowed her head and he saw her lips move faintly.

Ahmed remained standing in the aisle. His eyes searched the interior. There was a dankness in the air.

Twenty feet away a voice spoke in Arabic. The voice was addressing the stepfather of Jesus, His mother, and then went on in trembling awesomeness to address the Father.

Searching, Ahmed picked out the supplicant. He wore Arab dress and Arab burnoose.

In the pew Carolyn said softly, "Nazareth is a Christian Arab city today." Then she pressed her eyelids shut and was silent again. A long moment passed.

She opened her eyes, smiled faintly at Ahmed, and rose. She touched his arm as she came out of the pew. She held his elbow lightly as they moved to the door.

Outside, she removed the scarf from her head and held it in her hand.

"I don't think I am any less a Jewess for praying in His church," she said quietly.

There was a sharpness in his tone as he said, "Where now?"

Pain flashed across her face. "Back to the camp, I suppose."

"You came here just to pray in a Christian church?"

"No, I didn't ... " Her eyes flicked back to the church. "It doesn't matter."

"You said you had some shopping to do."

"I'm a fool," she said. "Trying to play the other woman's game."

She shook her head. "She looks at them and doesn't say a word, but they know what she wants. I guess you have to be born with that faculty. I wasn't."

"If it's any satisfaction, you're as much of a woman as she is."

"You were with her last night."

"I was with her."

"In Tiberias?" he did not reply and she went on. "Jacqueline talks about it whenever she can. When — when I'm too tired to escape outside. She . . . she goes into detail."

"She's got her eyes on you."

"I know," said Carolyn, shuddering. "It's . . . like a snake watching a mouse. I can feel her hands on me sometimes, even though she's across the room. One night . . . "

She whirled away from him and walked swiftly to the jeep. But she did not climb in. Ahmed approached.

"Keep a club handy." He clenched his right hand. "Or give her one right in the mouth. A few missing teeth will cool her off."

She kept her face averted from him. "There's been no one in the camp I can talk to. Mrs. Holterman . . . she hates my even being in the camp."

He saw her fist come up, dab at her right eye, then the left. He walked around the jeep and got in. He did not start the motor until she had climbed in.

He drove carelessly, his eyes, however, sweeping the sidewalks on both sides. The street lighting was woefully primitive and there were long stretches of dark streets, but there were people on them. Plenty of motor traffic too. Cars of all makes, manufactured in the cities of the world. American cars, Russian, German, Italian. He spotted two Mercedes Benz models, but neither was the car with the swarthy ones.

There wasn't a street, there was scarcely a block in which there was not a church. There were plaques on them, signs in virtually every language.

Many of the pedestrians on the street wore church or monastic garments. There were nuns in black habits and white. Some even wore purple and two were in yellow.

The streets of Nazareth followed the contours of the hillside upon which it had been built. Some ran parallel with the slope of the ground, although not necessarily straight. The cross streets were steep, although at times a driver could not be certain that the streets were cross streets. They frequently seemed to go in curves and circles.

Ahmed drove for ten or fifteen minutes up, down, and across, then gradually followed streets that led down. After a while he found one that seemed to point eastward and he followed it.

It led him to a lower street and this one definitely was familiar. He drove a little faster and they left Nazareth behind them. Carolyn had been long silent. Slumped in her seat, there was an air of listlessness, indifference, about her.

She roused a little when she saw the road ahead. After a moment she turned, looked over her shoulder.

"No," Ahmed said, "they're not following."

She drew a deep breath and exhaled heavily. "That's it," she said. "I'm all right now."

14

THE stone house occupied by the Holtermans dated back to late medieval times. It had apparently been built by a man of substance. It consisted of four large rooms. One Holterman used as an office and workroom. Another he had had furnished as a living room for his wife and himself. Modern European furniture was distributed about it. The other two rooms were bedrooms, for the Holtermans occupied separate bedrooms. There were no kitchen facilities in the house, the cooking being done by Druse Arabs in another building.

The food was brought to the living room and laid out upon one of the two tables.

This evening, Charles Holterman was sitting at one of the tables, writing in a leather-bound day book, or journal, that he always kept when in the field.

Across the room, Alice Holterman toyed with a Parisian magazine, but found little of interest in it. She sent glances across at her husband, saw that he was utterly absorbed in his work. She got her manicure set and began buffing her already buffed nails.

"Charles, my dear," she said finally, "do you mind if I ask you a question?"

"Of course not," replied Holterman automatically. His pen did not even miss a stroke.

"Thank you, love," Alice said, sweetly in the same conversational tone. "Were you as much of a bore twenty years ago as you are today?"

Holterman wrote a complete word before her question penetrated the small part of his brain that was not devoted to his journal work. He raised the fountain pen an inch from the book, but did not reply.

"Shall I repeat the question?" Alice asked.

He put down the pen and finally gave her his full attention. "You're trying to start a fight."

"We haven't had one in quite some time," she replied. "It's something to do. I can't just sit here night after night manicuring my nails."

"Have you been sitting here night after night?"

"I'm here tonight. And I don't like it. I want a divorce."

"We thrashed that out two years ago. There will be no divorce."

"You're awfully sure about that, aren't you?"

"My attorneys in Chicago have the evidence, including the photographs and the negatives. I can't prevent you from divorcing me, but I know you don't want the kind of divorce you can get in Paris, or Mexico or some of the places you've looked into."

"Dear husband," murmured Alice Holterman, "you're so awfully sure of yourself."

"On that subject I am. You like money too well and you won't divorce me unless I give you the kind of money you need."

"You're sure I can't get a man with money?"

"You've tried. Harvey Carlson had the money, but you found out that he didn't want a marriage."

"Harvey Carlson wasn't very much of a man. He was like you, my dear."

Holterman's eyes narrowed. "A man's ardor, or sexual prowess, if you wish, depends very much on the woman, doesn't it?"

She hurled the buffer across the room. It missed him by no more than an inch, but he didn't even blink as he saw it coming directly toward him.

"Damn you," she said venomously.

"Was Don Hill more of a man than I?" Holterman asked evenly.

"Ten times," she cried.

"And the Egyptian?" he pursued. "Are the dark-skinned ones more passionate?"

"You're asking for it," she said ominously.

"Where did you find him? You don't think I swallowed your story that he just happened to come along, immediately after Hill was so conveniently murdered."

She sprang to her feet. "What are you talking about?" she screamed.

"You quarreled with Hill the night before. In Nazareth."

"Your damned spies again! But you're not getting away with this. Accusing me of killing a man is a little too much . . . "

"But you did kill him, didn't you, my dear?"

She strode toward him. "I did not! You're not pinning anything like that on me."

She stopped before him, swaying a little from side to side. His calmness was undisturbed by her passion.

"I'm not trying to pin anything on you. I lied to the police, didn't I? I said you'd been here all night."

"I left him at ten o'clock," she said savagely. "I spent the night driving around."

"If you say so."

She stared at him. "I didn't kill him," she said earnestly. "If your spies followed me all night they'll tell you that."

"They told me that they lost you, but the last they saw of you, you were with him."

"Then they're not infallible, after all." Her composure was returning to her. "They haven't told you about the men from Chicago."

"What men from Chicago?"

"The Italians . . . " An icy smile came to her features. "You didn't spy on Hill when he wasn't with me. You don't know about Hill and the Italians."

"I know that you're not a very good liar. Italians from Chicago!"

"You're stupid, Charles. You're so very smart, but you're still a fool. You've spent millions of dollars digging all over this horrible country. For what? For a pile of broken vases? For a bunch of old bones and stones?"

"I'm an archaeologist."

"Archaeologist, my eye. Your father left you more money than you could count, but one thing he couldn't leave you was the guts to go out on your own and do something worthwhile. So you call yourself an archaeologist and you go around digging up old graves. It sounds so very genteel and cultural back there in Chicago. It impresses the other stuffed shirts at your clubs. It's better than bird-watching."

"You've got fangs for a tongue, Alice. Like a rattlesnake."

"A rattlesnake warns before he strikes and I'm warning you now, Charles. I'm going to make a laughing stock of you before the people you want to impress so much. Your own people."

She started away from him. He watched her. She headed for the door of her bedroom, but before she reached it she stopped. She stood with her back to him for a moment, then she turned.

"Give me the divorce, Charles!"

He shook his head.

"Then get ready for what's going to happen."

Holterman said, "You're playing a game, Alice. You're going to get hurt. More than you've ever been hurt in your life."

"Maybe," she conceded, "but somebody else is going to be hurt too."

"Meaning me?"

"I've said all I'm going to say."

She returned to the divan, plumped herself down, and scooped up the Parisian magazine. Holterman watched her a moment, then turned and picked up his fountain pen. But he did not begin to write.

15

AHMED stopped the jeep in front of the building where the archaeology team had their meals. He switched off the ignition and got out of the jeep.

Carolyn climbed out on the other side. "Good night," she said, and ran into the stone building.

Ahmed remained by the jeep. It was too early to go to sleep and too late to go to the workroom he shared with Miller Wood.

"A walk under the stars, Effendi?" purred the smooth voice of Sheik Yussuf.

He came out from the shadows where he had evidently been standing.

"I'm not an astronomer. The stars mean nothing to me."

The sheik chuckled. "When I was a young man, I raised game birds, Effendi. I had the best fighters in the Jezreel Valley. I trained the birds myself and one thing I learned was that no cock fought well unless he was blooded. I found that this was also true of women. A woman who has been blooded is much better."

"The trouble with spying," said Ahmed Fosse, "is that the spy has to keep his distance and he cannot always be certain of what is actually transpiring. He there fore has to manufacture things so that when he passes on the information his employer will deem it of greater worth than it is and pay him accordingly."

"Touché, Effendi! I will remember it when I dole out the weekly stipend. The Jewish girl is, of course, a nicely filled package. She will make some Jew a good wife and bear him many sons. Alas, I am an Arab."

"So am I," retorted Ahmed.

The sheik chuckled again. "I have given some thought to that. I thought at first, it is a pity, he lives in one world and is not a part of it, then he lives in the other world and is not a part of that either. But then I thought some more and I began to see the advantages. With women, for instance. The Western woman believes in monogamy. Good, you are a Western man. But the Eastern man is a polygamist — when he is a man of substance — so you are an Easterner when it is, ah, more convenient."

"I think I'll get some sleep," Ahmed said.

"My philosophizing does not interest you, Effendi?"

"You've the gift of talk, Effendi Sheik," retorted Ahmed. "It's your stock in trade and you're working at it all the time. Pry, probe, prod. The victim spills things and you pile it up until you can use it."

"But we are friends, Effendi," cried Sheik Yussuf. "We have a gentleman's agreement . . . "

"We have a business agreement."

"Very well, then, I am a merchant and you are a customer. I have things to sell. Tangibles, *intangibles* . . . "

Ahmed's eyes searched the dark eyes of the sheik, but in the dusk could see nothing there. He said: "What intangible have you got to sell?"

"Ah, that is more like it, my friend. You have some of those American engravings with you? The ones of the great patriot, Benjamin Franklin?"

"Suppose I had one or two. What would they buy?"

"One or two? My good wishes, Effendi. But if you had *five* such engravings . . . "

"You do not know anything for which I would pay five hundred dollars."

"Shall we take that stroll under the stars, Effendi?"

Ahmed hesitated, then began walking toward the tel. Yussuf hurried to catch up to him, but did not speak until they were out of earshot of anyone in the last buildings.

Then he said, "I can give you the name of the one who killed A. D. Hill."

"No sale. I'm not interested in a name. I'm not interested in Hercules Petrakis, either."

"The reason he was killed, Effendi . . . *that* is worth something!"

"Hill found something he was trying to sell Petrakis. Petrakis thought he'd get it for nothing. Or the thing Hill was trying to sell wasn't real. Either way, it isn't worth an agorot in Hebrew money."

"You are a difficult man to do business with," complained Yussuf. "You leap to conclusions and once you've got your conclusion nobody can take it away from you. You're wrong, Effendi. Those Italians you were chasing across the mountainside the morning, poof. They didn't kill the effendi Hill. Oh, they probably would have, if someone hadn't beaten them to it. And that article you say Hill was trying to sell to them, if they had it, they would not obviously still be spying here, would they?"

"I've thought of that. Hill hid it."

"Did he?"

"Don't bury it in oratory, Effendi Sheik. What you have to sell is the name of the person who *really* killed Hill."

"Yes."

"And the whereabouts of the article for which Hill was killed."

"No, Effendi. If I had that, I would not be here talking to you. Not for five of those American hundred-dollar bills. Not for five hundred of them."

"The name of the killer isn't worth five hundred dollars. Not to me."

"That is a pity."

"Then we've seen enough of the stars."

The sheik sighed heavily. "I am a Moslem, Effendi, as you are when it is convenient to you. But I am a Moslem *always*. The true Moslem believes that there is but one Allah and that Mohammed is his prophet. But we also accept the Jewish Jesus the Christ as a prophet. And did not Jesus say, after his own townspeople drove him out of Nazareth: 'A prophet is without honor in his own country'? That is my own circumstance. This is my country, but I am without honor in it. You, with a French passport, have more honor here than I have."

"You've been through my things," snapped Ahmed.

"No, no, that miserable cousin of mine, Fuad el Bakka, who cleans up your room found your passport lying on the floor. It was open and he chanced to note that it was issued to you in Paris in 1954. He mentioned it to me this evening."

"There is something wrong in a Frenchman being in Paris?"

"Effendi! I merely mentioned it, that is all."

"You've got something up that burnoose, Sheik. Let's see it."

The sheik turned to Ahmed and held up both hands palms outward, so that

Ahmed could see into the loose sleeves. "See, Effendi?"

"We still have no business transaction."

"The money need not be in your rucksack. The bills are of large denomination and a small packet of them can be carried conveniently."

"In my pocket," snapped Ahmed, "and if I see a Druse hand in the pocket, I'll cut it off."

"You probably would, Effendi. However, I don't believe there is a cousin of mine within, shall we say, a hundred yards who does not also have a knife."

"Do your business with effendi Holterman," said Ahmed. "He's got a million dollars for every hundred I've got. You can get more from him."

"But that is what I have been trying to tell you, Effendi. A prophet is without honor in his own country. The effendi Holterman regards me as a native. He does not talk to Arabs. Not about worthwhile things. You kick Arabs and sometimes you use a whip on them. As a Frenchman and as a, shall we say, executive of the organization, *you* can talk to Holterman about important things. You can sell merchandise to him for a large sum. I, alas, cannot. He would pay me with the kick or the whip."

"What you've got to sell isn't worth much."

"That is the basis of business, Effendi. The seller praises his merchandise, the buyer deprecates it. We negotiate. I will accept four of the engravings."

"Not even one."

For once the sheik hesitated. "We Moslems are fatalist. If it is written in the book there is no use trying to avoid it. Allah has so willed it, but the Franks do not believe that. They purchase insurance in vast sums. Would this not be in the nature of insurance? The, ah, the person has killed once. It may be necessary to kill again and what if you were the chosen one? Would it not be worth something so you can be on your guard to watch the, ah, person?"

"I may not be a believer in Allah," Ahmed said, "but I am an Arab and I, too, am a fatalist. What will be, will be."

"You see," exclaimed Yussuf, "when it becomes convenient for you to be an Arab, you become one. Let us not close our negotiations. Sleep on it, Effendi, and if you dream, dream with the Western half of your subconscious. Dream of the insurance value and tomorrow, perhaps, tomorrow, we shall conclude the deal."

They walked back to the camp. Before Ahmed's quarters, the sheik said, "Sleep well, Effendi — and dream."

Ahmed went inside. Miller Wood was stretched out on his cot, his hands laced under his head. He rolled his head sideward an inch or two.

"How was she?" he asked.

"That seems to be a subject of universal interest," Ahmed said. "I will put an announcement on the bulletin board in the morning."

Miller Wood grinned. "What will it say? That you struck out?"

"Struck out? Ah, baseball! No, the notice will say that I did not go to bat."

Wood chuckled. "Ah well, I never got to first base with her. And Don Hill failed to score." He shook his head. "I believe she's still a virgin, unless the Nazis raped her in one of the concentration camps she was in. Mmm, no, I guess not. She was too young at that time even for the Nazis ... I've always wondered what it would be like to really rape a girl, someone who put up a real fight. I've heard that it can't be done if the girl doesn't want it to be done. What's your opinion, Ahmed? Ever try it with one of your brown girls?"

Ahmed said: "My opinion of rape? I don't think I have an opinion on rape."

San Francisco – 1960

16

THERE were reporters on the Fort Mason docks in San Francisco, California, on the clammy, fog-patched day in June when Billy Krag got off the ferry that had brought him from Alcatraz Island. The reporters swarmed around him.

"How does it feel to be free after twenty-three years?"

"What're your plans, Billy?"

"You never talked at the trial, Billy. It doesn't make any difference now, you've done your time. Did you really do what they said?"

Krag's eyes did not go to any of the faces around him. He was searching for a taxi and he saw a stand ahead. He started for it. The reporters fell in on both sides of him. The bombardment of questions continued.

"How about a statement, Krag?" cried one of them. "My paper gave you the best of it twenty-three years ago. You owe us that."

"Television, Krag! I work for Paul Seuss and he'd like you on his program tonight. A hundred dollars. You can use the money."

Another: "How'd it feel going twenty-three years without a dame?"

A real stingeroo: "You goin' to carve up the next babe that won't put out?"

They had reached the taxis. Krag whipped open one of the doors, climbed in. A reporter tried to get in after him. Krag gave him a violent shove and pulled the door shut.

The cabby reversed, backed up the taxi, reversed and shot it forward. "Where to, Buddy?"

"The St. Francis."

"Not bad for a fella just got off the ferry. Them was reporters. You must be a big shot. I ever hear of you?"

"No," said Krag.

"I read the *True Detective Story* mags all the time. You ever been in one?"

"Just drive," said Krag.

The cabby shrugged. "Okay, okay. I was just makin' conversation. Don't make no difference to me. A fare's a fare."

Twenty-three years ago Krag had met

a girl in the lobby of the St. Francis Hotel, and as nearly as he could now recall, the place looked much the same. The furniture did not seem to have aged, but it had probably been replaced once or twice through the years.

He signed the register *William Krag, San Francisco, California.*

The clerk studied the signature, pursing his lips.

"I can give you an excellent room for, let me see, about fourteen dollars?"

Krag nodded.

"Your luggage?"

"There isn't any."

"I see." A tiny frown creased the clerk's forehead. "I'm afraid I must ask you to pay in advance. House rule ... "

Krag took out two worn ten-dollar bills.

"Fourteen dollars," the clerk said, "plus ten-percent tax ... fifteen dollars and forty cents."

He gave Krag four highly polished silver dollars, plus a half dollar and a dime. Krag recalled the idiosyncrasy of the hotel, which polished all its silver and never gave bills in change if they

189

could do it with silver dollars.

A bellboy took Krag to Room 821. Krag stopped him from opening the windows and performing the rest of his tip-building chores. He tossed him a half dollar. "That's all."

After the bellhop left Krag stepped to the window. Between two tall office buildings he could see the little island in San Francisco Bay.

Alcatraz.

The Rock, which had been Krag's home for nineteen years ... after four years in Folsom.

There was a knock on the door behind Krag. He turned.

"Yes?"

The door was opened by a white-haired man with a seamed face and a sagging body, a body that had once been muscular and well filled but now hung so loose that it was obvious that the spirit inside the flabby skin would not be there too long.

"I followed you from the docks," the white-haired man said. "You wouldn't remember me ... "

"I remember you," said Krag. "Your

name's Crowder. You're a policeman."

"I retired nine years ago." Crowder took an envelope from his breast pocket. "This came to me five months ago, when you went up before the parole board the first time."

The envelope was addressed to William Crowder, Yerba Buena Hotel, Sutter Street, San Francisco, California.

Inside was a sheaf of one-hundred-dollar bills and a slip of paper. On the paper was typed:

Give ten of these bills to William Krag upon his release. Tell him to find himself a deep, dark hole. Keep the other five bills for your trouble.

There was no signature. The envelope bore no return address but was postmarked Chicago.

Krag riffled the bills. "All fifteen are here."

Crowder shrugged. "I've got a pension." He paused. "And about two months . . . maybe three. It was a race — whether you'd get out first, or . . . " He left the sentence unfinished.

Krag put the bills and the note back into the envelope and tossed it to the bed. He turned his back on the former policeman.

Crowder stared at the back of the man who had turned away from him. His tongue came out, moistened his lips.

He said: "Thanks."

Krag turned. "You can take the money or leave it. It doesn't make any difference. Not to me."

Crowder said: "I watched you at the trial. You were eighteen years old and you were like ice all the way. You didn't give a damn if they gave you the cyanide or a season pass to Bay Meadows. You haven't changed." He exhaled heavily.

Abruptly, he turned and walked out of the hotel room, leaving the door open. Krag crossed, closed the door, and returned to the window.

After a while he undressed and took a hot tub bath. He lay in the water until it began to cool, then climbed out and, still wet, walked into the room and picked up the telephone.

"Is there a haberdasher or men's store in the building?" he asked the operator. "Ring it."

The operator gave him the men's store

and he told the manager what he wanted. He was toweling himself when knuckles massaged the hall door. It was too soon for the store delivery.

"What is it?" he called.

"Like to talk to you, Krag," said a voice outside the door.

"Go to hell," said Krag.

The door was opened and a heavy-set, puffy-faced man started into the room. "I'm Rafferty of the *Chronicle* . . . "

The was as far as he got. Krag struck him in the face with the towel. "I said, go to hell."

The man backed through the door. "That's no way to treat the press."

Krag slammed the door in his face and shot the night latch. The reporter banged the door and shouted a few imprecations through the thick paneling. Krag finished toweling himself and then threw himself on the bed.

It was fifteen minutes before there was a discreet knocking on the door. Krag draped the towel about his waist and opened the door. The manager of the men's store came in with an armful of clothing.

"I hope these are what you wanted."

"They'll do," said Krag. "How much?"

"It comes to two hundred sixty-two dollars and ninety cents."

Krag skimmed three hundred-dollar bills off the sheaf on the bed. He thrust them at the manager of the men's store. "Keep the change."

The man blinked at him. "The change from . . . " He clicked his heel together. "Thank you, sir."

He turned and marched out of the room.

Krag began taking pins out of shorts and shirts. He ripped off price tags and dressed himself, new socks, shorts, shirt, cuff links, necktie, and a gray pin-stripe suit. The suit was a little tight across the shoulders, but it would do.

He stepped into loose-fitting loafer shoes and looked at himself in the mirror. He saw a man who could have passed for a business or professional man, a hard-faced, extremely rugged-looking man of indeterminate age. Forty. Forty-five?

His hair was perhaps cut too short for a successful professional man. It would soon grow out, however.

He took the suit they had given him in Alcatraz and the remainder of his wearing apparel and threw them into the soiled towel container in the bathroom. He disposed with this of the smell of twenty-three years in prison.

He could not throw away what the twenty-three years had done to him.

He left the room and rode down to the lobby in the elevator. Rafferty of the *Chronicle* spotted him as he stepped out of the elevator. He came forward and three others of his ilk joined him.

"How's it feel to be free after twenty-three years?" one of the reporters called to him while still several paces away.

Another cried: "What are your plans now you've paid your debt to society?"

"Did you really kill the girl, Mr. Krag?" asked another.

"How'd they treat you in Alcatraz?"

"Is it true you spent eight years in solitary?"

"Did you take the rap for someone else?"

"Were you framed, Mr. Krag?"

The questions rattled at Krag from all of the four reporters. They waited for no answers. They sprang new ones, one question after the other. They overlapped each other.

They followed him out to the sidewalk, continued to shoot questions at him until the moment he stepped into a cab and slammed the door on them. They even yelled after him.

Krag gave no answers to any of them.

The cab roared away from the hotel. "The airport," said Krag.

"Them fellas was givin' you a rough time," observed the cabby over his shoulder. His head swiveled around. "Hey, ain't you Billy Krag? I seen your pitcher in the paper . . . " Brakes squealed as the driver slewed the cab toward the curb. "I ain't drivin' no kid murderer in *my* hack!"

Krag got out of the taxi. It was a block from the hotel. He was safe enough from the reporters. He walked away, rounded a corner, and stepped into a taxi in a cab zone.

There was a reporter at the airport. Krag looked through him as he introduced himself and, without a single word, walked past him. The reporter started to follow, hesitated, then headed for a phone booth.

Ten minutes later he was back, following Krag as he started for a plane. But he had no ticket and Krag had bought the last available seat on the plane, while the reporter had been telephoning his city editor for further instructions.

The plane took off and was soon flying over mountains. Mountains, desert, more mountains. The Nevada desert was blotted out by night by the time the plane landed on the outskirts of Las Vegas.

A taxicab dropped Krag at one of the casino-hotels on the Strip. There had been nothing like this in 1937, when Krag had passed through Las Vegas on his way to the coast. Las Vegas had been a lively little village then, with a population of perhaps two thousand. There had been gambling, yes, but it had been confined to a few saloons and honky-tonks on Fremont Street.

There had been no Strip then, no multi-million-dollar hotel-casinos. Krag had seen pictures of some of them, however. They had movies in Folsom and even in Alcatraz and two or three times through the years there had been pictures with Las Vegas backgrounds. And once he had seen a picture layout in a national picture weekly.

He went into the hotel and recognized two faces he had seen on motion picture screens.

There was a restaurant straight ahead. On the left was the hotel lobby, on the right the main casino. To get anywhere Krag had to pass batteries of slot machines.

He went into the casino, passed the blackjack tables, and watched for a moment at the first dice table. The rails were jammed with gambling patrons.

The second table had a little air around it and at the rear a third table had plenty of room.

Krag moved up to the table. A man sevened out and chips and silver dollars were raked in. A few were paid out. The next player got the dice; money was showered out upon the layout and the shooter threw the dice. He got an eight for a point and sevened out on the next roll. The dice were very cold.

A man on Krag's right got the dice,

made a point, and sevened. The dice were deposited in front of Krag by the stickman.

Krag put down a sheaf of bills. The stickman riffled them open with his stick. "Sorry, sir, two hundred is the limit."

Krag looked down at the money, then at the stickman.

"That's a thousand dollars," said the stickman quietly.

"I counted it," said Krag.

The stickman signaled to the pit boss. The man came over, sized up Krag, and nodded to the stickman.

"Shoot," said the stickman. He snatched up the bills, thrust them into the bill slot, and put out a single yellow striped check.

Krag shook up the dice, threw them out so that they bounced off the corrugated rubber cushion. They came up four-three.

The stickman scooped in the dice neatly, gave them a quick once-over, and dropped them to the table. He shoved them toward Krag.

"Your pleasure, sir."

Krag looked at him.

"Two thousand?"

The pit boss had moved back only a step or two. He moved forward.

"You're faded," he said to Krag.

Krag picked up the dice, threw them out. They came up six-one. Two striped yellow checks were added to the two before Krag. The stickman had to pay out quite a few other checks to other players.

The pit boss took over now.

"You're still faded, if you wish."

Krag waited while other players increased their bets, all riding with a big plunger.

He threw out the dice. He got a six and a four and there were audible groans up and down the table. But a few of the more rugged ones laid out checks for the odds. One even risked a hundred dollars for "the hard way."

Krag threw a four, box-cars, a nine, and then . . . two fives.

A rumble went up around the table.

Four more yellow, striped checks were added to Krag's stack.

"That's eight thousand," said the pit boss. He stared at Krag as the latter made no move to gather in his checks.

"One moment, sir."

The pit boss scurried away. Krag let the dice lay on the table. The pit boss located the casino manager, came back with him.

The manager said: "You wish to shoot eight thousand dollars?"

Krag nodded.

"And if you win?"

"That will be four passes," said Krag.

"And if you lose?"

Krag said nothing.

The casino manager exhaled lightly. "Shoot," he said.

Krag picked up the dice and threw a six-five.

The word had already gotten around the casino. The table was crowded and a roar went up.

Eight yellow checks were laid out beside the eight already there. Krag leaned over, picked up the two stacks of checks. As he walked away from the table the casino manager joined him.

"You wish to cash in?"

"Yes."

"You're a smart gambler, sir. So few people are."

They walked toward the cashier's window. Before they reached it the manager shot a sudden look at Krag's face. "Your face is familiar. Do I know you?"

"No," said Krag.

They reached the window. "Perhaps you'd prefer a check," the casino manager suggested.

"Hundred-dollar bills."

"Very good."

The manager watched the cashier count out one hundred and sixty hundred-dollar bills. As Krag put the packet into his pocket and turned away, the manager again fell in beside him.

"You're registered here, sir?"

"I'm going to register now."

The casino manager watched him walk off, but kept his eyes on Krag until he disappeared with a bellboy. Then he walked over to the registration desk and reached for the card that the clerk was about to file.

"Krag," he read, "William Krag, San Francisco . . . " Then his eyes narrowed. "Be damned!"

He dropped the registration card and reached for the telephone. He dialed one digit. "Billy Krag just checked in," he said, "right after winning fifteen thousand at the dice table. Yeah ... a thousand. Four passes. I okayed it. Thought you might want to know." He hung up.

In his room on the second floor, Krag gave the bellboy a dollar and waited a minute after he left. Then he came out of the room, walked down the corridor, away from the central staircase.

He walked swiftly, reached the end of the corridor, and found a flight of stairs going down. He came out at the rear of the casino, by the swimming pool, walked around the end of the hotel building, and rounded it to the front.

He signaled to the doorman and a cab moved up. He got in.

"Airport," he said.

At the airport he learned that a flight was leaving for Los Angeles in ten minutes. A jet would stop for passengers going east in an hour. Krag booked a through seat on the jet.

The jet settled down on the outskirts of Chicago at two-twenty, Central Time. It would go on to New York in a half hour. Krag got out and engaged a cab to take him to the Palmer House in the Windy City's Loop.

It was ten minutes after three when he undressed and went to bed.

The Chicago Tribune came with the breakfast tray. As he sipped his coffee, Krag began leafing through the newspaper. It was on page four, a one-column article of about four inches. It merely stated that William Krag, the rapist-murderer of San Francisco, had been released from Alcatraz, after serving twenty-three years. He had taken a plane to Las Vegas, and there disappeared into an unknown hideout.

The farther you got from the scene of the crime the less newsworthy you were.

That was the way Krag wanted it.

But the game still had to be played out. Life still had to be lived.

At eleven o'clock Krag paid off his taxicab at the corner of North Avenue and Clark Street. He stood for a moment or two on the street corner, then turned east on North Avenue and walked to Lake Shore Drive.

The mansions were still on Lake Shore.

They were interspersed with skyscraper apartment buildings, but some of the older millionaires were still holding out. The mansions were old-fashioned and some of them were grimy, but they still represented money. And, on the society pages of the newspapers, position.

Krag came to one of the mansions, which had a wrought-iron fence along the front. The gate was open and he walked up to the front door and pressed a pearl button. He had a considerable wait, before the door was opened by an ancient butler in plum-colored livery.

"Mrs. Holterman," Krag said.

The butler regarded him steadily for a moment, then he said, "I'm sorry, sir, Mrs. Holterman is not receiving callers today."

"Would you ask her if she has read the morning paper?"

The butler hesitated, then started to close the door. Krag said: "I will wait."

The door was closed. It was a full five minutes before it was reopened.

"Mrs. Holterman is in her upstairs sitting room," the butler said. "She has not been well."

He led the way to a deep-piled staircase and climbed slowly, heavily. He was very old and had been going up and down these stairs for a great many years.

Krag followed. On the second floor the butler opened a door and stood aside. Krag entered and the butler closed the door, remaining outside.

Before her marriage to Arthur Holterman, Phyllis Carmichael had been considered one of the most beautiful women in Chicago. She had matured extremely well and even now, in her early sixties, she was a striking woman. There was a regal quality about her that seemed to make her ageless.

She sat now in a wing chair, her white hair piled high on her head, her eyes clear and steady as she regarded Krag, who stood just inside the door.

The silence in the heavy, overfurnished sitting room was like a pall. Phyllis Holterman was obviously waiting for Krag to speak and he finally did.

"You know me."

She said, "What do you want?"

Krag took a sheaf of hundred-dollar bills from his pocket. Fifteen. He carried the money across the room and dropped it on a table beside her.

"Your messenger boy wouldn't take his fee. It's the full amount."

He turned and walked away from her. His hand was on the doorknob when she said sharply: "I sent you no money."

"Then Charles."

"He has been out of the country for almost a year." She hesitated, then shook her head. "Charles did not send the money."

He looked at her steadily. She tapped the floor with her rubber-tipped cane. "I do not believe there is anything else we have to discuss."

"No," said Krag, "there isn't."

"I have but one son," Phyllis Holterman said remorselessly. "I had two, but one died many years ago. I mourned for him then."

"How did he die, this other son?" asked Krag.

"You can find it in the newspaper files," she said sharply, "but I'll save you the trouble of looking. He was fond of boating and was on the lake when a sudden squall came up. The boat capsized."

"And the body was never recovered."

He drew in a short breath and exhaled. Then he nodded suddenly and turned away from her. Phyllis Holterman said: "The money . . . take it with you."

He went back and scooped up the sheaf of hundred-dollar bills. Crumpling them carelessly, he stuffed them into his coat pocket.

Phyllis Holterman watched him go and after he had gone she stared for long moments at the pattern of the carpeting of the floor. Her eyes remained dry, however; there was no creasing of her face, no quivering of muscles.

Only her mouth was formed in a straight, taut line.

Ordinarily, a man with a crewcut and beard is a conspicuous figure. But not in Greenwich Village in New York City. There, a clean-shaven man, wearing a shirt, necktie, and a suit with matching jacket and trousers would be an object of attention.

The man with the crewcut and beard was pretty much of a recluse, not uncommon in the Village. Wearing sandals, sweatshirt, and a soiled pair of slacks, he took the Sixth Avenue bus to Forty-Second Street almost every morning. There he walked to the library on Fifth Avenue and spent most of the day in one of the vast reading rooms.

Toward evening he returned to the Village, to his one-room apartment with a closet-kitchenette. He prepared his own meals. He spent the evenings reading. On rare occasions he went out late, and spent an hour or two at one of the taverns or cafés. He sipped black coffee.

Sometimes he talked to people, furtive-looking men usually, who were not regular Village habitués, but frequented the taverns for reasons peculiar to them. A hint dropped by one of these creatures led the crewcut man to upper Third Avenue, where a round of questioning brought him to a man who listened to him and said nothing in reply. But one evening the man came to the Village.

And so, in late July, the crewcut man boarded a transatlantic airliner. He carried a passport in the name of Peter Ostheimer. The following day the man with Peter Ostheimer's passport arrived in Paris.

He moved into a small *pension* and spent a day talking to a series of bland Frenchmen who expostulated and denied all knowledge of the things the man called Ostheimer asked them about.

Yet, after a week, the passport with the name of Peter Ostheimer was torn to shreds. The man who had brought it to Europe was now equipped with a "genuine" birth certificate, a *carte d'identité*, which proved that his name was Ahmed Fosse and that he was born in Cairo, Egypt, the son of a French father and an Egyptian mother.

With these documents, Ahmed Fosse left Paris. He arrived in a small village in Normandy two days later. He was now clean-shaven and carried an ancient portmanteau, which contained very few clothes, but a number of old books having to do with archaeology and the study of ancient languages.

Ahmed Fosse spent a night or two in an inn, then moved in with a Normandy fisherman and his wife. He spent much time on the beach, still littered with the rusting remains of boats and armament and now and then a whitened bone — the reminders of a war in which he had taken no part.

On the beach he usually doffed his striped jersey. He lay on the hot sands and let the sun burn and blacken his torso. He read books. In the evenings he sat with the fisherman and his wife and talked. He talked French, larded heavily with the Normandy dialect and idiom.

In September, Ahmed Fosse said good-by to the Normandy fisherman and his wife. Four days later he was in Marseilles, where he purchased a ticket on a French ship that left the following day. It was a cargo ship with only a few passengers and made stops at Malta, Genoa, Naples, and Palermo. Then it steamed across the Mediterranean and was finally berthed in a pier at Alexandria.

Ahmed Fosse had no difficulty with his passport and identity papers and, after a day or two in Alexandria, boarded a bus that carried him to Cairo.

A man born in Egypt, but who has spent most of his time in a foreign country, has trouble with his mother tongue, and Ahmed Fosse, in spite of his studies in Greenwich Village in New

York and on the beach in Normandy, had difficulty with Arabic. His books had not touched on the Egyptian idioms that were used by the native Egyptians.

His Arabic could have passed at Shepherd's Hotel, but it brought many a cocked eye, a suspicious look in the places Ahmed Fosse frequented. These were sometimes in the general vicinity of Shepherd's Hotel, but they were places against which the tourists of the hotel were warned. In them, however, Ahmed Fosse polished — rather, degenerated — his Arabic.

He spent the winter in Cairo.

He associated with disreputable *fellahin* and was once arrested with a group of them. He paid a small fine after spending three days in an airless, filthy cell.

In March he left Cairo and drifted southward. He was seldom more than a mile or two from the Nile and stopped for a day, sometimes as long as a week, at a village. He was seeking employment, but like many shiftless *fellahin*, when it was offered, he was chary of accepting it. How much work was involved? How difficult was the work?

In the Valley of the Kings, archaeological expeditions were engaged in sifting the ancient sands. Ahmed Fosse mingled with the *fellahin* who were working for the British and American archaeological teams. He accepted employment with one of the expeditions and worked and lived with the *fellahin* for three weeks.

The expedition used up its funds. Ahmed sat in the tents of the *fellahin* and cursed the foreigners who were despoiling and robbing the graves of the ancients ... and giving miserable wages to the real owners of the tombs and the land. And then, with the Nile rising, when other work could not be had, discharging them.

The Nile, as it had done from time immemorial, overflowed its banks in July and August. It deposited the rich silt of the upper Nile country, the mountains to the south, and it soaked the sands with its life-giving waters, and then the waters receded.

The *fellahin* planted their crops, the archaeological expeditions watched and waited for the sands to dry, and then, in the early autumn, their funds replenished from the rich overseas countries, they began to employ diggers once more.

By that time Ahmed Fosse was south of the ancient capital of the Upper Kingdom, Thebes. A small but well-equipped German expedition was probing the sands, after some promising discoveries the season before. They were hiring experienced diggers and Ahmed Fosse had experience, three years of it (three weeks which had been magnified into three years).

After a week's work, several of the German archaeologist knew Ahmed by name. He was the best worker of the *fellahin*, the first on the job in the morning, the last to put aside his shovel or sieve at night. He was that rare digger, an Egyptian, interested in what the sands held.

He could even be trusted to sift and sort without the eyes of a German on him.

One day the half-caste *fellah* went to the tent of Heinrich Klausner, the Number Two man of the team, and revealed to him a gold twelfth-dynasty amulet that he had 'found'. Questioned, he admitted reluctantly that he had found it in the blanket of a *fellah*.

The *fellah* was discharged the next day for loitering at his work. A few days later, Ahmed Fosse was put in charge of the *fellahin* who were sifting the sands brought to them by the team of diggers.

Working directly with Klausner and a woman member of the team, named Frieda Schultz, he learned very quickly. He talked to the Germans, expressed profound interest in the ancient history of his mother's people, and soon could talk intelligently about the eighteenth dynasty and the fourteenth and even the twelfth, eleventh, and tenth.

He identified objects found in the sieves, dated them precisely, and once, when even the archaeologists were in doubt, he hazarded a guess, which further study proved to be correct.

Heinrich Klausner gave the intelligent *fellah* some books to read. He read them quickly, avidly. He was soon studying hieroglyphics and mastered them in record time.

That he could read them ten years ago on the dank, bleak island in San

Franscisco Bay, the Germans did not know. The man who was now Ahmed Fosse had cut off his past. He spoke Egyptian fluently. He *looked* Egyptian. Very little of his French 'parentage' remained. He worked mostly with his shirt off and he was burned black as any *fellah* in the camp.

In April, Ahmed Fosse said to Klausner: "Mr. Klausner, in Egypt I am a *fellah*. I was born a *fellah*, I have lived as one, and I shall die as one. You have been exceedingly kind to me, but in that very kindness you have done me a disservice. You have made me discontented with my lot. I would like to go to another country, where my position in life is not set for me — where I can overcome my miserable beginnings and perhaps attain a better place."

The German shook his head. "You're doing excellent work, Ahmed. I can get you more money and perhaps a position of more responsibility."

"It would still be in Egypt and I would still be an Egyptian *fellah*."

"You do not have a university degree, Ahmed," the German said. "Still you have learned very quickly and you have a keen brain. I think you could overcome the disadvantages about which you seem concerned."

"I could do it easier in another country."

"Where?"

"I have heard of the excavations in Israel . . ."

"A trouble-ridden country."

"I would like to try my luck there. The British expedition is doing excellent work at Jericho."

"With potsherds. The language is different . . ."

"You said yourself that I have a flair for languages."

"Did I? You think you could learn the ancient Semitic languages?"

"If study and hard work can do it, I shall."

Klausner sighed heavily. "Your mind's made up?"

"I would appreciate references."

Israel – 1962

17

ALICE HOLTERMAN had gone to bed in her own bedroom, but her husband remained in the living room. He was still writing in his journal and the last paragraph he wrote read thus:

I have never shared the prejudices of my class. In my years of archaeological work in the Near East I have mixed with all sorts of people, all races, black, brown, white. I do not believe I have ever felt any prejudices against a person because of the color of his skin, or his religion, even lack of religion. Yet, today, I lashed out at a man with dark skin. Perhaps it was the man's attitude that brought out this trait in me. He claims to be half French, only half Egyptian, but he is all arrogance.

The fountain pen in Holterman's hand paused a moment, then continued to write:

221

Perhaps my prejudice against the Egyptian stems from the knowledge that he was out with my wife Alice last night. I presume the usual happened with them.

Holterman closed the journal. He put it in the drawer of the table and, locking the drawer, put the key into his pocket.

He was blissfully aware that Alice Holterman had long ago had a duplicate key made to the drawer.

The false dawn had barely lightened the window of the room in which Ahmed slept when he was out of bed, carrying his shoes and heading for the door. He opened it gently. It creaked a little and he cursed silently.

He pulled the door open quickly to lessen the squeaking and let it remain open after he went through.

Miller Wood sat up in his bed. He looked toward Ahmed's empty bed, then at the door.

Outside the building, Ahmed sat down on the ground and put on his paratrooper boots, sold throughout the Near East and

Europe as salvage goods. He laced them swiftly.

He got to his feet and headed eastward out of camp, passing the Druse area. None of the Druse were stirring.

He made the dry wadi and went along it swiftly, stumbling only a little in the dark. He came out of the wadi on the slope of the mountain when dawn was breaking in the east.

He kept to the shelter of the rocks, and had reached the place from which he had looked upon the tel diggings the day before, when the edge of the sun tipped over the hills to the east and brought full daylight upon the Tel Mas excavations.

Ahmed oriented himself, then with his back against a boulder, studied the hillside. It was roughest to the right; and be began climbing in that direction — an easy slope that had probably been gone over many times through the ages.

He found himself forced to climb in a little while. He was an amateur at mountain climbing, but he possessed the greatest essential of the successful climber. He was lean and agile and he had terrific strength in his arms and shoulders. With a bare fingertip grip on a ledge he could pull up his entire body with seemingly little effort.

He sought the roughest spots of the cliffside, where only a few patches of bush or shrubs had managed to find growth. He parted them and probed into them. And, finally, he was rewarded.

There was an opening behind one of the heavy shrubs — a hole in the face of the cliff. It was scarcely eighteen inches in diameter and had been choked entirely not too long ago. Someone had scraped away rubble.

Ahmed crawled into the hole. He sniffed the air, found it musty but clean enough.

Light penetrated only faintly through the heavy shrubbery outside, but he straightened gradually and found that he could stretch up from a kneeling position and just barely touch the rough ceiling of the cave.

He went in a few feet farther and struck a match. By its light he saw enough to tell him that he was probably in the right place.

He let the match fall and took out

a pencil flashlight that he had brought with him. He flicked it on and the tiny beam fell upon a mass of rubble and broken potsherds. He searched among the potsherds and found a sherd of glazed pottery, a sizable chunk from the rim of an ancient urn. There was faint writing on it. He put out the torch and polished the potsherd, then flicking on the light again, examined the writing. He made out a few letters.

The writing was Aramaic.

He sorted through the potsherds and then his hand found a rounded object. He drew it out from the rubble. It was a section of a human skull. He dropped it and moved back farther into the cave, some twenty feet from the mouth.

Here he found two or three more skulls and a number of bones. The cave seemed to have been used for burials. Either that or a number of men at some time in history had taken shelter here and had remained until they had died — either from starvation or self-destruction.

Suicide had not been uncommon during

the stormy days of the revolts of 68 – 70 A.D. and again in 132. The last "Messiah," Bar Kochba, had himself held out for three years in a cave in an inaccessible cliff along the shores of the Dead Sea. The few survivors with him had finally taken each other's lives, the last man killing himself. They could hold out no longer and refused to be taken alive by the Romans.

A similar situation might have existed here in Galilee. The remnants of a group from the village below could have taken refuge here and remained to the bitter end. In their fight they had probably taken the most valuable things they could readily carry.

A copper cylinder, containing . . . ?

The late A. D. Hill had gone exploring on his own time and had found the cave. Working alone he could merely sort out the surface objects, but he might not even have attempted a thorough search. The copper cylinder would have been conspicuous and he might have taken that and been satisfied.

On hands and knees, Ahmed crawled back to the cave mouth. He parted the bushes carefully and surveyed the valley below.

The camp had come alive. People were moving about and there were even figures around the excavations. It was time for Ahmed to get back, to clean himself and make a suitable explanation for his absence, if anyone had noted it.

The problem solved itself. As he forced his way through the thick shrubbery, his eye caught movement down on the slope. The Chicago-Sicilians were out bright and early. They were flitting from boulder to boulder some three or four hundred yards below and to the right.

Ahmed had the advantage of position. And surprise. They would be watching the valley below. This early in the morning, they would not be expecting anyone to be behind them.

Ahmed moved downward. He went swiftly fifty feet to a ledge. Now he was in an awkward spot. He had to lower himself, hang from the edge of the ledge and find a footing below, then another and another. There was twenty feet of almost sheer cliff before he could again find footing.

He lowered himself and his groping boots found a projection. He let go of the ledge above and, flat against the face of the cliff, bent forward. There was an outcropping three feet to the left. He had to fall toward it, but his hands gripped it and he was sprawled for a moment in an arch, his feet to the right, his upper body to the left.

A chunk of the projection broke off and clattered down the slope. Ahmed moved swiftly then, swung his body to the left, and kicked about with his feet. One foot found an inch or two of rough rock, took hold.

He did not hear the report of the gun. But inches from his hands, a bullet chipped out stone. Ahmed let go of the roughened spot, let his body slide down the face of the cliff.

He went down twenty feet, struck a ledge, and ricocheted off. His clawing fingers slowed his pace, but could not stop his fall entirely. He went past the ledge and landed sideward of a shelf another dozen feet down. The wind was almost knocked from his body and he lay still.

Then he turned on his side and looked

upward. A bullet kicked out splinters five feet above him. Painfully, Ahmed thrust a skinned hand into his right trousers pocket. He touched the warm metal of the flat automatic and drew it out.

He rolled over on his other side and peered over the edge of the shelf.

The Sicilians were out in the open, separated by a score of yards. They were looking upward, searching for him. Both men were at least two hundred yards from Ahmed. Their shooting had been wild, but they had sent a couple of bullets too close for comfort.

Ahmed thrust the automatic over the edge of the shelf, aimed as well as he could in the awkward position, and fired once at the man on the left, then switching quickly, sent two bullets in the general direction of the second man.

He drew up his arm, then, and waited for retaliation.

It did not come immediately, and after a few moments he peered over the edge.

The Sicilians were in full retreat. Their position was poor — an armed man above them, a camp below. Time would work against them and they did not intend to give their enemies that time.

They were scrambling down the easy slope, going pell-mell in the direction they had fled the day before.

18

AHMED put away the automatic and got to his feet. He had covered the worst of the terrain and had no trouble making the descent.

He had scarcely reached the floor of the valley than he saw a delegation headed toward him. It consisted of Miller Wood, Charles Holterman, and a half dozen of the Druse. Sheik Yussuf was with the Druse.

Holterman made a signal to the others and went ahead.

"What the devil's going on here?" he snapped the moment he was close enough for Ahmed to hear.

"I spotted them yesterday," replied Ahmed. "I thought they might be spying again today and climbed up early to get above them."

"Who asked you to do that?" snapped Holterman. "If you saw anything out of the way yesterday why didn't you report it to Dr. Sando? Or to me?"

Ahmed shrugged.

The color began to rise in Holterman's face. "You fired back at them. That's a violation of our rules. No member of the team is permitted to possess a firearm."

"I wasn't given a copy of the camp regulations." said Ahmed carelessly.

"Were you allowed to carry a gun in Egypt?"

"In Egypt I was a native."

"Well, you're not here. You're an alien, in Israel, by the sufferance of the Israeli government. Hand me that gun."

Ahmed hesitated. His life might depend upon having that gun later, but he knew that if Holterman made an issue of it, he would be dismissed from his job and the camp.

He drew out the gun and handed it to Holterman.

Holterman snorted as he glanced at the automatic. "This is a pretty fancy gun. Where'd you get it?"

"A man who wants a gun can always get one."

Holterman thrust the automatic under the waistband of his whipcord trousers. "I'm not happy about this, Fosse, I'm not happy about it at all. I'm beginning to wonder if it wasn't a mistake giving you a job. Things were quiet and orderly around here, but since your arrival there's been an unrest and commotion that I don't like at all. I'm not at all certain that you fit in here."

"You hired me," said Ahmed. "You can fire me."

For a moment Holterman looked as if he would accept Ahmed's challenge. Then he looked over his shoulder in the direction of the camp, and when his eyes came back to Ahmed, they were uncertain.

"I'll let this pass," he said grudgingly, "but I'm warning you — your extra-curricular activities will be watched from now on. Understand?"

Ahmed nodded and walked past Holterman. Miller Wood grinned crookedly at him as he passed. A few feet farther along, Sheik Yussuf beamed at him.

"The insurance, Effendi," he murmured. "Don't forget it."

Ahmed went on to the camp. He washed his hands and face, brushed his clothes, then went into the mess hall.

A Druse was gathering up the breakfast dishes.

He was not happy about serving a late breakfast to Ahmed, but Ahmed spoke sharply to him and the Druse brought him some cold gruel and half-stale bread. The coffee was muddy, but Ahmed drank it without complaint.

Finished with his breakfast, he adjourned to the translating workroom. Miller Wood was at his desk.

"What was all that about?" he asked.

"Hasn't anybody around here been aware of the spying that's been going on?" countered Ahmed.

"I don't know about the others, but I've known about it ever since it started," replied Wood.

"And you haven't been curious?"

"It wasn't any of my affair. Don Hill . . . " He broke off.

"Hill knew about it?"

Wood hesitated. "If he did, he didn't confide in me." He cleared his throat, then his voice rasped out: "What's your game, Fosse? You're supposed to be an archaeologist, but you're acting like some kind of spy yourself. Snooping around in the middle of the night, asking questions."

"I've got a sensitive skin," retorted Ahmed. "It's especially sensitive around my back. In the general area where A. D. Hill got the knife. I don't want one in the same place."

"How the hell do you know *where* he was stabbed?"

"The Israeli police just happened to mention it. I was questioned by them, you may recall. I didn't have an alibi about being here, at the time. As a matter of fact, I was on the road not too far from where Hill was killed, at just about the time he died. The police weren't very happy about that."

"If the idea of a policeman being able to read Aramaic wasn't too ridiculous to entertain, I might suspect you of being a policeman yourself."

"One thing I'm not," said Ahmed grimly, "is a policeman."

"Then stop acting like one. Mind your own business and stick to your work. Sando made a few cracks at breakfast about our department being behind."

Ahmed went to his worktable and

attacked the mass of papyrus fragments. He worked for an hour and found three pieces that seemed to fit together. He was conscious several times that Miller Wood was watching him covertly, but ignored the other language man until Wood finally spoke to him.

"The Herr Doctor Holterman was more interested in chewing you out than he was in what the Chicago boys were doing up on the hill."

"That occurred to me," Ahmed said. He pushed two fragments of papyrus about, then added: "They're after the manuscript that Hill found in the cave."

There was dead silence behind him. Then Ahmed heard a chair pushed back. Wood came to his table.

"What manuscript, what cave?"

"The cave up on the cliff. That's where Hill found the manuscript, isn't it?"

"You've *found* a cave?" Wood snapped.

"Yes. But someone was there ahead of me. I assumed it was A. D. Hill."

Wood was standing beside the desk. He came around now so that he could look directly into Ahmed's face. "I've been in these diggings more than a year. I've been over every inch of the valley and just about every foot of the hills around here and I never found a cave. *You've* been here two days and you say you've found one."

"I was looking for one," said Ahmed. "Were *you*?"

"Not necessarily. But I'm an archae-ologist; I've always got my eyes open for things like that. I know what they found in caves down at the Dead Sea." He stabbed a stubby forefinger at Ahmed. "Why in hell were you looking for a cave?"

Ahmed leaned back in his chair. "A member of this archaeological team was murdered by a person or persons unknown. There are whispers and innuendoes all over the camp that he found something valuable. There are Chicago gangster lurking around. What conclusions would *you* draw?"

"I'm interested in *your* conclusions."

"Hill was killed south of Nazareth. It was early in the morning, just about dawn. There was a copper cylinder in the car with him. What was he doing that far from here, at that time of the day, or night? Was he making a run for it?"

"A run — where?"

"Away from here, out of the country."

Wood stared at Ahmed a moment, then shook his head. "That was the wrong way to go. He would have had an easier time of it going north, to Syria, or east to Jordan."

"You're forgetting the Chicago chaps," said Ahmed. "They've been hanging around here, before Hill was killed and since. Why? Because they *thought* something valuable might be found here? Uh-huh, they *know* it's been found. They know who found it, too. They weren't too far from Hill when he was killed."

Wood swore roundly. "Damn it, Fosse, you know too much. Your finger's in the pie somewhere. It's *got* to be."

"What about *your* fingers, Wood?" Ahmed asked. "You and Hill were buddies. You've spilled that much yourself. You say he didn't confide in you, but you lived together, you slept in the same room. You couldn't help but know about his comings and goings. An interested observer might even suggest that you were partners."

Wood snarled at Ahmed, "Next thing you'll be saying that we had a falling out and that I was the one who killed him!"

"Were you?"

Wood took two quick steps around the table and cocked his fist to throw it at Ahmed. He caught himself in time, however.

"I've tried to get along with you, Fosse. You won't let me. If *that's* the way you want it . . . "

"I don't want a damn thing, Wood," Ahmed replied wearily. "Just let me alone, will you?"

"That goes double." Wood whirled away from Ahmed, then winced as his eyes went toward the open door.

Carolyn Caxton stood there.

"I'm sorry," she said, "I should have knocked, but the door was open . . . "

Miller Wood was in too savage a mood to talk to her. He stormed past her, out of the room. Carolyn looked anxiously at Ahmed.

"I'm sorry, Mr. Fosse . . . "

Ahmed made a gesture of dismissal. "I've been getting into the porridge all morning."

"I know," she said. "I — I have a pair of field glasses and I was watching you. Even before those men . . . shot at you."

Her head turned involuntarily to the door. Ahmed got up, crossed and closed the door.

"How'd you know I was up there?"

"I saw you leave camp."

"Before dawn?"

"I couldn't sleep. I was just coming out of my room when I saw you leaving camp."

"It was dark; how'd you know it was me?"

"I — I knew. I had an idea where you were heading. It was the way you went yesterday and when it was light enough I watched from behind the building. I saw you climb the cliffs . . . You found a cave."

"I was inside for quite a while."

"I know."

"You knew about the cave before?"

"I suspected there might be one. There usually are in those limestone cliffs. Of course, I couldn't explore the cliffs myself, but I've often thought I would like to do so, if I were a man."

"Hill climbed them."

"He spent a lot of his spare time exploring and I know he liked the mountain."

"He found the cave before I did. That's where he got the manuscript."

Her eyes clouded at mention of a manuscript. "There *is* a manuscript, Mr. Fosse?"

"Isn't there?"

"We're back where we were last night. You're questioning me again. I — I just came here to warn you."

"About what?"

"Dr. Sando said something about — about being displeased with your activity here. It wasn't so much what he said, but the *way* he said it, and I gathered that Mr. Holterman had talked to him about it."

"Holterman doesn't care for me. He's told me so himself."

"I know. If you'd just kind of take things easy. You're very good in your work; even Dr. Sando admitted that. It's just that . . . well, your way of going about things, the way you talk. Miller Wood's complained about you, too."

241

"The feeling about me's pretty general ... "

"No!" exclaimed Carolyn. "*I* don't feel that way. I — I wouldn't want you to lose your job. And Mrs. Holterman ... "

"Yes," said Ahmed, "let's not forget *her*."

"I'd like to," Carolyn said tartly, "but I know that she likes you and she has a great deal of influence with her husband."

"She's my friend at court," Ahmed said mockingly. "As long as I sleep with the boss's wife, my job's good."

"That's a terrible thing to say!"

"It's true, isn't it?"

There was the trace of a quiver in her jaw, then she whirled and headed for the door. Ahmed watched her go out.

19

A SMILE played about Alice Holterman's lips as she read the final entry in her husband's diary. She closed the book, put it back in the drawer, and locked the drawer with the duplicate key she had had made only a short time after her arrival in Israel.

She took a quick turn about the room, then drew a deep breath and went to her husband's office.

Holterman was seated at his desk, staring into space. He did not even seem to be aware of his wife's arrival. She stopped some six feet from his desk.

"I hope you're thinking about Subject A," she said after a while.

He roused himself, blinking."Eh?"

"Last night. We talked."

He exhaled heavily. "Please, Alice, it's bad enough in the evening. I've got other things to do during the day." He grimaced. "That Egyptian you forced down my throat. He's become impossible."

243

"You mean he's stood up to you?" Alice said mockingly.

"That damn fool was out on the hillside this morning having a gun battle with a pair of Europeans."

"I thought I heard a commotion." Then she suddenly regarded her husband sharply. "On the hill, you say?"

"He was climbing around up there right after it got light. The fool climbed up while it was still dark."

"The Europeans," said Alice. "What did they look like?"

"How would I know? They were too far off." He glowered at her. "Some of your friends probably."

"Of course," retorted Alice, "cast-off lovers."

"I've had about all of *that* I can take," snapped Holterman. "When you start taking up with Egyptians, you're going too far."

"You know, dear," Alice Holterman said sweetly, "that's a very good idea . . . taking up with Egyptians."

"I'll throw him out of this camp if he so much as looks in your direction again," snarled Holterman.

"Why, I do believe the man's jealous," taunted Alice. "Let me know when you throw him out. You did mean it literally, didn't you?"

"Damn you," said Holterman savagely.

She blew him a kiss, then walked out of the room, swishing her hips deliberately.

Outside she went directly to the building where Ahmed was working. Ahmed had only minutes before had his scene with Carolyn. He had reseated himself at his worktable, but was not working.

Alice came in and closed the door behind her. "Good," she said, as she took note of Wood's absence, "we can talk. I've just heard about your little adventure this morning. What were you looking for up on the cliff?"

"A cave," said Ahmed. "The one A. D. Hill found."

"You found it?"

"Yes."

"And?"

"And what?"

"What was inside?"

"About ten thousand broken potsherd. A few skeletons."

245

"What else?"

"I was inside some twenty minutes altogether. I'd need a month to make a thorough search."

"You know what I'm talking about, my fine Egyptian friend," retorted Alice. "Did you find the manuscript?"

He shook his head.

"You're lying."

"I'd lie if there was any reason to."

"Yes, you would," said Alice Holterman thoughtfully. "You'd lie and cheat and probably kill. I've had a strange feeling about you ever since I first saw you. There's a strength in you that I don't think anyone has ever plumbed. And I don't mean just physical strength, although I imagine that you're strong enough." She paused. "Just *how* strong are you?"

"How strong do I have to be?" countered Ahmed.

"That's what I'm trying to find out." She hesitated, then added: "Is there anything you've ever been afraid of?"

"Everybody's afraid of something."

"I wasn't talking about everybody. I was talking about you."

"Mrs. Holterman," said Ahmed patiently, "you're asking childish questions."

"So it's Mrs. Holterman again."

"Your husband's made it plain that he doesn't want me talking to you. He comes in, I'm out of a job."

"The hell with your job, my friend. I've got a better one for you."

"I'm no good at that kind of work."

"Now you're being insulting."

"Am I, Mrs. Holterman?"

"What would you do if I slapped your face?"

"A man who lived in this part of the world said on a mountain not too far from here: 'If a man strikes you in the face, turn unto him the other cheek.'"

She stepped up to him and struck him with her open palm, hard. Without a change of expression, he turned the other side of his face to her. She raised her hand to strike the cheek. But before the palm could land, Ahmed had struck her with his own open hand, a blow so hard that it bowled her over.

The expression on his face was still the same.

He said: "He said *turn* the other cheek.

He didn't say to take the blow."

She got to her feet. There was a trickle of blood escaping from her mouth. She dabbed at it with her hand.

"That was the answer I wanted from you. Now we'll talk business. How would you like to earn a million dollars?"

Ahmed looked at her steadily. "The manuscript, I suppose."

"What else? A. D. Hill was asking two million for it. I think we can get three million, maybe more."

"I get one million out of three?"

"No, laddie-boy," said Alice Holterman, "we're not going to start dickering. I can *hire* strong men, you know. I'm not without resources, even without Charles Holterman."

"He's not in this?"

"Don't *you* become childish. Charles *has* a million dollars. In fact, he's got a great many millions. But *I* want a couple of million of my own. I want them without Charles. Are you following me?"

"I get a million . . . and you."

"The second half remains to be seen. You get a million dollar, American."

"Why do I get the million? You already

248

have the manuscript."

"You help me get it out of the country. That isn't very much, is it?"

"Wasn't that what Hill was trying to do when he got the knife in his back?"

"You're not Hill."

"The price is right," he admitted. "I've got a little personal business to take care of first."

"Personal business? You're not referring to the little Jewish girl . . . ?"

"No," he said, "it's not the girl."

"Look, Buster," snapped Alice, "if we're going to be in this together, you'd better come clean. We're going to have enough trouble getting that little piece of parchment out of this country. The minute we start away from here, all hell's going to break loose. I know one fat Greek who's going to bust a gut and he's got some Italian boys working for him who don't play with marbles. The Israeli government's going to take a sudden interest in us, too. And there's a husband of mine that you don't want to write off. He's been hunting for fame and glory for a good many years and we're snatching it out from under his hot grubby hands. He won't like it a little bit. So don't you go complicating things with 'personal business.' We get the manuscript tonight."

"You've got it nearby?"

She held up a cautioning finger. "I didn't stop your little game awhile ago, Buster, but we're not playing any more now. You know very well where the manuscript is."

"Where?"

Her face set in hard lines. "In the cave, where else?"

"You've seen it there?"

"I haven't been in the damn cave. I'm not an eagle. I can't fly. Hill put it back where he found it."

"If it's hidden in that rubble, it's going to take a few days or weeks to find it. Unless he told you exactly *where* he put it."

"Now wait a minute, Mr. Ahmed Fosse, or whatever your name is. You were right around Hill when he died. In fact, the Greek thinks you *took* the manuscript from him. I don't. I think he put it back in the cave before he made a run for it. But I think he told you where when he knew he was dying." She looked at him sharply. "Otherwise, how would you have known about the cave?"

She drew in a deep breath and let it out slowly.

"Find the manuscript, Egyptian," she said ominously. She glanced at her wrist watch. "You've got until evening. Have it by then, will you? It'll be so much nicer all round. Nobody'll really get hurt and we can be on our way and perhaps be out of the country by morning."

She went to the door and turned the knob but did not open the door. She said: "I'd rather have you for a partner, but if you force me, I'll throw in with the Greek. I won't like it, but you won't either. Don Hill didn't like it, not one bit, when he got that knife in his back."

She went out.

20

MILLER WOOD did not return to work. He was in the dining room, however, when Ahmed entered shortly after twelve o'clock. Carolyn Caxton was also there, as was Jacqueline.

"Hi, Sheriff," the Amazon said, giving Ahmed a salute. "Been doin' any more pistol practicin'?"

Ahmed took a seat opposite Carolyn Caxton.

Jacqueline persisted: "The bad man take away your six-shooter, Sheriff?"

Carolyn Caxton exclaimed, "Please, Jacqueline!"

"Whoa-ho, Nellie!" cried Jacqueline. "Annie Oakley's sidin' up with Sheriff Whosit — Wyatt Earp. Tell me, Sheriff, how long's it take you to draw from the hip? Eight-tenths of a second, or is it ten minutes? I haven't been watching television lately and I've kinda lost track of those things." She shook her head.

"Won't talk, huh? Yup, that's our strong silent man of the Old West. Yup, nope. Say! How would you translate 'Yup' into Egyptian?"

"Yup," said Ahmed.

"And Hebrew?"

Dr. Sando came in the dining room. His face showed that he was in a foul mood. He sat down at the head of the table without acknowledging even Miller Wood's nod. Jacqueline Dietrich gave him a once-over and decided that silence was the better part of valor.

The lunch proceeded in silence. They were about halfway through when Miller Wood finally essayed a conversational gambit.

"That sun's really bearing down today."

Sando continued eating and that ended the conversation.

There was dessert, dried apricots, soaked in water, but Dr. Sando did not wait for his portion. He finished his mutton, drank his tea, and went out.

The minute he was gone, Jacqueline uttered a whoop. "That's the grandaddy of all grouches! Big Poobah Holterman must have given him wherefore."

"Jacqueline, my love," said Miller Wood. "It's awful hot outside. Why don't you cool off? Get a bucket of water and dip your head in it three times and take it out twice, will you?"

"I'll do that for you, Woody," said Jacqueline sweetly, "right after you climb into the sack with little Carolyn."

Carolyn cried out and sprang to her feet. "You . . . you monster!" she cried and rushed out of the dining room.

Jacqueline smiled a vinegary smile. "From that," she said, to Miller Wood, "I gather it's going to be a little while." She shifted to Ahmed. "Mmm, I wouldn't make the same deal with our sheriff. Little Carolyn's mighty sweet on him." She bobbed her head. "It could be any time now, Sheriff. Or have you already crawled in with her?"

Ahmed Fosse picked up his saucer of apricots and walked around the table. Jacqueline watched him, her eyes narrowed. She was half expecting something, but not quite sure what it would be.

Ahmed started to hand the saucer to her, then suddenly raised it high and upended it over her head. He pressed the saucer down on top of the mess.

Jacqueline was screaming curses at him as he went out of the dining room.

Miller Wood got up from the table. His face was twisted in a huge grin and he was chuckling.

"That's the best thing I've seen since James Cagney shoved a grapefruit into a woman's face in an old movie."

Jacqueline was clawing apricots and syrup out of her hair. She hurled a handful of the sticky mess at Miller Wood. It missed him and he beat a hasty retreat out of the room.

The Druse were permitted two hours for their midday meal and a nap, but the members of the archaeological team usually took an hour longer. The midday temperature in the valley was seldom below one hundred degrees and frequently it was much higher.

Ahmed adjourned to the room he shared with Miller Wood, after depositing the apricots on Jacqueline's head. He stretched out on his cot and closed his eyes when Wood entered.

Wood shuffled around in the vicinity of his own bed, then Ahmed heard the bed creak as he lay down upon it.

Alice Holterman had given Ahmed until nightfall to produce the manuscript. Ahmed was not underestimating her. She was quite capable of . . . anything.

She would stick to her bargain with him as long as it was to her advantage. She might even give him the million dollars, once the manuscript was disposed of. If it suited her purpose.

He was not concerned about that. There was something in Ahmed's character that she still had not plumbed. She did not know what his personal business was.

The man who had called himself Ahmed Fosse had come to Israel for one reason.

To kill a man.

Ahmed intended to do precisely that.

He was going to kill Charles Holterman. Nothing had weakened that determination. Only . . . something had been added — a new element that he had not been aware of before.

He had not known before coming here how strong the desire was in Charles

Holterman to achieve fame in his chosen profession.

That ambition in Charles Holterman *could* be fulfilled. The elements of it were here. They were in Charles Holterman's grasp. He could close his hand on them and they were his. The only thing that mattered to Charles Holterman that was possibly more important to him than life itself.

Fame.

It would justify Charles Holterman's life.

It was in Ahmed Fosse's power to reveal that fame to Charles Holterman, to dangle the possibility of it before Holterman, and then . . . to destroy it. Just before he killed Holterman.

In that one awful instant when he knew he was dying, Holterman would know that he was dying . . . *defeated!*

He would know, too, *who* had defeated him in the end.

Ahmed wanted that.

He had earned it.

Ahmed swung his feet to the floor and headed for the door. As he went out, Miller Wood raised himself from his cot.

He stared at the closed door and shook his head.

Heat waves were shimmering outside. The camp was quiet. The archaeological team members were all inside. The Druse were under their canvases.

Sheik Yussuf was under canvas, but he sat in his chair, looking toward the camp as Ahmed Fosse approached him.

He said: "You've decided to buy the insurance!"

"I want to talk to effendi Holterman and I don't want the woman to know it."

"She spent a little while with you this morning. The time was well spent?"

Ahmed took a crumpled hundred-dollar bill from his pocket and dropped it in the sheik's lap. "Send one of your cousins to him. She doesn't understand Arabic and she'll think some camp business has come up. Have your man tell him that I want to talk to him . . . on an extremely important matter."

"Where, Effendi? Eyes are everywhere."

"The diggings. I'm not worried about the eyes. Just the ears."

The sheik smoothed out the crumpled bill. He caressed it fondly. "The Americans make such beautiful things, Effendi. You could not add one more?"

"I could not."

"And the insurance? Surely you have considered that, in view of what happened to you this morning."

"That hundred dollars is clear profit to you, Sheik."

"A man must earn his livelihood, Effendi." He nodded. "The message will be delivered."

21

AHMED walked between the buildings toward the tel. Eyes would be spying from the buildings, but he was walking openly. They would merely think he was mad, walking about in the midday sun. Mad dogs and Englishmen . . . and Egyptians.

He reached the tel, but did not enter the trenches. The heat would be stifling without the slight breeze that was above ground.

He did not look toward the camp. Everyone in the camp knew of his trouble with Holterman that morning. They could understand that he was concerned about his job, that he was meeting Holterman to apologize to him, to beg for forgiveness.

Holterman took his time. The Druse had not put the message across strongly. Perhaps the sheik was at fault there. For a hundred dollars he should have known how to coach his man, how to make Holterman understand the urgency of Ahmed's midday request.

It was twenty minutes when Ahmed finally heard the crunch of boots on sand. He turned.

Holterman's face was set in hard line. "What the devil's so important that you could not come to me?"

"Your wife, Effendi. I thought you might want to talk to me without her hearing."

"We could have spoken in Arabic," snapped Holterman. Then he stabbed a well-manicured finger at Ahmed. "You didn't summon me here to talk to me about my wife. I warned you about that . . ."

Humility was still in Ahmed's tone. He said quickly, "No, Effendi. I wanted to tell you about the manuscript."

"What the devil are you talking about?"

"Surely you have heard about the manuscript that Professor Hill found!"

Holterman's eyes narrowed. "This is it, Fosse! You talk now and you say something, or it's your finish."

"If you will permit, Effendi. You are aware that Hill made a discovery of great magnitude."

"I've heard the talk, yes. But I have yet to hear one concrete, valid statement by one competent person."

"The manuscript exists."

"You've seen it?"

"Not precisely. But someone . . . "

"There we go again!" cried Holterman. In his fury he clawed savagely at Ahmed's arm. Ahmed struck sideward, dislodging Holterman's grip.

"I've had enough!" Holterman raged. "You've been snooping around, sticking your nose into things that don't concern you. You've gathered up every damn bit of rumor and gossip and you come to me with it. Do you take me for a fool, Egyptian? Do you think you can win favor from me for gossip that I've heard too much of myself?"

Ahmed took a step back, away from Holterman, so that the latter would not again attempt to grab him. He said, and now without humility: "You said yesterday that if you could prove John the Apostle lived here, you would be satisfied." He turned suddenly and pointed toward the limestone cliffs. "His bones are up there, Holterman. What do you think I was doing up there, practicing mountain climbing? There's a cave there. John's bones are in it."

Holterman's eyes were upon the cliffs. The rage was seeping out of him, but he was not yielding. "The cave I'll accept. I'll even concede that there might be skeletons there, artifacts surely. But proof of John's existence?"

"Hill found the cave. He also found the manuscript."

Holterman stared at Ahmed. "How do you know?"

"I can't tell you that. You've forbidden the subject . . . "

Holterman's face twisted. "My wife again!" The muscles of his jaws played. "I'll concede this much and you'd better justify it . . . I know my wife was — friendly — with Hill . . . " He grimaced again. "She took you to Tiberias the night before last. She told you about Hill?"

Ahmed nodded.

"Damn her!" swore Holterman. "She doesn't draw the line anywhere. A man she'd just met . . . " He paused. "I've been thinking about you, Fosse. Did you just *happen* to come to this camp? Or did you have a particular reason? I mean, did you know my wife before you came here?"

"I did not." Ahmed paused now. "I knew another member of the expedition."

"Who?"

"I'll give you that answer later. Right now, accept my word that Hill did find a manuscript, that it's quite possibly the most important artifact that's ever been found by any archaeologist anywhere. It's more important than the discovery of Tutankhamen's tomb. It would make you more famous than Breasted."

Holterman was breathing heavily. "I would not be telling the truth if I said I hadn't considered the possibilites of the rumors being truth. I've even thought of there being a letter — or document — in John's own handwriting . . . a document that would be authentic, that could not be disputed . . . Yes, Fosse, I know what such an artifact would be worth."

"It would be worth everything, wouldn't it? To a man like you."

"To *anyone*, not just me."

"It would be the second most valuable

artifact that could be found by any archaeologist."

"Second most valuable?"

"I was just speculating. What if the manuscript was a letter *written* to John? Signed by . . . "

Holterman cried out hoarsely, "By whom?"

"John's leader."

"No!" cried Holterman wildly. "That — that would be too much!"

"Would it, Mr. Holterman? Have you considered the value of such a document? It would be quite a treasure, wouldn't it? To use the late A. D. Hill's very words: 'the greatest discovery ever made by man.'"

Holterman was stunned into silence. But Ahmed knew that thoughts were running pell-mell in the other's mind. Thoughts of fame, power. All else now was gone from Charles Holterman. If the thing that Ahmed was dangling before him could be acquired, could be snatched . . .

Yes, Holterman would do anything to acquire the thing that he was thinking about.

Holterman said: "My wife has seen that manuscript?"

"She says so."

Holterman shook his head. "There's been an air of triumph about her these last two days. It's been in her attitude, her voice, when she speaks to me. She's been making threats ... " He nodded slowly. "That would account for it." He turned and looked toward the camp.

"No, Effendi," said Ahmed quietly. "You couldn't choke it out of her. She's stronger than you are."

"I wonder," mused Holterman.

"The prize is too rich, Effendi," cautioned Ahmed. "Don't let it slip away because of a hasty move."

"You're right." Holterman turned back to the cliff. "Is it up there?"

"I don't think so."

"You don't really know *where* it is?"

"Those men who were shooting at me this morning, Effendi. They're the ones Hill was dealing with."

Holterman was aghast. "He intended to *sell* the manuscript to ... to *gangsters*?"

"He was asking a million dollars. But there was a slip in the negotiations.

266

I don't know precisely what. Perhaps Hill decided he wanted more money. Perhaps the others could not come up with the actual cash. They had a falling-out ... and Hill made a run for it. Somebody killed him, but then found out that Hill didn't have the manuscript with him. Only the container in which he had found it."

"Then he hid it! While he was being pursued?"

Ahmed nodded.

"My wife was with him," Holterman said, a note of triumph in his tone. "I know that much. The Druse reported ... " He scarcely even grimaced at the revelation. "Yes, they follow her and report to me. How do you think I knew about the two of you going to Tiberias?"

"Of course," said Ahmed. "You were saying ... your wife was with him that night."

Holterman groaned. "Hill knew he was being shadowed. He lost the Druse in the vicinity of Nazareth. I don't know where they went, what happened after eleven o'clock. But Alice knows. She was with him when he eluded the Druse."

"She says they quarreled and she left him."

"Damn! Did she say he had the manuscript with him at the time?"

Ahmed shrugged. "Mrs. Holterman does not tell everything."

"Who does?" Holterman fixed a steely look upon Ahmed. "You haven't told me why you've come to me about — about this."

"I've got an offer," Ahmed said. "I was hoping you would like to improve it."

"I should have expected that, knowing what kind of a man you are."

"What kind of a man am I, Effendi?"

Holterman made a gesture of dismissal. "My wife's made you an offer, I suppose. To help her smuggle the manuscript out of Israel . . . " As he made the statement, the significance of it struck Holterman with full force. "No!" he cried. "She couldn't do that to me." His eyes rolled wildly. "Fosse! Anything! You can name your own price."

"Her offer is a million dollars."

"Money! Bah! I wasn't even thinking of money. If that's what you want, you can have it. More than she'd ever pay you, more than anyone else can put up. One thing I've got is money . . . "

"The plumbing business is good in America?"

"What the devil are you talking about?" Holterman grimaced and made a contemptuous gesture. "You've read that my father made his money manufacturing plumbing supplies. He made money — what's the difference *how*? He didn't steal it, which is more than you can say about some of the fortunes that were made in America — and elsewhere, for that matter. I've no time to discuss that with you. Just get me that manuscript, Fosse. You can write the check yourself and I'll sign it."

"And Mrs. Holterman?"

"The hell with Mrs. Holterman," roared Holterman. "She can have her goddam divorce, anything she wants. Just get me the manuscript, that's all."

Ahmed said quietly, "I'll get it, Mr. Holterman. I'll put it into your hand and then we'll make a settlement."

"When? How soon?"

"Tomorrow, perhaps."

"Not perhaps. Tomorrow — without fail!"

"You are not concerned *how* I get it? What I will have to do?"

"No. Keep the details to yourself. Don't tell me a damned thing. Just hand me the manuscript. That's all I'm interested in."

Charles Holterman's thirst for fame was even greater than Ahmed Fosse had counted upon.

22

HOLTERMAN left him. Ahmed remained by the tel. His eyes roamed about the mound, the excavation. Now and then he looked toward the cliffs.

He paced back and forth and once or twice he thought about the field glasses that might, or might not, be watching him.

Ahmed returned to the manuscript workroom before the Druse went back to their own work. He became engrossed in the jigsaw puzzle on his table and found two pieces that fit into the group. He could then read several words and proceeded with his task. He was aware by mid-afternoon that Miller Wood had not returned to the room, but he was just as well satisfied.

Around four o'clock he set a small fragment of parchment beside a fairly large one and then within minutes put two more pieces with them. He found

271

now that one edge of the second pattern fit with the larger one he had already created and moved the two segments together. A large new piece then fit into the space between and by five o'clock he had a rough segment of pieces put together that measured more than eight inches in diameter.

He read the result. It was a decree issued in Jerusalem, from the Sanhedrin itself, although apparently written by a scribe. It told, in carefully couched terms, of the desire of the Sanhedrin to resist the Romans and to give support to Bar Kochba, if it could be done without exposing the people of Beth-el-Arkam to unnecessary grief. The date, while not given, was undoubtedly at the beginning of Bar Kochba's revolt, which would put it in the Christian year of 129 A.D.

The document, when put together, would be of historical significance. It would account, perhaps, for the fate of the village. Resistance had been stiffened toward the Romans. The Romans, first defeated by Bar Kochba's army, had brought in new legions, and had then started on a campaign of extermination.

This village, having aided Bar Kochba during the early stages of the revolt, was on the Roman death list.

The village had been destroyed. Bar Kochba had met his own end some distance to the south, on a cliff overlooking the Dead Sea.

Yet the document, while important, had nothing to do with John the Apostle.

The early Christian writers had made mention of the longevity of John's life. It he was approximately the same age as Christ, he had lived to the ripe old age of 102 and would therefore have died in 98 A.D. Some Christian authorities, however, held that John had been a mere youth when chosen by His Master, a boy no more than sixteen or seventeen. If he had served Jesus for approximately three years he would have been not more than twenty at the time of Jesus'crucifixion.

Counting the error in the calendar, which had been rectified in modern times from historical date not available to medieval church archivists, Jesus had been born in 4 B.C. and had died in 29 A.D. John, thirteen years younger, would then have lived until 111 A.D.

Or if he was Jesus' age, until 98 A.D.

He could not have lived in Beth-el-Arkam at the time of its destruction, circa 132 A.D.

The manuscript in the cave could not be genuine.

But Ahmed Fosse had not seen the manuscript. He did not know of its written content. He knew of it only from whispers, from rumor. Hill had thought highly of it, enough to risk his life for it. He had died, extolling it as the "greatest discovery ever made by man." A dying man seldom lies with his last breath.

However, Ahmed had done a good day's work here in the manuscript room. He had dated the fall of Beth-el-Arkam. He had even determined the cause. As far as he knew, no one else with the Lake Shore expedition had done more.

It was still more than two hours until nightfall.

Alice Holterman's deadline.

He went outside and stood under the awning that had been stretched over the door to partly cool the doorway. He could see the Druse area from where he stood, and, as usual, he saw Sheik Yussuf seated in his canvas chair, watching.

It was his sheikdom, his domain. He ruled the Druse from that chair. From it he hired and fired, extracted his toll. From it he conducted his espionage. That, Ahmed had learned, he performed impartially. His men spied for whoever paid for the espionage. He probably worked it both ways, taking money from the one who wanted information, from the one he was spying upon.

Yussuf knew everything that went on in the camp.

Almost everything. His men had been lost by A. D. Hill in the archaeologist's last stage.

Or had they? Had Yussuf's 'cousins' followed to the end? Had they reported in full to him?

Ahmed started toward the sheik.

The Arab chieftan watched him approach. "Your talk with the Great One was satisfactory?"

"That insurance, Yussuf. Spell it out again. What do I get for it?"

"The name of the person who killed A. D. Hill."

"What else?"

"The name of the person who — "

"You said that."

"I am saying it again. The information is valuable. For six hundred American dollars . . . "

"Four, you said."

"That was yesterday. The price has gone up." He smiled brightly up at Ahmed. "However, I will make a concession. Four hundred dollars . . . and a small consideration."

Ahmed looked at him sharply.

"That you tell me," said the sheik, "how an Egyptian *fellah* acquired so many American one-hundred-dollar bills?"

"I stole them," snapped Ahmed. "What else?"

"You didn't steal them in Israel. Nor in Egypt."

"Why not Egypt?"

"Surely, Effendi, you do not underestimate me. I am an Arab. I have cousins, well, friends, in Egypt. I have had two days to investigate you."

Ahmed regarded him steadily. "I haven't underestimated you, Yussuf. I know that you don't sit here all night and I know that you're the sheik of your people and that they come and go. They could have telegraphed, or talked by telephone via Cyprus and Cairo. You could have verified that I really worked for Munich's expedition . . . "

"A year and three months," said the sheik. "Dr. Klausner, who wrote you the letter of reference, still speaks well of you."

Ahmed reached into his pocket and brought out a thin sheaf of folded bills. He skimmed off four of them. Yussuf leaned forward, took the bills.

"Allah is merciful, Effendi. You will tell me now how you got this money."

"I will not."

"Then the price is still six hundred dollars." The sheik beamed again. "Please, we will both profit. I will not have to spend money checking on you in France."

"There's a child's fairy tale in France," snapped Ahmed. "The moral of is it that you shouldn't kill the goose that lays the golden eggs."

"Ah, yes, very good, Effendi. I believe I heard that story myself . . . in England. It is an English fairy tale, isn't it?"

"By now it's international. You've got your money."

"The woman," said Yussuf, then as Ahmed showed no surprise, "not Mrs. Holterman. The big one."

"Jacqueline Dietrich."

"You are very self-disciplined, Effendi. You show little emotion. Is not the information startling to you?"

"I live in two worlds, Yussuf, the Arab world and the world of the Franks. I have lived long enough to distrust both."

"That is interesting to know, Effendi. It is no more than I suspected, however. You are always on your guard. It would be interesting to watch you in a real crisis, a matter of life and death . . . of extreme pain. Would you break, Effendi?"

He shook his head.

"Were you in the war, Effendi? The big one."

"You've a reason for asking that."

The sheik shrugged. "Not really. I have so much time that I think about people. In my mind I try to put together puzzles. My cousin Sidi bel Roumi chanced to be passing your window last night — just chanced, mind you — when you were preparing for your couch. You were, ah, taking off your shirt at the moment he happened to look in. He says that your back is scarred to a considerable degree. In my musings, I thought you might have been a prisoner of the Boche during the war. Floggings were not unusual. The Germans do those things very thoroughly."

"Those cousins of yours," said Ahmed meaningly. "Do you lose many of them?"

"Lose? Ah, I see. No. We are a numerous family. We are seldom out of sight or hearing of one another." The sheik chuckled. "It is a comfort, is it not? To have one's family about him in times of, ah, stress or peril?"

Ahmed nodded thoughtfully. "You've seen that I have only one or two of the bills left, Yussuf. But suppose, just suppose, that I could obtain another supply of them. How many would you want for the name of the person who took the manuscript from Mr. Hill?"

A frown actually came to the sheik's face. "Alas, no one is infallible, Effendi. Not even my numerous cousins. They saw the actual placing of the knife into Professor Hill's back, but the professor did not die at once. He lived, apparently, long enough to drive fifteen or twenty kilometers. Unfortunately, he drove extremely fast and there was no one with him when he died. Not that my cousins know of. The woman wielded the knife, but she did not get the manuscript. That I can tell you with certainty." He sighed heavily. "How many of the engravings can you obtain, Effendi?"

"None, if I cannot get the manuscript."

"I wish that we could do business but, alas, we cannot. There may be, however, other things for which we could barter. I will think of some things. Allah be with you, Effendi!"

The last as Ahmed walked abruptly away from him. The sheik looked after him, shaking his head. "There," he said, under his breath, "goes a man who will not live to a ripe old age."

The Druse laborers were coming en masse from the excavations. It would be dinner-time in a few minutes and in an hour the sun would dip the Galilean hills. Darkness would settle swiftly upon the valley of Tel Mas.

Ahmed had not yet formed a plan for the evening.

He went to his sleeping room. Miller Wood was not there. Ahmed left the room and headed for the manuscript room. Wood was not there either.

He judged it to be within minutes of dinner-time.

He decided to be the first in the mess hall.

He was.

A Druse was setting the table. He exclaimed in Arabic, "You are too early, Effendi."

Ahmed seated himself at the center of the table, facing the door.

He waited.

Carolyn Caxton came into the hall in less than two minutes. She walked around, sat down beside him.

For a moment she did not speak, then, with her head bent forward, she said quietly, "I did not get the things I needed last night."

Ahmed shook his head. "I shall be busy tonight."

"Please," she said, "everyone is talking. There will be trouble if you go with her."

He said cruelly: "*You'll* be the one who has the trouble if you chase after me."

She drew in her breath sharply.

"I don't want you. Can I make it any plainer?"

A sob was torn from her throat, but Jacqueline Dietrich came in then.

She stopped on the other side of the table and fixed Ahmed with a porcine stare. "I haven't forgotten, my bucko! I haven't forgiven, either."

She pulled out her stool and sat down. There was a certain amount of grace in her movements that belied her huge proportions. She was not as much fat as she was muscular. Ahmed, however, had already taken note of that during previous observations of her.

The Druse waiter brought in a platter of the inevitable mutton. With it he brought canned tomatoes and stale bread. Dr. Sando entered as the others were helping themselves. He took his seat at the end of the table.

"Mr Fossay," he said, "I chanced to drop in at the scriptorium on my way here. I noted the work you had done in assembling the parchment fragments.

My Aramaic is not of the best, but the message I could make out was of interest. Could you translate it?"

"It was dictated by the Sanhedrin, Mr. Sando. It is, in effect, an order to the village of Beth-el-Arkam to give assistance to Bar Kochba."

"Capital, my dear sir! That was what I thought it was. I recognized the name of Bar Kochba."

And that's about all you did make out, thought Ahmed. He said, however, "A few fragments are missing, but if I find them, I believe I can give you a written translation by noon tomorrow."

"Splendid. I shall so inform Mr. Holterman. He will be pleased." Sando grimaced. "I, er, meant that it will do much to offset the difficulty of this morning."

Holterman had already spoken to Sando to release the pressure on Ahmed.

Jacqueline said: "You are to be congratulated, Mr. Fosse." She looked about pointedly. "And where is our dear friend, Miller Wood? Was he present this afternoon when you assembled the fragments?"

"He was around," replied Ahmed. "In and out."

"In and out, eh? Come to think of it, I haven't seen hide or hair of him since noon."

Dr. Sando stopped in the act of ladling mutton upon his plate. "Wood's taken time off? He did not inform me."

"He may be ill," said Jacqueline heartily. "Is he in his bed, Mr. Fosse?"

Ahmed shook his head. Damn the woman. "He said something about working outside this afternoon."

"Indeed?" said Sando. "He was not at the tel. I spent an hour there just before dinner." The scowl was back on his face. "I wish the members of this team would keep me informed of their activities. At least during working hours. Miss Caxton, we have not heard from you. Have you seen Mr. Wood this afternoon?"

"No, Dr. Sando," replied Caxton.

"He gave up?" chortled Jacqueline. She winked at Dr. Sando. "Perhaps he went to Nazareth to get what he could not get here. Correction. Tiberias." She turned to Ahmed. "Isn't there a night club in Tiberias that is called *Salome and the*

Seven Veils? I thought I heard you mention it yesterday."

"Miss Dietrich," Sando said severely, "drop the subject, will you?"

"As you say, Effendi Doctor. I'll finish my dinner and retire to my bed with a good book. And that's all I'll take to bed with me." She looked at Ahmed and Carolyn with an expression that indicated she did not believe they spent their evening reading.

Ahmed finished eating. He pushed back his stool, bowed to excuse himself. Beside him, a quick look of anguish flitted across Carolyn's face. He saw it.

He went outside.

Alice Holterman was standing in front of the house she occupied with her husband. The Cadillac was not too far away.

Ahmed stood in front of the mess hall for a minute or two, then began strolling toward the Druse area. For once, the sheik was not in his canvas chair. Ahmed caught a glimpse of him seated under the awninged table with a number of his 'cousins.' They were having their evening meal.

Ahmed continued on, apparently out for an evening stroll. He was soon, however, going down the rutted road that led to the highway.

He had gone a hundred yards when he heard the Cadillac. He moved to the side of the road.

The Cadillac pulled up.

Alice looked at him inquiringly. He nodded.

He opened the door and climbed in beside her. She sent the car hurtling forward. It bounced and jolted over the rutted road, swept through the cut between the two ridges, and headed for the Tiberias-Nazareth highway.

"Which way?" she asked, then.

"Tiberias."

She sent him a quick look. "I thought it would be Nazareth."

23

SHE made the turn into the main road. Behind them the sun was setting. There were shadows on the pavement. Alice kept her foot heavily on the accelerator and the big Cadillac purred smoothly.

Ahmed saw a signpost ahead. "Slow down."

She took her foot of the gas pedal, braked lightly. The signpost loomed up on the right. Lettered in Hebrew and Arabic was the legend: *Shobetha 8 kms.*

The road did not cross the pavement. Alice turned into it. There was only desert ahead. And desolation. She looked sideward at Ahmed.

"Stop," he said.

The ruts were lights. The road was seldom used by vehicles. She pulled to the right, braked to a stop, and shut off the ignition.

"Go ahead," she said ominously.

"I don't know where it is."

"You don't, eh? I want a cigarette." She reached for her bag on her left side. Ahmed was not quite fast enough. She got the bag before he could stop her. Her left hand snapped it open, groped inside, and came out with a .32 automatic that could have been a twin to the one Holterman had taken from Ahmed that morning.

Perhaps it was the same automatic.

She crossed her hand in front of her, pressed the automatic against Ahmed's side. "You've got about five seconds left," she said savagely. "And don't think I won't shoot."

"I know you will," Ahmed replied. "You're as much of a killer at heart as Jacqueline Dietrich . . . "

"That fat cow," snapped Alice. Then she stopped. "Jacqueline?"

"She killed A. D. Hill."

"She was in Nazareth that night." Alice's eyes slitted, then suddenly she opened them. "You found that out and you're using it to stall. If that's all you can do . . . "

"Pull the trigger," said Ahmed, "and you'll never see the manuscript again."

She stared at him in the failing light.

The pressure of the gun against his side did not relax. "The Greek would make you talk."

"Do you think so?"

She looked at him again for a long moment. "I think he would, but I'll admit that I'm not certain. But if *he* can't make you talk, I can't either. I'll have to make my deal with Petrakis."

"He doesn't know where it is. I don't either, but I think I can find it."

"In how long a time?"

"Tonight."

She said coldly: "Anything to get this gun out of your side. Anything to keep me from pulling the trigger!"

"I want that million as much as you want your two."

The pressure of the gun was relaxed. But only a trifle. She said: "Do you know where to search?"

"With your help — yes."

"My help? I told you I didn't know where it was. I had a quarrel with Hill and he threw me out of the car."

"Mrs. Holterman," Ahmed began and was interrupted by her.

"Formal to the end!"

"I've trained myself to think," he went on. "I can concentrate as few people can. You think *you* can concentrate. You can't. It takes years of practice. You have to learn to shut off all of your senses, except the power of concentration. I can do it. I want to take you through your last night with A. D. Hill. I want to know every tiny thing you did, I want to know everywhere you went. You may have been places, done things, or seen things that barely touched your subconscious. I'll bring it out and somewhere along the line I'll find the answer. Believe me, I will."

The pressure of the gun muzzle relaxed again. For a long moment Alice was quiet. Then she nodded.

"I've heard that they can do it in India, in the Himalayas. I don't think those people are any stronger than you."

"You've got to help. Concentrate as hard as you can. We'll begin at the beginning of the evening. You drove to Nazareth in your car to meet Hill."

"How do you know that?"

"Hill was in his own car. You picked me up the next morning in yours. You said you'd been driving around all night ... Where did you meet Hill in Nazareth?"

"Our usual place. In front of the Nazareth Café."

"Keep thinking hard. Was he there before you?"

She nodded.

"You parked your car where?"

"A block away. I walked to his car and got in with him."

"Think again. He had the copper cylinder with him?" As she nodded: "Did you open it?"

"Not then. Later ... "

"Where was that?"

"Where we went."

"*Where?*"

"Where could we go?" she asked tartly. "There's only one lousy hotel in Nazareth. Twenty-four rooms and two baths. You've got to fight off the cockroaches with clubs. We drove to a road north of Nazareth. It runs along the mountaintop and there isn't much night traffic."

"What did you do there?"

"Damn it, what do you think we did?"

"All right, you said you saw the

manuscript. Before or after?"

"Before. I wanted to make damn sure he had it."

"He showed it to you. Did he read it?"

"What was the use of that? I'm not a Jew. I wouldn't have understood it. He told me what was in it."

"And?"

"It was a letter." She hesitated. "We've gone this far, all right. Hill said it was addressed to John the Apostle."

"There was a signature?"

He could see the shudder that ran through her. "Yes. It was signed . . . Jesus."

"What did Hill say the letter was about?"

"Nothing much. Just a friendly letter that Jesus wrote when He was in Nazareth and John was in Jerusalem. Greetings and that sort of thing. He wanted John to see some relatives of both of them. Give them His blessing. Hill said the contents weren't important. What *was* important was that it was written by Jesus Himself, that He had signed the letter."

"He was *sure* about the letter? It wasn't . . . a forgery?"

"Don't be a fool." She cocked her head to one side. "He did say that it was strange . . . that it looked not new, but not old either. But he said the cylinder was authentic, that he'd had a hard time removing the lid. It was — fused — he said. And the writing was correct for the time. He was an expert on those things. I checked with Charles about — about Hill. He said Hill, in spite of his faults, was the best man in the world on the — the Aramaic language."

"He may have been right. I've read his articles on the subject. He knew what he was talking about. Concentrate again now . . . You saw the letter . . . "

"I had it in my hands."

"Hill told you what was in it. Then what happened? Did he fold it again and put it back in the container?"

"Fold it? It was rolled . . . "

Ahmed nodded. "I threw that in just to see if you were concentrating. It *had* to be in a roll. He put it back in the container?"

"Of course."

"You're sure of that? It's important."

Her forehead creased in thought. Then

293

she nodded. "I remember it distinctly. He had to bang the lid a couple of times to make it fit on the cylinder."

"And then?"

"We made love. You want a description of that?"

"Skip it. Afterward?"

"A car came along. It passed us and Don got panicky. The Sicilians and the Greek were in the car."

"They'd followed you?"

"I don't see how they could have. But Don thought so. He was supposed to meet them in Nazareth later. About two hours later. When he saw them on the road, he said they were going to try a double-cross. Kill us both and steal the manuscript. We got out of there in a hurry. He practically ran them off the road. They followed, but they couldn't catch us, not the way he was driving."

"Where'd you go?"

She hesitated. "To Nazareth. We drove around, stopping a few times. We talked . . . "

"Wait a minute. You drove around. Where?"

"The city. No place special."

"Once to get some cigarettes. Another time he wanted to get away from the car, see if anybody was watching us. The third time, same. Then again, later."

She leaned away from him, staring at the darkening sky. She had forgotten about the gun. It rested on her lap now, although she still held it in her hand. But loosely.

She was thinking over something she had said.

"The cigarettes. He lit one and gave me one later. The package was more than half-filled."

"Where'd he go to buy the cigarettes?" exclaimed Ahmed.

"A little *Hall neer Ka-Khat* — drugstore. A dirty little store."

"He went in alone?"

She nodded. "He wasn't gone long, but . . . "

"Think, Alice," he urged. "Do you remember where the store was?"

"The damn places all look alike to me. It's a dirty old city. I wouldn't buy a newspaper in any of the stores if they were back home. Here it's about what you expect."

He leaned across and turned the ignition key. "We'll find the store and when we do, we might get our answer."

She started the motor, made a sharp U-turn, leaving the rutted road, then swung back onto it. She switched on the lights and sent the car toward the paved road.

She headed the car toward Nazareth. The gun was lying on the seat between them. Ahmed glanced at it. "Put it away, if it makes you feel better to have it. Otherwise . . . "

She reached for the gun, scooped it up, and switching it to her left hand, managed to put it back into her purse. She stepped harder on the accelerator.

She passed the Tel Mas turn-off without slackening speed. There was fairly heavy traffic on the road, but she zoomed in and out of her lane. She was utterly oblivious about the rights of other drivers and drove as if she were the only driver on a central Nevada highway.

24

THEY passed Kfar Kana. The lights of Nazareth glittered ahead, but she did not slacken her speed until the streets narrowed and then she slowed down only after a narrow escape, almost striking an Arab, who was riding a donkey.

She may have despised the city of Nazareth and been little aware of the streets and the landmarks, but she had no difficulty finding the drugstore. She brought the Cadillac to an abrupt halt outside the store. She withdrew the ignition keys and started to get out of the car.

He touched her arm. "Better if I go in."

"I want to know every damn thing that goes on," she retorted. "You're not going to pull any double-cross on me . . . "

"You go in with me and we'll get nothing." He nodded toward the store. "I'm an Arab. They'll talk to me. They'll freeze up as they always do with tourists."

She hesitated, but saw the validity of his statement.

"I'll be watching," she warned.

He got out of the car, went around it, and strolled up to the window. He looked in, saw the place was empty of customers. He opened the door.

A bell jangled at the rear. A young Arab made his appearance from an alcove at the rear of the prescription counter."

"Good evening, Effendi," he said, bowing.

"May you be twice blessed by Jesus," said Ahmed in Arabic.

The Arab brightened. "You are a Christian? The fez ... for a moment I thought ... "

"I have lived in Egypt and the fez is an old habit. We are few in numbers in Egypt, but we try to make the pilgrimage to the home of Our Savior."

"Can I be of service to you, Effendi?" asked the young Arab.

"A man I came to see in Nazareth, a Frank; I was with him three nights ago and he excused himself to come in here to make a purchase ... "

The Arab was listening, but his

expression was blank.

Ahmed went on. "He asked me to drop by this evening and purchase the same thing. For him. Alas, I have forgotten what he told me to buy."

"A razor? Toothpaste? We carry a complete line from America. Soap. Perfume . . . something for a lady?"

Ahmed shook his head. "Perhaps I'd better describe the man. He was about forty-five, tanned from the sun. He was wearing khaki trousers . . . "

"You are talking about Professor Hill?" exclaimed the Arab.

Ahmed exclaimed, "You knew him?"

The Arab shrugged. "The Israeli police are very thorough. They had been to every store, every church in Nazareth. They had a picture of him . . . " He grimaced. "They forced open his eyelids, but he was dead when they took the picture. It was not a pretty sight."

"What did they want to know about him?"

"The police do not tell things. They ask questions, they ask a thousand questions, until you do not know what you are replying."

"Did they want to know what he bought here?"

"If they asked that once, they asked it twenty times."

"What did you tell them?"

"Nothing."

"You told them nothing, or he bought nothing?"

"He bought nothing. A five-agorot roll of . . . " He walked to the right a few feet, scooped up a roll of Scotch tape, with its tin dispenser. "A roll of this . . . Scotch tape, it says here in English, which I do not read very well, but I know from the trade name."

Ahmed took out a coin and dropped it on the counter. He picked up the Scotch tape. "May Jesus bless you," he said and started for the door.

Outside, Alice watched him come toward the car. He got in beside her.

"Well?" she asked.

"The next stop — after you left here."

"Don't tantalize me. What did you find out, if anything?"

He tossed the Scotch tape into her lap. "That's what he bought."

She picked up the Scotch tape, stared

at it, then at Ahmed. "It doesn't make sense." Then suspicion came back. "You're holding out . . ."

"We haven't got time," Ahmed said grimly. "Drive on to the next place you stopped."

She tossed the tape dispenser to the seat between them. She started the car, headed for the next corner, and turned left. She drove downhill for two blocks, then swung to the side of the street. They were in front of a church.

"He got out and stood there under the lamppost. He wanted to see if we were being followed."

"You stayed in the car?"

"Most of the time. I got tired,then got out and went over to him. He didn't like it and he snapped at me. I gave it back to him and then we got in the car again."

"While he was by the post, did you keep your eyes on him . . . every minute?"

She hesitated, then nodded. "He wasn't exactly by the post. He stood three or four feet from it. He watched the cars that went by, the people."

"He never touched the post at all? You're sure of that?"

She thought a moment. "He never touched the post."

"The next place."

He was not to surprised a few minutes later, when she parked her car about a half block from another church. It was the church into which Ahmed had gone the evening before with Carolyn Caxton. The Church of Joseph.

"He went inside?" asked Ahmed quietly.

"Yes." Then she added, "I followed him. I'm not a Catholic, but I resented the idea of being left outside. We'd already had words . . . "

"Stop for a moment," Ahmed said. "He went inside and you followed. After how long an interval?"

"Right away. He wasn't even inside. I called to him and he stopped by the door. We — we talked. Then he went inside. I followed . . . a half minute afterward. No, it couldn't have been more than ten or fifteen seconds."

"The copper cylinder? He took it with him?"

"Of course. He gave it to me inside to hold while he . . . while he prayed."

"Hill prayed?"

"I was as much surprised as you are. You could have knocked me over with a ... " She laughed shortly without humor. "He wasn't praying much up there on the mountain."

Ahmed said: "Let's do it step by step. I'll get out of the car. You follow at the distance you followed him. Call to me and I'll stop, then we'll go inside and do exactly as you did the other night."

She exhaled heavily. "If this concentration business pays off, it'll be the first miracle this town's seen in about nineteen hundred years."

He waited until she had stopped talking. Then he got out of the car and walked toward the church entrance. He walked easily, with direction.

He was a dozen feet from the church door when he heard her call. "Ahmed!"

He stopped, turned. She came up quickly.

"You said he was at the door when you called him."

"I missed by a few feet. I don't see how it matters."

"It may matter a great deal. Keep your

mind on it. I'm going in alone. You wait, as nearly as you can determine, the time you waited before. Then come in. Inside, do what you did the last time."

"All right," she said, "we'll play it out."

He opened the church door and went in.

He had to remind himself not to stop inside, but to go ahead, as Hill had probably done. Automatically.

The holy water font was at his right. He moved toward it, dipped his fingertips into the marble font and touched his forehead, then made the sign of the cross. He paused a moment, as Hill had probably paused, then went forward.

His ears were attuned to the sounds about him. He felt a puff of fresh air on the back of his head, heard heels clicking. Then she said, sharply behind him:

"Wait!"

He stopped. He was still three feet from the first row of pews.

He said quietly, "This is where he was when you caught up?"

"We're not off an inch," she said. She

looked around. "I'm not used to churches. They give me the willies . . . "

"Keep your mind on the subject. What pew did you go to?"

"Right here. The last one."

Ahmed stepped to the pew and stood aside for her to enter first. She touched his arm. "He went in first . . . "

He entered the pew, kneeled, and made the sign of the cross. She sat down beside him and whispered, "I thought you were a Moslem."

"I'm doing what Hill did. He knelt when he prayed, didn't he?"

"Yes, but *I* didn't. I sat here."

"How long did he pray?"

"About long enough to say the Lord's Prayer."

He mouthed the words silently, looked up at her. She shook her head and he repeated the mouthing. She nodded when he looked at her again.

He started to his feet.

"That's when he gave me the cylinder to carry."

He pantomined the movement and she moved out of the pew. Ahmed followed, turned toward the altar and genuflected as

Hill must have done. He caught up with her by the font.

He stopped. The holy water font was a massive piece of marble or carved stone. It was almost black from cleaning or polishing through the ages. It rested on a square pedestal. The font itself was routed out of the native stone. It was a good two feet across, although the pedestal itself was only half that thick.

Ahmed stepped past Alice, groped suddenly underneath the font. He ran his hand along the stone. He moved around past Alice, who was watching him narrowly.

He was in front now, facing the interior of the church. His hand went under the font . . . and he touched it!

An electric shock seemed to run through Ahmed's arm and he was surprised that he could feel such a stimulated triumph.

The roll of parchment was not more than eight inches long, perhaps an inch and a half thick. It was attached to the bottom of the font . . . with Scotch tape.

He wrenched it loose. The tape had not adhered too well. Hill had been in a hurry. There were only seconds between the time he had come into the church and the arrival of Alice. He had guessed that she would follow him.

Ahmed whipped up the parchment roll, thrust it quickly between two buttons of his shirt against his stomach.

Alice's eyes gleamed. They walked together out of the church without speaking.

Ahmed pulled open the door for her and let her go out first. He followed, allowing the door to swing shut.

They walked silently, swiftly to the car. Neither spoke a word. Not until they were in the car and the door was closed. Then Alice said: "The miracle happened!"

"The Scotch tape was the tip-off. The minute I learned what he bought at the drugstore, I knew it was only a matter of finding the place where he'd hidden it. You crowded him close and he had to get rid of it at the first place where he could lose you for a moment."

"No," she said, "he planned it. He stopped in at the church twice . . . two nights before the last one. In fact, now that I think back, he went through the whole thing. The mountain ride . . . " She shook her head. "All except the drugstore bit. That was new. He was always sure we were being followed and he pulled all sorts of stunts to catch whoever was following us. We never saw anyone who knew us, except . . . " She said, sharply then, "The Dietrich woman! She was walking by, right here, when we came out. She tried to talk to us, but Hill wouldn't have any of it. I wouldn't either. We cut her dead and got into the car. And then we started the fight all over."

She stopped.

"Let's have it," Ahmed urged.

"He threw the Jewish girl at me. Said he'd rather sleep with her than . . . Oh, what's the difference? We had one helluva fight while we were driving . . . "

"While you were driving?"

"You can yell and drive. Then . . . he threw me out. The car was still moving when he opened the door on your side and shoved me out. He went off like a bat out of hell and I picked myself out of the gutter and found my car. I wasn't in any mood to go back to the camp. Not when I got time to think. I smelled a double-cross. The damn quarrel was a phony. He knew about my temper and he forced it on me, so he could get away with the manuscript . . . "

"No," said Ahmed soberly. "If he planned it that way, he wouldn't have been compelled to hide the manuscript in the church. Not for that reason alone. He knew someone was following . . . "

"Dietrich?"

Ahmed hesitated. "You ran into her after you came out. Did you see her before . . . ?"

She shook her head.

"Anyone? The Italians . . . ?"

"Not after the mountain. But we lost them up there."

"You said you'd gone through the routine two nights before. On those occasions did you really see anyone who knew you?"

"No. No one following us."

"But you *did* see someone?"

"We met Petrakis the night before. At Kfar Kana. He had the Italians with him. But at that time Hill was still dickering with them. Everything was nice and friendly . . . "

"Let's go to Kfar Kana."

She started to drive off, then looked at him.

"We've got the manuscript. We don't have to go back over the trail any more."

"When I'm running," Ahmed said, "I like to know where the hounds are before they start barking."

"They'll be after us soon enough. Which way do we run, north, east, south — west?"

"You've got a road map?"

She indicated the glove compartment. "Everything I need is in the trunk. I'm traveling light."

He was silent a moment. "I need a half hour back at the camp."

"Don't be a fool! We've got everything that matters. I've enough money for expenses. There isn't a damn thing back there that's important."

"I've got to settle some personal business . . . "

"The hell you have. I've got everything she's got and more."

"I'm going back," Ahmed said, "with or without you . . . "

She reached for the bag at her left side,

but this time Ahmed was too swift for her. His arm snaked out, caught the bag. She clawed at him, almost running the car into a building. She swerved away in time and by then he had taken the automatic out of the purse. He tossed the purse to her lap. The automatic he kept in his hand away from her.

"Our partnership's getting off to a swell start," she said savagely.

"It'll work out," he offered by way of peacemaking. "You can wait for me outside the camp if you want. I'll be a half hour, no more, no less."

"And those bloody Arabs'll be snooping all over the place. There's always one around everywhere you turn."

"You've a great contempt for them?"

"Now don't go taking things personal again. I don't think of you as an Arab. If I had, I'd never have picked you up on the road, right about here. Buster-boy, we're in this together. All the way. We're not going to fight. Hill and I did that and trouble came out of it, that's all. I'm not against Arabs. I just don't like them crawling all over me. Spying."

"Spying," said Ahmed. "Have you ever

bothered to talk to one of them, the
Druse? I mean, aside from your house
servant."

"They can't talk English, I can't talk
Arabic."

"Some of them speak excellent English.
Their sheik, for instance."

"I've seen him. Lazy, good-for-nothing."

"He's a graduate of Cambridge."

"What? Why, he looks as filthy as the
rest of them."

"That's what he wants you to think.
I'm going to tell you something about that
particular Arab. He's the hereditary sheik
of his people. His father and his father's
father, and a good many generations
before them, all ruled his particular tribe
of Druse. They were here for a good
many hundred of years before there were
any Jews in Israel. I mean during the
thousand or more year that Hebrew were
away from this country."

"So what? I read all that in guide book
before I came to this damn country."

"You're missing what I'm trying to
tell you. The Druse are intermarried,
interrelated. They're a clannish lot. It's
one for all, all against the Jew . . . against

the outlander. You, me . . . every European and American who comes to this country."

"They're glad enough to take our money."

Ahmed shrugged. "That's your husband's viewpoint. The Druse are a colored race — to him. He doesn't understand them, never will."

"And you do? Because of the Egyptian blood in you? This isn't Egypt . . . "

"I don't understand them much more than you do. But I speak Arabic. I've had some talks with the sheik. I've given him money . . . "

"Agorots, or whatever the hell they call the local money . . . "

"American dollars," retorted Ahmed. "They're potent, here as well as anywhere in the world. The sheik knows every single thing that happens in the camp, a great deal that happens outside. His cousins, as he calls them, all work for him. They report everything to him and they watch everything . . . and everybody. They watched you and Hill."

"What?"

"In camp and outside. Yes, in Nazareth.

You didn't know they were watching you, because you're not even aware of the Druse. That man you almost ran down on the donkey, when we came in, he was a Druse. But they don't all ride donkeys. Quite a few of them drive cars."

"You mean to tell me that we were being watched, mmm, up there on the mountain the night . . . "

"Yes. As a matter of fact, I paid Sheik Yussuf for that information. His men followed you until Hill threw you out of the car. He drove away so fast then that he lost them."

"They followed us into the church?"

"Perhaps not. At least not closely enough to see where Hill hid the manuscript."

"Why are you telling me all this now?"

"So you don't make any wrong moves when we get back to the camp. Just wait for me. Stay in the car, don't talk to anyone. Don't go anywhere where you don't want to be seen."

"All the more reason we ought to cut out now. We can be in Jordan in an hour . . . "

"Syria. Jordan's too close. They'll be expecting us to go that way. Tiberias is too close to Jordan."

"All right, Syria. But let's go now. No one's following us . . . "

"Don't be too sure."

She looked over her shoulder, then into the rear-vision mirror. "They're keeping their distance, if they're following . . . " She stepped heavier onto the accelerator and the Cadillac began to purr loudly.

Ahmed waited a moment.

Then: "Ease off. We're almost there."

She held her foot down on the accelerator. He said: "In three seconds I'll take the wheel from you."

She waited two of the seconds, then raised her foot. She shot him a venomous look.

The car slowed and Ahmed saw the Tel Mas road sign ahead.

Alice braked the car, suddenly twisting the wheel. The car made a sharp right turn, threatening for an instant to turn over. It was during that instant that Ahmed saw the police car, blocking the rutted road.

Alice almost hit the car, but came to a

BOS21

stop a foot from it. Two Israeli policeman came trotting toward the Cadillac. One of them had been with the previous police expedition. He recognized Alice Holterman and touched his hand to his cap.

"Mrs. Holterman," he said. He gestured to the other policeman.

"Let them through."

"What's the idea?" she demanded.

"We're trying to keep outsiders away," the first policeman said. "I'm afraid there's been a little trouble . . . "

"What kind of trouble?" asked Ahmed quickly.

The policeman was chary of replying. But he had not been specifically coached by his superior at the camp. "A man's been killed . . . "

"A man?" cried Alice. "Who . . . ?"

"I believe his name's Wood."

"Miller Wood," said Ahmed.

Alice Holterman screamed. "Oh, *no*!"

"Would you like me to drive?" asked the policeman.

She covered her face and began to sob violently. But even as she sobbed, she moved out from under the wheel.

The policeman got into the car, took the wheel.

She was pressed against Ahmed. He could feel the sobs wracking her body. She did it extremely well. She had sized up the situation quickly and had decided that the frail woman act was called for. It would prevent much questioning, much supervision of her acts and movements.

The policeman had probably never driven an American Cadillac and he handled the machine as if it had been made of precious metals. He eased it along the ruts, increased the speed only slightly over the smooth parts of the road.

They reached the camp. Several police cars were parked around. There were three or four uniformed policemen about. A searchlight or two had been set up, and the area between the Druse tents and the buildings housing the team members was brightly lighted.

The main activity was around Dr. Sando's building and it was to this that the policeman moved after shutting off the motor of the car.

Alice stayed in the car, sobbing. In between sobs she whispered to Ahmed:

"We've got to get away."

He replied quietly, "It's going to take a while."

"Make it as soon as you can. I'll be ready any time you are. Quick now, hand me the manuscript. They won't search me."

"No," he said. "I'll hold onto it."

"You fool, they're liable to search you."

"I don't think so."

"You double-cross me, I'll crucify you," she threatened.

He got out of the car. She remained in it, her face buried in her hands. Ahmed joined the policeman at the door. He looked toward the car.

"Perhaps it will be all right for a while," he said.

Ahmed went inside.

25

D R. SANDO was at his desk. Charles Holterman stood nearby, beside Jacqueline Dietrich. The sheik was in one corner. The rest of the room seemed to be filled with officials and policemen.

Dr. Sando exclaimed as Ahmed entered, "Here he is now!"

One of the officials turned upon Ahmed. "Your passport, please!"

Ahmed handed it to him. "You looked at it three days ago. It hasn't changed."

The official gave him a sharp look. "The Egyptian, yes! You know, of course, what our attitude is toward Egyptians?"

"The passport is French," Ahmed reminded.

"So it seems. We shall check it." He closed the book and put it into his pocket.

Ahmed said: "You're keeping it?"

"Until this is cleared up." The official added grimly: "You won't need it, since you won't be traveling for a while."

"I'm under arrest?"

"No one's under arrest. Not yet. Two members of this expedition have been murdered within three days. That is a major calamity, Mr. Fosse. Even in this country. There will be an exhaustive investigation. We shall not rest until we have the criminal in custody."

Holterman said suddenly: "Where's Mrs. Holterman?"

Ahmed did not reply. The policeman who had come with Ahmed said: "Outside in the car, sir."

"What's she doing out there?"

"I'm afraid she's, ah, crying, sir," said the policeman.

Holterman blinked.

The Israeli official said to Ahmed: "Are you prepared to make a statement of your movements for this evening?"

"Why not? I left here shortly after six o'clock . . . "

"Alone?"

"I started out alone, but Mrs. Holterman was going into town and gave me a lift."

"What town, Mr. Fosse?"

"Nazareth."

"Not the *Seven Veils* tonight?" chirped in Jacqueline Dietrich.

"Please!" the official turned to her. "Seven Veils?"

"That's where they went night before last. *Salome and the Seven Veils*. It's a joint in Tiberias."

"I know the place."

"I figured they were going for an encore tonight," went on the Amazon.

Dr. Sando could not restrain himself. "Miss Dietrich — please!"

"Uh-uh, Sandy, old boy," chortled Jacqueline. "These lads are cops and you talk to them when they ask you questions."

"They haven't asked you . . . "

The official reasserted his authority. "If you don't mind, I'd like to pursue my duties. Mr. Fosse, you said Mrs. Holterman gave you a ride to Nazareth. Did she drop you anywhere?"

"Not exactly. She merely wanted to get some aspirin at the drugstore. I went in and bought it for her, then we started back and decided to stop and have a cup of coffee."

"Where?"

321

"I don't know Nazareth. Just a place. Couldn't tell you precisely where it was, what its name was."

"And that is all you can tell me?"

"If I told you more, I'd be making it up."

"Gentlemen," said Charles Holterman suddenly, "would it be out of order if I went out and talked to my wife?"

"I must apologize," exclaimed the official. "It was thoughtless of me. Of course you may go to her. I will not question her until she has recovered somewhat from the shock. You may assure her of that."

"Thank you. I will."

Holterman went out.

Jacqueline Dietrich snickered. "Yes, sir, Mrs. Holterman needs a bit of comforting. She certainly does."

Ahmed said: "How was he killed?"

The official hesitated. "You have a right to know, I think. His neck was broken. His head was twisted around . . . "

"Took a strong man to do that," opined Jacqueline.

Ahmed said: "Or a strong woman."

"Whoa-ho, laddie-boy!" cried Jacqueline.

"We gonna play rough?"

"Miss Dietrich, please," expostulated the official. "I must ask you not to interfere." He turned back to Ahmed.

"He was dead for some hours when his body was found. The doctor estimates that he died some seven or eight hours ago."

"Where was he found?"

The official indicated with his head. "In the old river bed, a hundred yards or so to the east."

"To think that I spoke harshly of him only this noon," exclaimed Dr. Sando. "I had been told that he had not been at his work and assumed that he was shirking his job. All the time he was lying out there . . . "

The Israeli official looked at his watch. "It is getting late. Unfortunately, most of our staff is off for the day and it would not be convenient to bring secretaries and recording machines here. I'm afraid I must ask you all to remain in your quarters tonight. Then in the morning I will ask you to come to the police station in Nazareth. Statements will be taken there."

"You want every member of the

expedition to come to Nazareth?" asked Dr. Sando.

The official hesitated. "The non-citizens. Our interpreters will question the Arabs here."

He signaled to one of the policemen. "The camp will be under close watch. For your protection I must ask that you obey the police. No one is to leave camp for any reason whatsoever. Is that understood?"

"Of course," replied Sando. "No one will *want* to leave."

"You will remember to stay close to your quarters. Only in that way can we give you real protection."

He signaled again to his men and they began to file out. Ahmed watched them, expecting that one policeman would perhaps remain, but none did.

Jacqueline exclaimed then, "It's me for the hay regardless."

Ahmed stretched out his left arm to block her. "Just a minute."

"Don't pick a fight with me, laddie," she snapped. "I was only telling the truth."

"You pointed at me," Ahmed said.

"You're as strong as any man in this camp."

"Me, I'm a woman. Miller Wood was no pansy. I say what's in my mind and I don't take any sass from any man or woman, but twistin' a full grown man's head, uh-uh!"

"She's right, Fosshay," snapped Sando. "Things ran smoothly here up until the day you showed up. Since then there's been nothing but fight, fight, shooting and murder." His tirade suddenly got the best of him and he sprang to his feet and pointed a quivering finger at Ahmed.

"It's time Holterman knew the truth. You've been playing around with his wife and she's been the cause of the trouble, first with Hill, now with you. I'm fed up and I wish to Christ you'd never come here."

He stormed past Ahmed, out of the room. Jacqueline Dietrich chuckled and, winking at Ahmed, followed Sando.

That left Ahmed in the room. And the sheik. The sheik remained in the corner. He said: "Your money was well spent, Effendi. You know the score, they don't."

"She killed Wood?"

"One murder or two, what difference, Effendi? You paid to know about the first; I won't charge you for this one. Who else?"

"None of your cousins was watching?"

"Effendi Wood did not seem important enough."

"He was close to Professor Hill."

"They shared the same room, as you do now. Effendi Wood drank and I do not think that effendi Hill would confide in a drinker. Not about important things and the manuscript is important, is it not?"

"Two dead people said it was."

"Effendi," the sheik went on, "I am still in business. It is good business custom for a merchant to throw in a little something extra now and then. You are a newcomer to this country. I just want to caution you . . . the Israeli policemen are extremely thorough. Competent and thorough."

"You mean something by that."

"Their sheik — he has no real title, but he is an important official in the government . . . Rosenstock is his name, I believe . . . he kept your passport."

"It's a good passport."

"Excellent, Effendi, then it will be all right. You have nothing to fear. You did not kill effendi Wood and your passport is in order. I must go to my cousins now. They become restless when the Israeli masters are about. I would not want them to do anything rash."

He bowed elaborately and headed for the door. Ahmed went out with him.

The Cadillac had been moved to the front of the Holterman building. Two policemen were in front of Sando's building; four or five others were stationed at strategic spots. There was a gaggle of them in front of the Druse tents.

"May Allah sleep with you," the sheik said outside, for the benefit of the Israeli police.

Ahmed nodded. He walked to his own building. A policeman was in front of the door.

"I sleep here," Ahmed told him in Hebrew.

"Ahmed Fosse," said the policeman. "Ah, yes, the Egyptian." He smiled thinly.

Ahmed went past him into the building.

The lights were on in his room. His few belongings had been thoroughly searched.

The bed had been stripped, the blankets and sheets folded and deposited on the floor.

Miller Wood's bed had also been stripped. His private possessions had been taken out of the room. Including his clothing.

Ahmed looked at the window. There was no curtain or shade and there was probably a policeman outside watching him from the dark.

He was conscious of the manuscript between his shirt and skin, but he was not going to take it out now and examine it. He knew that.

He made up his bed and, with the light still on, stretched out upon it.

26

IT was not good.

Rosenstock was an official of the Israeli government. It would not come out of his own pocket. He would telephone to Paris to check Ahmed Fosse's passport.

How soon before he would learn that the passport in the name of Ahmed Fosse had belonged to a man dead five years?

Would Rosenstock send cables to other countries? Or make telephone calls? The United States?

That was all right. He knew nothing about Billy Krag. Not without fingerprints.

Ahmed had lived in this room for three days. He had handled many articles.

Had fingerprints been taken from them?

Ahmed got up. He looked quickly toward the window, but could not see anyone outside. That did not mean that there wasn't someone out in the dark, looking into the lighted room.

He picked up his rucksack from the pile of clothing beside the bed. Several pieces of leather were sewn into the canvas. Ahmed ran his hands over the leather, looked at his fingers.

They were blackened.

Lampblack, or whatever it was they used for dusting for fingerprints.

Yes, they had his fingerprints. If routine cablegrams were sent to the leading countries of Europe ... and the Western hemisphere ... it was quite probable, since the Israeli police were so competent, a reply would come from the Federal Bureau of Investigation in Washington, D.C.

The fingerprints were of Billy Krag, an infamous rapist-murderer who had been paroled from Alcatraz only two years ago, after serving twenty-three years.

A subsequent phone call from Rosenstock to the United States would elicit the information that the rapist-murderer, Billy Krag, had studied archaeology and dead languages for most of the twenty-three years he had been in prison.

Rosenstock would seek no further for his double murderer.

How long did he have? Twenty-four hours? Forty-eight?

The sheik had cautioned Ahmed Fosse. The Israeli police are extremely efficient.

Twelve hours?

In twelve hours Ahmed, under police escort, would be going to Nazareth for official questioning. He would probably be in the police station when the reports came in from the countries.

The Federal Bureau of Investigation ran fingerprints data through gigantic machines. An identification could be made in as little as a half hour, two hours at the most. The result of the identification would be so startling that the reply to Israel would be made immediately.

Perhaps there were not even twelve hours.

It had to be now.

27

AHMED got to his feet and left the room and the building.

Outside, the police guard confronted him. "You are to remain in your quarters," he said.

"I have to see Mr. Holterman."

"My orders were to . . . "

"Mr. Holterman's the head of this camp. I work for him. I have just thought of something extremely important that he should know . . . "

The policeman hesitated and lost. Ahmed walked past him, striding swiftly to Holterman's building. A policeman on guard there frowned at him, but did not try to prevent his entry.

A short hall inside opened onto Holterman's living room-study.

Holterman was at his desk, his journal open before him. Alice Holterman was not in the room.

"You, Fosse," snapped Holterman, "you had to be the first to disobey the police order to stay in your quarters."

"It couldn't wait."

"You've something to tell me . . . about the murder?" There was a note of anxiety in Holterman's voice.

"No," said Ahmed, "who killed Wood isn't important, but if you must know, it was Jacqueline Dietrich."

"Dietrich!" cried Holterman. "You're insane, man!"

"She also killed Hill,"

"Stark, raving mad," cried Holterman.

"There's no time for that. Believe it or don't. It's no skin off my nose. There's some business between us that has to be settled . . . "

Holterman's face made a quick transformation. The anger disappeared, was replaced by eagerness. "You . . . you've found the . . . ?"

He could not finish the sentence.

"Yes. I've found it."

Holterman shoved back his chair so violently that it crashed to the floor. "Where is it?"

"In due time."

"I must see it. Now! Nothing matters, nothing — "

"I said wait. There's a matter more important than the manuscript."

"Nothing is more important than that . . . "

"Look at me!" said Ahmed Fosse savagely.

Holterman stared at him.

The door of the adjoining room was torn open. Alice Holterman reeled in. There was froth on her mouth, dribbling down her chin. Her eyes were wild. She was clawing at her throat with one hand.

"Charles!" she gasped. There was so much poignancy and anguish in her cry that Holterman wheeled. He reacted violently.

"What's wrong with you?" he cried hoarsely.

"Poison!" gasped Alice. She screamed and clutched her stomach. "It — it's terrible. The pain . . . " She screamed like a lost soul.

Holterman rushed to her, started to catch her, but drew back. "A doctor . . . "

"Where?" asked Ahmed quietly.

"Nazareth! We've got to take her to Nazareth . . . " Holterman looked wildly around, saw a blanket on the sofa. He rushed to it, scooped it up, and threw it about his wife's shoulders. It fell to the floor and he stooped to pick it up. It was then that Alice caught Ahmed's eye. She made a quick gesture toward to door and for an instant there was no pain on her face.

The woman was a consummate actress.

Ahmed ran to the door, whipped it open, and dashed outside. The policeman on duty was in the act of lighting a cigarette.

"Mrs. Holterman's taken poison," Ahmed exclaimed. "We have got to rush her to a hospital . . . "

"Mother of Moses," cried the policeman in Hebrew. He rushed past Ahmed into the building.

Ahmed followed.

Holterman had draped the blanket about his wife's shoulders. Her face was smeared now with the froth from wiping it from her mouth. The policeman took one look at her and groaned.

"There won't be time," he wailed.

Holterman paid no attention. Clasping his wife about the shoulders, he rushed her to the door, colliding with Ahmed, coming in. Ahmed squeezed aside, let them through, then followed. The policeman was hard on his heels.

Outside, Holterman half-ran, half-dragged Alice toward the Cadillac. The policeman came out, yelled to one of his mates, the one in front of Ahmed's building.

"Jakob!"

The second policeman came running over. While the first stood by impotently, Ahmed helped Holterman bustle Alice Holterman into the back seat of the convertible.

He started to close the door, evidently intending to get into the front seat and drive, but Ahmed pushed him in beside Alice. "I'll drive."

Ahmed slammed shut the back door, opened the front. The policeman grabbed his arm. "I will drive."

Ahmed brushed his arm off his own. "Get in your police car. Lead the way. Use your siren and give us a free run. Every second counts."

Without waiting for a reply, he climbed in behind the wheel. The policeman hesitated. A moan, rising to a scream, from Alice Holterman decided him.

He yelled and rushed away.

Ahmed switched on the headlights, turned the ignition key. He backed the car, twisting the wheel, then sent it forward into a U-turn.

He kept his foot lightly on the accelerator, idling the motor.

"Drive, man!" cried Holterman.

Ahmed waited. The police were piling into one of their own cars. Ahmed wanted them ahead of him.

The headlights of the police car came on. Ahmed moved the Cadillac. The police car was headed in the right direction. The siren wailed and it was off.

Ahmed kept close behind the police car.

They roared across the flat plain, bounced and jolted onto the ruts, then whipped through the cut between the two banks. Ahead was the pavement.

The police car reached it, turned left. The siren wailed loud and clear.

The Cadillac reached the pavement . . . and Ahmed turned right.

Holterman yelled, "You're going in the wrong direction!"

"No, we're not," said Alice Holterman savagely. Ahmed heard her grunt, heard the startled exclamation from Holterman.

"What are you doing?"

"Holding a gun in your side, my love," sneered Alice Holterman. "I asked you for a divorce and you said no. A bullet'll do the job quicker and more neatly . . . "

"You're mad!" cried Holterman. "You . . . you planned this together."

"We didn't *plan* it. We just work well together," replied his wife.

The Cadillac was already doing sixty. In the rear-vision mirror, Ahmed saw red lights flashing . . . then white, as the police car turned.

"Hold on," he said over his shoulder.

He jammed the throttle down to the floor board.

Holterman made one last attempt. "You've got the manuscript. You're running away with it!"

"Bingo!" cried his wife. "You got it right on the nose!"

Ahmed heard a slight scuffle in back, was about to turn, then a twinge of pain was forced from Holterman.

"Sit still, love!" sang out Alice. "A

bullet the next time . . . Step on it, my Egyptian friend."

Ahmed risked a look into the mirror. The headlights were straight behind . . . but were they less bright?

"Keep going," said Alice. "Watch out for a road to the left in about a mile. It's dirt, but the Cadillac will take it better than their dinky jalopy."

She paused, then: "Comfy, darling?"

Holterman did not reply this time.

The Cadillac was doing eighty. Eighty-five. The needle went up to ninety and then Ahmed eased off. His eyes scanned the left side of the road.

Headlights coming toward him blinded him for a moment. Then the car was past him and he saw a post on the left side of the road. He took his foot off the accelerator, touched the brake, lifted his foot, touched down again . . . then harder.

Tires screeched and Ahmed took the turn. The car careened so violently that he thought for an instant that it would turn over. He righted it, however, and pressed again on the gas.

The road was no more than a track. At

sixty miles an hour, Ahmed could scarcely hold the wheel. But he fought it. The car hit a rut, then a depression. Ahmed was jolted six inches from the seat. Behind them he heard Alice gasp.

Holterman cried out, "Stop it, man! You'll kill us all."

The speedometer said sixty-five.

Lights flickered behind Ahmed. The police car was making the turn. Would their car be able to keep the speed?

Ahmed missed a right turn, skidded off the road into the sand.

The wheels churned, but did not take hold instantly. It was then that Holterman made his move. Ahmed, intent upon getting the car in the back seat. He shifted into reverse, forward, then back again.

The wheels took hold just as Alice screamed.

The rear car door was opened. Holterman was plunging out headlong. "Goddammit," swore Alice wildly.

The car leaped back onto the pavement, almost went off on the far side. Ahmed whipped the car back onto the pavement and then it was too late. Alice, scrambling on the floor board for the automatic, found it. She sent a wild shot through the car door.

Ahmed braked savagely.

"No," screamed Alice, "let him go. We don't need him."

"*I* need him," snarled Ahmed. He tore open the car door at his side and scrambled out.

He was aware that Alice was still screaming at him. He started after Holterman, running into the darkness. Behind, on the road, headlights were looming up.

He might catch Holterman, but he would not catch him in time to get back to the car before the policemen roared up.

He had lost the game.

He ran back to the car, slammed shut the rear door, and piled into the front.

"Damn you," cried Alice. "You'd risk everything for a man I don't want to see again as long as I live."

"I want to see him," Ahmed said grimly. "And I will."

"Get going!"

It was high time. The headlights behind

were looming large. Ahmed slammed his foot down hard on the gas pedal. The Cadillac took off with a smooth roar.

The road was straight for a mile or so.

28

THE headlights, in the rear-vision mirror, seemed to be suddenly steady. Of course — Holterman had run back to the road, had flagged down the policemen.

It was the head start Ahmed needed.

He made good use of it. Alice climbed over the back seat into the front beside him.

"That was the first time I ever saw you with your guard down. You hate him, don't you?"

"I hate him," Ahmed said, again with the mask over his features.

"Why? Because of me . . . ?"

He did not reply. Alice studied him from the side. Ahmed kept his eyes on the road. It was necessary, for the car was climbing a hill, and the road had become a winding lane.

Ahmed drove heedless of oncoming vehicles. It would be too bad if a car came around a turn toward them. He took the turns on screeching tires, sometimes almost missed a turn.

The police, who had only their lives to consider, would not dare drive as recklessly as he did. In five minutes there were no longer any headlights even on the turns.

Ahmed crossed the hill, got down on level ground, and for a minute or two let the car go past the ninety-mile-an-hour mark. There were hills again, then off to the right, he caught sight of shimmering lights.

"Migdal," Alice said. "That's four or five miles north of Tiberias."

"Take a look at the map," he said.

He continued his reckless driving while she studied the road map from the glove compartment. She used the tiny map light on the dashboard.

She said, "The main road runs along the lake. A place called Tabgha is next, three-four miles. The road turns straight north then, between Tabgha and Capernaum. Five-six miles from the look of this, the road splits, one goes north to Lebanon, the other turns east to Syria. Not more than four or five miles."

"We're about thirty miles from Lebanon, perhaps fifteen from Syria . . . " Ahmed frowned. "Doesn't the Jordan River run parallel to Syria?"

"Yes. It doesn't seem to be more than a mile or two from the border."

"That's when our troubles begin." He shook his head. "The police know which way we're going. They can't be fools enough not to use the radio in their cars. If they do, the border guards will be waiting for us."

"I've still got the gun," Alice reminded.

"That's a cap pistol," retorted Ahmed. "The guards will have rifles, machine guns. Probably bigger stuff. There's no love lost between the Jews and Syrians. They're always shooting at each other along the border."

"The rough stuff is your department," said Alice. "I've done my share. I got us away from the police."

"Don't worry," said Ahmed grimly, "we'll get out of the country." Then, as an afterthought: "Did the police take your passport?"

"They wouldn't dare. I've got it in my purse."

"That takes care of you with the Syrians. They'll pass an American."

"You shouldn't have any trouble with them. You're an Arab."

The road ahead seemed to peter out suddenly. No, there was a pair of ruts winding up a hillside. They were little traveled, however. But they pointed in the right direction and Ahmed followed the ruts.

He reached the top of the hill. Down below was a ribbon of black macadam. Off to the left were shimmering lights.

He tooled the car down the ruts toward the pavement. A minute later he turned onto the macadam road.

He pressed down hard on the accelerator. The shimmering lights grew rapidly. Headlights came toward the Cadillac. Ahmed did not even bother to dim his own headlights.

They swished past the approaching car. The town of Tabgha was ahead of them. He eased off, slowing the car down to seventy, to sixty. He hit a hole in the road, was jolted off the seat, but still kept his foot on the gas pedal.

A car coming out of a cross street

swerved violently away from him, almost collided with a corner building. Ahmed was heedless.

They were through the village then. He kept his eyes alert now for the turn-off that would take them straight north.

Signposts showed up ahead. He did not even glance at them, but swept into the left fork of the road. There probably were no police at the village of Tabgha behind them.

There would be police ahead. Soldiers, too.

He shifted in his seat, gripped the wheel harder. Beside him, Alice braced herself for a mad ride.

He gave it to her. He took the straight stretches at better than ninety, seldom eased off below eighty for the curves. A winding hill road he took at seventy.

In ten minutes they came to the final fork in the road. Here he read the signs. They were in Hebrew, Arabic and English. The English said: *Lebanon* with an arrow pointed to the left, *Syria* with an arrow pointed to the right.

He turned right.

Alice said suddenly, "You've got the manuscript?"

He nodded. He had been conscious of it throughout the wild ride, had once or twice wondered if his exertions would damage it. The manuscript was vellum and it felt smooth and warm against his skin. He hoped that it would not be damaged.

There were things more vital to him than the manuscript. His accounting with Holterman. It had been delayed. But it would come, of that he was determined. To make it come eventually he had to get to safety, from where he could make further plans.

Syria.

The road gradually dropped. He made a turn and caught a glimpse of lights ahead and a shimmering band which reflected the man-made lights as well as the moonlight.

The Jordan River.

He suddenly began braking.

"You're stopping!" Alice cried.

There were zigzagging red lights ahead. There was a patrol station on the near side of the Jordan River.

Ahmed pulled the car off the road, stopped it, but kept the motor running.

"It's too late to risk it. The police can't be that stupid."

"Isn't there another crossing, a smaller road?"

"There wouldn't be a bridge."

She hesitated. "I guess we leave the Cadillac then."

"You can swim?"

"For two million dollars?"

Ahmed shifted into forward, switched off the lights, and turned right off the road. The car hit a bump, caught the gear box on a stone, and with a grinding roar, tore loose. The car rolled to a stop.

"That solves that problem," said Ahmed.

He got out of the car. Alice got out on her own side, came around to join him. "They'll find the car and be after us too soon."

"Let's take that little swim, then!"

They struck off, down the incline toward the river, walking swiftly, toward the river and away from the bridge and the police checkpoint.

They had covered about half of the

distance to the river when Ahmed stopped. He pointed down.

"A soldier," exclaimed Alice. "He's got a rifle slung over his shoulder."

The soldier was walking along easily, perhaps twenty feet from the river bank.

Alice thrust the little automatic toward Ahmed. He grunted. "What do you think I am, Dead-eye Dick? At this distance I couldn't hit him with six tries. But his rifle will get us." He shook his head.

"You can sneak up on him."

"There's fifty feet of beach. He'd hear me before I got close enough."

Even as Ahmed spoke, a searchlight from the direction of the bridge lit up the beach. The soldier whirled, removed the rifle from his shoulder.

"They've been alerted," Ahmed said quietly. He crouched low, looked off toward the river. "There's another soldier a few hundred yards down the river."

Alice exclaimed petulantly, "We've got to get across."

"Not here, that's certain."

The searchlight moved to the right. Ahmed caught Alice's arm and threw her to the ground with him. The light moved over them, continued on a few yards, then moved back toward the beach.

Ahmed got to his knees. "Let's get out of here."

"But the car's broken, you said."

"We've still got our legs."

They both rose to their feet and began walking to the right. Back at the Tel Mas camp, Alice had changed her shoes. But the ones she wore now were still not walking shoes. The Cuban heels sank into the ground and she stumbled every few feet.

"Damn these heels," she exclaimed.

"Take off the shoes."

"I'm no peasant. I can't walk on my bare feet."

"You're not going to move very fast in the shoes."

"Never mind me," she snapped. "I'll keep up with you. I'll keep thinking about my two million dollars . . . "

Yet in a short time she was falling behind Ahmed. He was compelled to slow down. They were climbing, but after a while they reached a ridge and went southward along it. Off to the left, Ahmed could still see the Jordan.

Ahead, on the right, a few blinking lights appeared. They became steadier, larger as they proceeded along.

"Maybe we can get a car there," Alice said.

"It's not more than five miles from the Sea of Galilee," said Ahmed. "We'd have to ditch the car there."

"It'd be worth it."

He shook his head. "It would give away our position."

"I can't go much farther," she protested.

He did not reply.

They skirted the edge of the village. From a sign, Ahmed made out that it was called Kfar Hanasi.

A mile past the village, a brilliant light appeared on the left. It was a searchlight down by the river. By it's light Ahmed, searching, saw two soldiers patrolling the beach.

They would not be able to cross the Jordan at this point. Where the river flowed into the Sea of Galilee, there was probably an even stronger guard.

Ahmed began to bear to the right, descending the easy slope. They reached a lush valley dotted with farmhouses.

Some were darkened, but a number were lit up.

They crossed fields, but Ahmed gave the houses a wide berth. He did not want to rouse dogs.

Alice suddenly sank down on the ground. "I can't go another step," she said.

"Nothing much will happen to you," he said. "You can go back."

"Don't be a fool!"

"Your husband's got more than two or three million," said Ahmed. "He told me so yesterday."

She swiveled her head up to peer into his face. "What got you onto a subject like that?"

"I told him I was going to find the manuscript tonight. He made a deal with me."

She struggled to her knees. "You didn't . . . ?"

"He thinks I did. I had something else in mind."

She managed to get to her feet and tried to read his face in the half-light that was shed by the moon and stars. But if she had difficulty reading anything in his face in broad daylight, it was now virtually impossible.

She said: "I've read my share of books and I've heard about the inscrutable East, but I know my way around people. Especially men, and the more I see of you the less I know about you. You don't give out, Mister. Not a damn bit."

"We'd better get along," he said.

"I can't go another step without a rest. I want to talk. You've thrown out a couple of hints about yourself and Charles. What's between you?"

"According to your own figure, I've got three million dollars under my shirt. If you want to get caught here in the open and lose that, it's all right with me. But I'd like to get my third share . . . "

She groaned. "What's the use just wandering around in the dark? You don't know where you're going."

"I know one place we're not going. Syria."

"You've got to have some objective."

"Jordan. It's on the other side of the sea."

"And you just happen to have a little boat tucked away in your pants pocket?"

"The Sea of Galilee has been a fisherman's place ever since people lived here. Most of Christ's Apostles were originally fishermen. They're still fishing the same waters in the same old way. Small boats, nets. We might be able to get one of them to take us across."

She brightened. "How far is it to the sea?"

"Four miles. Possibly five."

She groaned again. "I've got to have a rest."

"Not here. It's too open."

"Where?"

He nodded to the south and east. "Up in the hills there."

"I can't make it."

"You've got to."

She started off, limping, her jaws clenched. He fell in beside her. She stumbled after a while and he caught her arm to keep her from falling. She caught hold of his hand, but finding no response, no pressure in it, let it go again.

He walked a little faster and she had to hurry to catch up. He kept a fairly brisk pace and she had to use her fast-vanishing strength to keep up with him.

They began to climb and she fell behind. "Wait . . . !"

"Keep quiet," he warned. "We're conspicuous enough without anyone hearing you yell."

"You're not going to leave me behind," she snapped. "I've still got the revolver."

"It's an automatic," he replied. "Not a revolver."

"Who cares? It's got bullets and I know how to pull the trigger."

"Use the gun," he said, "and there's no going back. You've still got that ace in the hole. Your husband. He'll use his money to hush the scandal."

"You don't know Charles!"

He paused a moment and she caught up with him. She wanted to sink down to the ground again, but he pushed her ahead of him. He remained behind her then as they toiled up the steepening slope.

Halfway up the rugged hill, they did rest for a few minutes. Again near the summit.

Finally they reached the crest of the hill.

Galilee was unfolded before them then.

Galilee in the middle of a bright, moonlit night.

The Sea of Galilee shimmered before them. Ahmed could make out its shape. It curved on the left around toward the Jordan. The far shore was dark. His eyes went to the right. Capernaum was almost directly ahead of them, no more than a couple of miles. On the right shore, the western, was the village of Tabgha, which they had skirted on the mad drive northward. Beyond Tabgha was another small place, Migdal, and then, a few miles beyond and slightly to the east, was the largest city of Galilee. Tiberias.

"A five-mile sea trip would do it," said Ahmed.

29

THERE was no reply from Alice Holterman. He looked around. She was on the ground, lying flat on her face. He looked down at her. There was no tenderness in him regarding her. She was hard, vicious, and utterly unscrupulous. She had probably never actually killed anyone, but he knew that she would if she were driven to it. She would kill him without compunction for the parchment roll that was pressed against his stomach.

She was physically exhausted, a pitiful sight at the moment . . . if there had been any pity in him.

He walked away from her. Some thirty feet away he sat down. He was inured to physical exercise and the exertion he had gone through in the past two hours had scarcely winded him. He did not know what lay ahead and it was just as well that he rested.

He stared out across the village that lay

below, at the sea beyond.

After a moment an idle thought occurred to him. This hilltop on which he was sitting, this was the Mount on which a Man had preached a sermon more than nineteen hundred years ago.

He had laid down His belief to a multitude, beliefs that had been taken up by the people and had endured for nineteen hundred years; that had inspired countless millions of persons.

Yet the Man had not been able to forestall His own savage end. He had been compelled to allow Himself to be scourged, forced to carry a tremendous cross, and then had been nailed to the cross and raised up until He had died in His final anguish. He had not been able to stop mortals from doing those things to Him, although He had proclaimed Himself immortal.

Perhaps He had stood upon the very spot on which Ahmed was now sitting.

Ahmed unbuttoned his shirt and took out the roll of ancient vellum. It was soft to his touch, warm . . . from his body temperature. It was smooth vellum, with none of the stiffness of age that was customary for old vellum. It had been well preserved in the copper cylinder.

Had it been written by the Man who had preached the Sermon on the Mount?

He unrolled the vellum and held it up. He could make out there was writing, but it was too dark for him to read it. It would have to wait for another time.

He stared at the parchment.

The vellum was still warm in his hand. Too warm to be natural.

What was it He had said after descending from this mount?

"Foxes have holes, and birds of the air have nests; but the Son of man hath not where to lay his head."

Ahmed Fosse had spent twenty-three years of his life behind bars, walled in by stone. More than half of his life. He was free now, but for how long? How soon before the net would encircle him?

The burning desire for vengenance had sustained him through those years behind bars. Had it been worth it? Was it *still* worth it?

Birds had their nests, foxes their holes in the ground. The man who called himself Ahmed Fosse and whose real name was Fredrick Holterman had no place he could call his home.

His mother had denied him. His brother . . . ?

His brother had not only placed him behind the walls, but had let him remain there. For twenty-three years.

Was there a Master Plan by which one person was meted out misery and hardship and another luxury, ease . . . and happiness?

Yet Charles Holterman was not happy. He was prematurely aged and his last few years had been made miserable by his wife. Through the years . . . in the quiet of night, in the moments or hours he was alone, he must have thought . . . of what he had done to his brother.

Or . . . had it never given him concern? Did he sleep blissfully of nights? Had he never wakened in the darkness of his room?

Fredrick Holterman had paced the concrete floors of his little cell countless nights, countless hours.

Fredrick Holterman was dead. He had been drowned in Lake Michigan a quarter of a century ago. His memory was dead.

Ahmed Fosse lived.

He got to his feet and he paced back and forth, on ground that another had trod once in torment. Here ... and in His Garden of Gethsemane. He had not sinned Himself, but He suffered for the sins of others.

Ahmed had suffered for the sins of another.

His immediate predicament now had *not* been caused by another. This Ahmed Fosse had done himself.

He had lived with death in his heart. He had lived *for* death. He was enduring all of this now because he wanted to kill a man. His brother.

He clutched the vellum in his hand.

Why would it not cool?

He looked toward the woman on the ground. She had rolled over onto her back. Deep breathing caused her chest to move up and down. She was fast asleep. From exhaustion.

She was able to sleep.

The man who had become Ahmed Fosse could not sleep. Sometimes, on other nights, after an unusually trying period, Ahmed had been awakened by a voice. The voice of vengeance.

The voice he seemed to hear now was not as harsh.

It was a soft voice. It called softly.

"Ahmed!"

The voice in his dreams had never called him Ahmed.

There was a figure down the hillside. It moved.

A voice came from the moving figure. "Ahmed! Are you here . . . ?"

He shot a quick glance over his shoulder. Alice Holterman had not stirred. He went down the hillside.

She was carrying a bundle in one hand. She dropped it to the ground and ran uphill swiftly, lithely.

He met her a hundred feet from the top of the hill.

"How'd you know where to look?"

She stopped five feet from him, staring into his face, lit up by the moonlight. "I — I don't know. I have a transistor radio and I listened to it. They found the car near the bridge that crosses the Jordan. I knew you couldn't cross the river and I didn't think somehow that you would go north. It seemed natural that you should backtrack, come down to Tiberias and try to get across the sea in a boat. It's what I would do."

"It's a good thing the police don't think like you do," said Ahmed grimly. "This isn't Tiberias, though."

"You didn't have time to get that far. I — I thought you'd be here. On the Mount."

"What made you think that? I'm not a Christian. The Mount doesn't mean a thing to me."

"I'm not a Christian either," she said, "but I've read the New Testament. I . . . I thought a man in travail . . . "

"Who's in travail?"

"Please," she said, "we're wasting time quarreling. You've built a wall of steel around you, but there are holes in it. I — I've caught glimpses through the holes. I've sensed the torment you've gone through . . . "

"There are no holes in me," he said harshly. "There's nothing in me to see, nothing that would interest a girl like you."

"I want nothing from you, Ahmed," she said soberly. "I expect nothing."

"As long as you understand!"

"I brought some clothes for you. A burnoose and djellaba. The zone across the lake is demilitarized. There are two or three kibbutzim there, that's all. If you reach the shore, you can run for the border. The Jordanians will let you in . . ."

Ahmed half turned. "Mrs. Holterman's up there."

She reacted visibly. "That complicates things. I — I hadn't thought about her."

"She wouldn't think of you. She wouldn't of me, if it meant any inconvenience to her. Besides, she can go back to her husband. He'll protect her just to protect himself."

"Then come!"

She hurried down the hillside, scooping up the bundle she had dropped. When he caught up with her, she pressed the bundle toward him. "You can change on the other side. They — they wouldn't let you on the boat if they thought you were an Arab . . ."

They reached the village at the foot of the Mount and in a few moments were on the seashore. There were boats all along it, boats of all sizes. But there were people there, too, fishermen, townspeople. It was one o'clock in the morning, but the fishermen were already preparing to put out to sea to get the early catches.

Carolyn took his arm, stopped him by the edge of a building. "Wait here," she whispered. "I'll try to arrange for a boat."

He moved back deeper into the shadows and she ran down to the shore. He saw her accost a fisherman, who shook his head. She went on to another. The second fisherman listened. Carolyn seemed to be talking earnestly to him. Then she reached into a pocket and drew out money. She handed it to the fisherman, then came running back toward Ahmed.

He moved out from the heavy shadows.

"It's arranged," she said excitedly. "I told him you were an American who had lost his passport. You had to get out of the country and couldn't afford the delay of getting a new passport."

She took his hand and in her eagerness began to pull on him. He followed.

The fisherman was a leathery-faced man of indeterminate age. He said in

Hebrew: "This man is in trouble? He has the eyes of a hawk." He wrinkled up his nose in disgust and spat. "He is a Gentile."

"I've paid you," cried Carolyn.

"Yes, you've paid for a catch of fish . . . "

"A good catch."

"We will go," said the fisherman. He eased a looped rope from a stanchion and clambered aboard his vessel. It was not more than twelve feet in length, about five in width. It smelled of fish.

Carolyn climbed easily into the boat. Ahmed followed. The fisherman picked up an oar and, leaning over the end of the boat, placed it against the stanchion. He shoved hard and the boat moved a few inches. The fisherman kept on pushing, then almost fell over the boat into the water as it moved swiftly away from the wharf.

He dropped the oar and ran to the sail. Shouting, "We sail!" he raised the sail.

The wind caught the little sail and the boat began to pull away from the shore. Carolyn, who had been crouched in the bottom of the boat, found a box and sat down on it.

"There won't be any problem on the other side. Just go through the kibbutz and you'll be at the border in no time." She frowned. "Do you have any money?"

He nodded.

"You may have to bribe one of the Jordanian border guards," she said. "I have some Israeli pounds. They don't like us over there, but they'll take the money."

"I have enough of my own," said Ahmed. He sat down in the bottom of the boat. He was facing her but kept his eyes averted from her.

"Did Holterman get back to the tel before you left?"

"Oh, yes," she said. "The police came out again from Nazareth. They're all over the place."

"But you were able to get away."

"I am a Jew," she said simply.

The fisherman began to chatter. One of the passengers was a Jew, the other a Gentile. They were talking in a language he could not understand and he was not happy about it. He regretted having agreed to take them across the lake. He could, he averred, have done better fishing.

Carolyn listened to him for a while, then spoke sharply, "I am a doctor at the Hebrew University in Jerusalem," she told him. "I have met our prime minister, Ben Gurion . . . "

"The High Priest!" exclaimed the fisherman, shuddering disdainfully. "Is he a better Jew than I am? Has he earned his food by the sweat of his brow? A politician. He lives from the sweat of men like me."

Ahmed said suddenly in English: "Do you believe that Elijah rode to heaven on a chariot?"

Carolyn replied simply, "I believe in the Bible."

"You believe that Moses talked personally to your Yahweh?"

"The Old Testament is accepted by Christians, Mohammedans, and Jews," she said.

"What about the New?" he demanded. "Do you believe any of that?"

"I believe that Jesus was a great teacher, a rabbi."

He swept a hand about the sea. "Do you believe that He stopped a storm on this sea by waving His hands? Do you think He *walked* on the waves?"

She groped for the proper words. "In his lifetime Jesus spoke before multitudes of Jews. He performed miracles . . . "

"If you believe that you've got to believe that He was a God!"

She was silent a moment, then with her head bowed: "I do not think that He was the Messiah. But I do not quarrel with the beliefs of Christians or Mohammedans." She hesitated. "I feel sorry for those who do not believe in *anything*."

"You feel sorry for me?"

There was a catch in her throat as she answered, "I feel sorry for you, yes."

He lapsed into silence. He looked out over the water, toward the lights of Capernaum, of Tiberias to the south.

They sailed for ten minutes across the smooth water. Then she said softly, "Ever since I first saw you, something has bothered me . . . something I can't place my finger on. You look like . . . " She shook her head. "It is ridiculous, but I cannot help it. You look, at times, like

Charles Holterman."

"Holterman would fire you for that," snapped Ahmed. "He doesn't like dark-complected people, especially *poor* ones."

He was aware suddenly that he was revealing more of himself to this Jewish girl than he had ever before to anyone. Certainly more than to Alice Holterman, who was sleeping on the Mount where He had preached His memorable sermon.

The fisherman began to mutter again. Soon, he was complaining loudly. Carolyn took some money from a pocket and bent over, moved past Ahmed toward the fisherman. She thrust the money at him.

"This will help you to hold your tongue," she said tartly.

He spat over the side of the boat, but clawed for the money. As he stowed it away in a pocket, he growled in Hebrew: "Jew and Gentiles don't mix. Have you slept with this Gentile?"

"You're a filthy old man," Carolyn cried.

"It is the young who are filthy," he retorted. "Their bodies control their appetites and they will go to bed with whoever . . . "

Ahmed said suddenly in Hebrew: "You will be still from now on or I will throw you in the sea and sail the boat myself."

The fisherman gawked at him. He started to speak, then thought better of it. He shot angry, suspicious glances at Ahmed and at Carolyn, but he spoke no more.

After a while Ahmed snapped again at him: "You're headed for Ein Gev. Turn left."

The fisherman half rose in protest, but he sat down again and turned the tiller. The boat made a sharp turn to the left.

The darkness of the shoreline showed up. In a few minutes the keel scraped sand.

The fisherman said then: "We are here and I shall have to spend the rest of the night cleaning the stench from my boat."

"Pay no attention to him," said Carolyn quickly. She stood up in the boat. "I will not go ashore." She held out her hand. "It's good-by now."

Ahmed apparently did not see her extended hand. He picked up the bundle of clothing she had brought for him, leaped over the side of the boat into a few inches of water. He strode ashore and stopping, turned.

She said softly in English, "Good-by, my love!"

He suddenly strode back into the water. Drawing the rolled-up manuscript from under his shirt, he said: "I don't know what I'll run into. I want you to keep this for me."

She took the vellum roll.

"You know what it is?"

She nodded.

"Will you meet me in Jerusalem?" he asked.

"Oh, yes," she replied. "When?"

"I don't know. A week, perhaps two. I will be there."

"I will wait. You tell me where and I will wait." She paused. "Forever."

"You'll keep that for me? No matter who tries to take it from you?"

"I will keep it. I promise."

"I'll find you in Jerusalem. Be sure of it," Then he added: "I haven't trusted anyone since — since I was eighteen years old. I'm trusting you now."

The moonlight was full upon her face.

There was a wan smile upon it.

He turned from the boat and plunged toward the darkened shore. He did not look back, but it was only minutes before he was regretting having given her the manuscript.

It was still time to turn back, to call to her.

He came to a stop, but he did not turn.

30

THERE were lush fields ahead of him, fields of grain. Olive groves. This was one of the famed kibbutzim of Israel, one of the numerous communal farms on which lived one-tenth of the Jewish population. The Jews who had come from all the countries of the earth had found their peace on these farms; they had turned to the soil from which they had been too long. Working with their hands they earned their daily bread and with it the peace they had never found as overintellectualized people of the great cities of the world.

In the distance a dog barked. Ahmed walked through a field of waist-high wheat. Beyond was a fringe of olive trees. He reached them and stopped.

He unrolled the bundle of clothing Carolyn had given him, donned the burnoose and jdellaba, and continued on through the olive grove.

He crossed a farm road, thought he

saw a flicker of light through trees, and began to run swiftly through the olive grove. The Arab costume was not meant for running, but he did not slacken his pace.

He ran easily, steadily, at a distance-consuming pace.

He ran for a mile, then paused. He had crossed through the olive grove and was now in what seemed to be a banana field. The plants were ten feet high, heavy with green fruit and foliage. The trees were set closer together than the olive trees and afforded better shelter for him.

He walked swiftly, getting back his wind. He did not know what lay beyond the banana patch.

He burst through the edge of the field and saw it then. A strip of bare earth, fifty yards wide. On the far side of it a barbed wire fence.

He stopped, looking around.

There was no living thing in sight.

Bent low, he ran swiftly toward the barbed wire. Reaching it he threw himself on the ground. The lowest strand was less than a foot from the ground. He would have to raise it, to crawl under.

But was the wire charged with electricity? Or wired to an alarm system.

He had to play it safe.

He scraped away dirt with his hands, dug furiously until he had scooped out a shallow trench six feet long, a foot deep. Stretching out he rolled into the trench, turned, and crawled out on the other side.

He was out of Israel, in Syria.

He got to his feet, began brushing the dirt from his enveloping garb. A rifle bolt clicked nearby; and an Arabic voice commanded: "Do not move an inch!"

A Syrian soldier appeared from behind a heavy shrub. A rifle was pointed at Ahmed from less than twenty feet.

"You will clasp your hands over your head and turn around," the soldier ordered.

Ahmed obeyed. The soldier came up, prodded him sharply in the back with the muzzle of the rifle.

"The reward will be paid to me," the soldier said in satisfaction.

"I have money under my burnoose," said Ahmed. "I will pay you twice the reward if you will let me go."

The soldier was quiet a moment. Then the muzzle poked Ahmed harder.

"March!"

A footpath led through the brush. Ahmed padded along it, the soldier's boots crunching behind him a few yards. Ahmed considered making a break for it, but he knew that the soldier would fire instantly. If the bullet did not strike him down, the report of the rifle would bring down immediate pursuit. It was still a long way to the Jordan border, and with the Syrian army after him, Ahmed did not think that he would be safe in Jordan.

He was still thinking it over when he came out of the brush and saw a hut ahead, a hut with two soldiers outside and a dim light over the door.

"Sergeant," the soldier called from behind Ahmed, "I have a prisoner. A border runner."

One of the two soldiers came forward. He peered into Ahmed's face.

"Your passport," he said, holding out his hand.

"I have no passport," replied Ahmed. "I can explain it to the officer in charge."

"You came into Syria without a

passport?" asked the sergeant pleasantly. He suddenly cuffed Ahmed on the side of his face. "You are probably a Jew passing as an Arab!" Then to the guard who had brought Ahmed up, "Shoot him if he moves."

From the door of the hut, the voice of authority spoke: "What is going on here?"

A man, obviously an officer, came forward. "Did I hear this man say he would explain to me?"

He lashed out at the sergeant, returning a blow harder than the one that the sergeant had given Ahmed.

"You will come inside, please," the officer said, politely to Ahmed. "I am sure there will be no difficulty about the passport." He winked hugely.

He went back into the hut. Ahmed followed. It was furnished inside as a combination bedroom and office. There were two chairs in the room.

"I am Lieutenant Fuad," the officer said, indicating one of the chairs. "Will you sit down, please?"

Ahmed seated himself on one of the chairs. The lieutenant looked down at him.

"This is a poor time of the night to be conducting business, but there is an urgency in your case, I suppose?"

"There is, Captain."

"Lieutenant, please. I am not yet a captain, although I hope to be as soon as I can save enough money to make the, ah, small payment to the colonel who is in charge of the border patrols. Your passport now. You must have one to come into my country; or you must have the equivalent." He smiled brightly, closing one eye in a wink.

"Ah, yes," said Ahmed. He started to reach under his burnoose, then looked at the lieutenant. Fuad's hand had dropped to the butt of the revolver in his holster.

"I am reaching for the equivalent of the passport, Lieutenant, Effendi."

"But of course."

Through a slit in the burnoose, Ahmed reached into a pocket and brought out the sheaf of bills he still had. It was a thin sheaf of hundred-dollars bills.

There was a table beside him. He counted out two of the bills and looked up at the smiling lieutenant's face.

"American money," said the lieutenant.

"How much is that in Syrian pounds?"

"Eight hundred, roughly, counting four pounds to the dollar."

"I regret, Effendi," said the lieutenant, "that is not the equivalent of a passport."

Ahmed added two more bills.

The lieutenant's smile now reached from ear to ear. "One more?"

Ahmed added a fifth bill to the pile on the table. The lieutenant reached past him, scooped up the money, and thrust it quickly into a pocket.

"I will be a captain within a week," he said.

"I am sure you will be a good one," Ahmed assured him.

"May I now be of assistance to you?" asked Lieutenant Fuad.

"I want to get into Jordan."

"There should be no difficulty about that," said the lieutenant heartily. "There is a road two kilometers east, which will take you to the border. If you will ask there for my good friend Lieutenant Feisal, there will be no trouble. You will need to give him only two of those passport equivalents. He is not ready to be a captain, alas."

The lieutenant followed Ahmed outside. He saluted and then snapped at his men: "Attention, dolts! The Effendi is leaving and is not to be bothered again. Effendi, may Allah go with you."

Ahmed left the guard post, heading eastward along a beaten path between the heavy brush that grew in the swampy ground. He walked less than a mile before he came to a well-traveled road. He turned south on it.

Dawn found him plodding along the dusty road. The swampland had been left behind and the desert was beginning. He passed an Arab riding a donkey, with a woman walking along behind, carrying a child.

The chugging of an automobile came from behind on the road. Ahmed stepped to one side, watched a drab, dust-covered Opel churn along the dusty ruts of the road.

He held up his hand to stop the car, but the Arab driver did not even look at him.

The sun came swiftly over the eastern horizon. The countryside was desolate, barren. A few miles to the east there were fertile kibbutzim. Here the land was parched, uncultivated.

This was Arab country, backward country.

A cloud of dust appeared out of the dust. As it bore down on Ahmed he suddenly realized that the car was a Mercedes Benz.

It was too late to hide; the country was too open to run. They could leave the rutted road and drive across country almost as fast as upon it.

He stood to one side and the car stopped. The two Italians climbed out of the front. From the rear piled Hercules Petrakis and Jacqueline Dietrich.

She was wearing skintight trousers and her khaki shirt was at least two sizes too small for her.

She strode past Petrakis and stopped about eight feet from Ahmed.

"Lo, the poor Arab!" she said mockingly.

One of the Italians snapped, "Clap your hands behind your head and turn around!"

"Mesheer," said Petrakis oilily, "this is indeed a fortuitous meeting."

"For you."

The Greek shrugged. "All of this could have been settled amicably. There was no need for anyone to get hurt."

"Your lady friend likes to hurt people," said Ahmed evenly. "Ask her if she got pleasure from twisting Miller Wood's neck ... and putting a knife into Professor Hill's back."

"They were stubborn," snapped Jacqueline. "Like you."

One of the Italians moved in close. He thrust the stubby-nosed revolver within a foot of Ahmed's stomach. "Turn!"

Ahmed turned and started to raise his hands to close them behind his back. He never completed the movement. The Italian smashed the back of his head with the little gun. He put his last bit of strength into it and Ahmed went down like an ox struck by a sledge.

31

A LANCET of pain shot through Ahmed's head. It began at the base of his skull and pierced the skull and seemed to reach its apex in the region of his right eye. The pain jolted him back to consciousness. He opened his eyes and peered at black earth just two inches away. He was lying on his stomach, his head only slightly turned sideward. He tried to move his hands and found that they were tied behind his back with a rawhide thong. His legs were similarly tied.

The voice of Jacqueline Dietrich cried out: "He's awake!"

Rough hands caught him, whirled him over on his back. The two Italians stood over him. One of them bent over, caught him under his armpits, and jerked him up to a sitting position, slamming him back so that Ahmed's head struck the bole of a tree.

The pain almost caused him to lose consciousness.

Through a miasma of pain and anguish he saw movement before him ... the Italians, Hercules Petrakis, and Jacqueline Dietrich. Most of all Jacqueline.

He was aware that something was being put about his wrists and he knew that he was being pulled upward so that his heels were resting on the ground. He could not maintain his balance, but he found that it was not necessary. His body was being raised taut, so that his boots barely scraped the ground.

A little pressure was released on his arms then and his feet rested more securely on the ground. His eyes cleared and he saw that he was in a swamp or morass. Swamp grass grew lush all about, but there were only a few trees in his range of vision. He was hanging from a tree.

A rope had been thrown over a limb and he had been pulled up so that he was more or less dangling from the branch.

Jacqueline Dietrich came around, caught his hair in one savage fist, and jerked up his face. Holding her own ugly face less than eighteen inches from his, she spat at him.

"How do you feel now, Egyptian?"

"I feel fine," said Ahmed, "as long as I don't have to get in bed with you."

It was the worst insult he could think of at the moment and it produced an instantaneous response. She smashed her fist into his face.

"Is this better?" she snarled. She drew back her fist again, but Hercules Petrakis sprang to her side.

"Please, Miss Dietrich! There is no reason to abuse him unnecessarily. There are things we must find out from him."

"He'll talk," said Dietrich. "I promise you that!"

"Then let him talk." The flabby Greek appealed to Ahmed. "We have searched you, Mesheer. The manuscript is not on your person. You must have given it to the woman last night. All we ask is that you tell us her whereabouts. Please!"

"Find her," said Ahmed simply.

The Amazon drew back her fist, measured the distance carefully, and let Ahmed have it squarely on the jaw. He sagged, the weight of his body hanging solely on his wrists.

He did not lose consciousness entirely, but his head was swimming in a haze

387

of fog. He was only partly conscious of movement about him, was aware that voices were exclaiming all around. He could not make out the words, however. Somebody was doing something to his person, but he did not know what and did not care.

Suddenly he gasped. A cascade of water was dashed against his face. He recovered full consciousness. Blinking water out of his eyes, he saw that Jacqueliine Dietrich was again in front of him. She held a six-foot length of one-inch manila rope in one hand and was straightening out a kink in the rope with her other hand. He was aware that the burnoose had been stripped from him.

"The shirt too," ordered Jacqueline.

One of the Italians, behind Ahmed, caught the shirt in one hand and ripped it down. A whistle of awe came from his lips.

"Lookit this!" he exclaimed.

Petrakis shuffled over. "Mother of God!" he murmured.

Ahmed's back was a criss-cross pattern of ridges and welts, old, white, some still angry-looking, having never healed properly. There were more than twenty jagged, irregular white scars interspersed with the welts and ridges.

"You have been flogged before," Petrakis said.

Jacqueline Dietrich came swiftly around. Her face showed satisfaction as she examined Ahmed's back. "Looks like you got the grandaddy of all whippings awhile back. With a cat-o'-nine-tails."

"Cattails?" asked Petrakis.

"It's a whip with strips of rawhide. Little chunks of lead are tied to the ends of each strip."

The face of Petrakis showed concern. "He had endured such a whipping? There is nothing we can add to that . . . "

One of the Italians said suddenly, "I knew a fella once in Chicago. They put little slivers of wood under his fingernails, pushed them in . . . and then they lit the slivers."

"That is barbarous!" cried the Greek.

"He talked," shrugged the Italian.

"This little man's going to talk now," said Jacqueline Dietrich. "Ask him the questions!"

Petrakis moved around to get in front

of Ahmed. "The stakes are very high, Mesheer," he said, pleading in his tone. "I do not like these harsh measures, but there is too much at stake. Great wealth. When you left the Tel Mas diggings with the woman you had the manuscript with you. The woman is gone now, and so is the manuscript. Where are they, Mesheer? The woman and the manuscript?"

Ahmed remained silent.

"You will meet her somewhere, Mesheer? Where?"

He waited for an answer. Suddenly he groaned.

The rope whistled and Ahmed had to clench his teeth to keep from crying out. His back muscles quivered spasmodically.

The rope was laid on again and again. Jacqueline gave him ten strokes, each like a white-hot bar of iron thrust across his back. He knew that blood was streaming down his back.

Jacqueline shifted her position then so that the new blows would criss-cross the others.

She said: "Is he talking, Hercules?"

He shook his head sadly. "He is mute."

"Good!"

She lashed Ahmed again.

The Italians stood to one side impassive, but the Greek was watching the lashing. His face was flabby, quivering. He was not enjoying it at all. His lips moved as he counted the lashes.

"Fourteen . . . fifteen . . . sixteen . . . "

His eyes went to Jacqueline's face. Her eyes were glazed, shining. Her mouth was parted, spittle drooling from the corners of her mouth.

"Nineteen!" cried Jacqueline furiously. She gave her finest effort to the next blow.

"Twenty!"

The Italians reacted. They had put away their revolvers, but one of them now went for his. A shot rang out and he thought better of it. His hands went into the air. The other Italian promptly threw up his own hands.

"Enough!" cried the voice of Sheik Yussuf.

Ahmed twisted around, forced up his head, and saw Yussuf striding toward the group around the tree. Seven or eight Arabs, most of them with rifles, advanced in an open fan formation.

Jacqueline Dietrich was the last to see the Arabs. When she saw them, she began screaming foul imprecation.

"Hold your tongue, woman!" ordered the sheik. He signaled to one of his followers and snapped in Arabic, "Cut him down!"

A man with a gleaming, curving scimitar ran forward. He gently cut the rawhide above Ahmed's head with a flash of the scimitar, then caught Ahmed as he collapsed. He lowered him gently to the ground on his stomach. He sawed at the ropes that bound Ahmed's wrists and ankles.

Through the fog that threatened to envelop Ahmed he heard the voice of the sheik. "It is not good for a woman to beat men . . . " Then, as she began to call him foul names in English: "Tie her up. She wears pants, treat her like a man."

Ahmed was aware of a furious struggle near him, but then the struggle gradually ceased and he heard only heavy panting.

Sheik Yussuf knelt beside Ahmed. "Effendi, this is a terrible thing they have done. It is barbarous." His finger touched a spot lightly. "You were flogged once before." He spoke to his followers and one of them came and knelt on the other side of Ahmed.

He was aware that the Arab was washing the blood from his back. Soothing ointment followed and took out some of the fire of the wounds. Finally, one of the Arabs tore clothing into strips and wound them about Ahmed's torso.

Yussuf tapped Ahmed's shoulder. "It is the best we can do, Effendi."

He helped Ahmed to a sitting position. Ahmed gained his feet on his own power.

He looked down at Jacqueline Dietrich. She was trussed up like a pig for roasting. She glared at him, venom gleaming in her eyes.

A little pile of weapons — three revolvers, a sawed-off shotgun, and three knives — was on the ground.

The Italians and their employer were off to one side, watched by a pair of alert Arabs with rifles.

The sheik said: "You made a sudden departure last night, Effendi, and not too much later the Amazon met with the Franks and she, too, left the country. I decided to follow. After all, we have had profitable business transactions together and one does not like to lose a good customer."

"This is going to cost me," said Ahmed wearily.

"You offend, Effendi. This was an act or mercy. To accept money for it would be unthinkable."

"I'm glad to hear it," said Ahmed grimly.

"Of course," continued the sheik, "one has retainers and to maintain them, baksheesh must be distributed. If you wish to distribute a small amount to these miserable cousins of mine ... " The sheik shrugged expressively.

"I paid out my last hundred-dollar bill to a border guard," Ahmed said. He hesitated, then seated himself carefully upon the ground. Leaning forward painfully, he grasped the thick heel of his right paratrooper boot.

He wrenched the heel violently and a tightly folded packet of green paper fell to the ground.

"Ingenious!" exclaimed the sheik.

Ahmed unfolded the packet of bills,

took of one and held it up. "Can you change this for me?"

The sheik started to reach for the bill, but his hand froze in mid-air. "A thousand-dollar bill? There — there *are* bills of such denomination?"

"Doesn't every rich American carry them?" Ahmed asked sarcastically.

"Allah be praised!" exulted the sheik. He took the bill, examined it lovingly, and even held it up to the light. Then he stooped suddenly to peer at the bills still in Ahmed's hand.

"They are all like this. There must be, mmm, five, no six . . . seven?"

"Eight, counting that one. How much baksheesh is required, Sheik?"

The sheik's eyes were back examining the bill. "A few agorot will suffice . . . " Then he caught himself. "What am I saying?" He groaned. "Effendi, could we step aside and discuss a small matter . . . a matter of business?"

Ahmed got to his feet and walked to one side a few yards. The sheik kept up with him.

"I do not know your private affairs, Effendi," the sheik said earnestly, "but one knows that you left Israel in a hurry. Without your passport. You are in Syria, but is Syria your destination?"

"What if it isn't?"

"That is the point I should like to discuss with you, Effendi. Without meaning to pun, you are not yet out of the wilderness. You wish to get back to Israel? Perhaps to meet . . . someone?"

"Who?"

The sheik shrugged. "The Jewish girl also disappeared last night. She cannot come to Syria because she is a Jew. Jordan is even more out of the question. I am an Arab, Effendi. The borders mean nothing to me or my people. We have grazed our goats and sheep wherever there has been grass. From time immemorial. Goats cannot read border signs. Neither can my people."

"But you can read, Yussuf."

"I am the sheik of my people. Where they go, I go. Alas, the same is not true for you. You are in a, shall we say, unfriendly country. Without a passport. You wish to cross another border . . . "

"I got into Syria without too much trouble."

"Getting back into Israel will be more difficult. The Jews are a dedicated people. You cannot bribe them. Besides, the Israeli police are very anxious to apprehend you. Your flight, last night, indicated guilt. The hue and cry, alas, is in full voice."

"What are you suggesting?"

"A business transaction, Effendi. I will travel with you. My cousins and I. You will wear our clothes, you will be one of us. You will not be troubled by border guards. Police will not, ah, detain you. Name your destination and we shall deliver you there. Safely."

"For how much?"

"I am a poor sheik," said Yussuf sadly. "I am the nominal ruler of an impoverished people. They look to me for aid and succor and I must provide it to them. The money you have in your hand, Effendi. It would be a boon to me . . . and to my people."

Ahmed came to a decision. "I'll admit that you helped me out of a spot and I'll grant that you could probably take me wherever I want to go." He peeled off one of the thousand-dollar bills and handed the rest to Sheik Yussuf. "It's a deal."

"Allah be praised. My people thank you, Effendi. I myself thank you." His eyes strayed to the single bill in Ahmed's hand.

Ahmed shook his head, refolded the bill, and sitting down on the ground, returned the bill to the cavity in the heel. He snapped the leather back into place and got to his feet.

"The destination, Effendi?"

"I'll give you that later. South."

"Into Jordan! Excellent . . . " He raised his hands to signal his Arabs, then turned back to Ahmed. "The Frankish offal, Effendi! What of them?"

"Let them go back to Israel. They'll hang the woman, and the others — they'll probably deport them."

"That would mean testifying against them in court." The sheik shook his head. "One tries by all means to stay out of the Hebrew courts." He bobbed his head. "The automobile. We will destroy it and they will be afoot. I do not think they will fare well in Syria on foot. They probably do not have entry visas and they will probably wind up in a stinking prison. Yes, that is what we shall do. Baba!"

A huge Druse came trotting up. The sheik gave him specific instructions and the Druse trotted away.

32

IT was mid-afternoon when a wandering band of Arabs arrived at the Syria-Jordan border just east of the Jordan River. There were nine men in the band and four donkeys that carried their possessions.

Their sheik conversed with a bored sergeant of the Syrian guards, who waved them on. The Jordanian guard, a short distance away, was seated in a chair tilted back against the guard office. He yawned and did not even bother to speak to the Arabs.

A hundred yards from the border, Sheik Yussuf fell back and said to one of the Arabs who was leading a burro, "You see, Effendi, there is kinship among all Arab people. You are buying that kinship, Effendi."

"The price I'm paying is good."

"I am not complaining. I only wish I could do it for friendship alone. But one has responsibilities to his people . . . "

"Sure, sure, Sheik."

They camped that night at the edge of the desert and Ahmed sat around a dungfire and ate *cous-cous* from a cooking pot. Afterward he stretched out on his stomach and tried to sleep.

And could not because of the pain in his lacerated back. After an hour of sleeplessness, he climbed painfully to his feet and, going off a short distance, stared south into the wasteland. The moon was almost full and the stars were bright overhead.

"Foxes have holes, and birds of the air have nests; but the Son of man hath not where to lay his head."

The words ran through his mind.

The Son of Man had been weighed down with the sins of humanity. He had been in torment, because He had known the mortal fate that was to be His.

Yet, in His final anguish He had cried out to His Father in Heaven: *"Father, forgive them; for they know not what they do!"*

The man who called himself Ahmed Fosse did not believe.

He was alone.

There was no solace for him, no hope of redemption, of absolution. Or peace.

He had suffered as few men have suffered. He had suffered for twenty-three years and he had suffered this day. He had received physical pain such as few men have endured in their lifetimes. Yet the pain was not physical alone.

The pain was within him. In his breast, in his brain.

Only once, the night before, for a short time had he felt any peace.

That was when he paced back and forth upon the Mount, where He had once paced back and forth.

Had that been peace?

Ahmed did not believe.

A shadow moved across the sand and stopped before Ahmed Fosse.

Sheik Yussuf ben Adhem said: "One cannot sleep because of the wounds? Perhaps we should look at them and put on some more of the healing ointment. It is a special preparation, used by my people . . . "

"It's all right," snapped Ahmed.

"Your thoughts are not pleasant,

Effendi? You are thinking of the little Jewish girl . . . "

"To hell with you, Yussuf!"

Ahmed stalked away from the sheik and, returning to the dead campfire, stretched himself out upon the sand. And this time, in spite of the wounds on his back that he knew were bleeding again, Ahmed turned over on his back.

After a while he slept.

The little band of Bedouins followed the snakelike course of the Jordan River. It wound back and forth across the wasteland and by following it, the traveling was slow and the distance covered was twice as much as if a more direct southward path had been followed.

But Ahmed Fosse seemed content with the leisurely travel and the Bedouins preferred to be close to the river, for they were always within reach of the most priceless thing in desert travel — water.

On the third day they reached the most ancient city in the world. Jericho.

The British Archaeological Expedition, under the direction of a woman archaeologist, Kathleen Kenyon, had spent years on the dig and seven successive layers of the old city had been exposed, photographed, and recorded to the nth degree.

"Will you visit with them?" asked the sheik of Ahmed Fosse, as they stopped at some distance from the magnificent tableau before them.

Ahmed shook his head and the sheik showed disappointment.

They made camp a dozen kilometers south of Jericho.

That night, around the campfire, the sheik said, conversationally: "There is talk, Effendi, that the British have discovered proof that the walls of Jericho actually did tumble about the time that the Hebrew Joshua blew his trumpets."

"The walls probably fell," replied Ahmed carelessly, "but if they did it was because the Jews undermined them . . . or there was an earthquake during the siege."

"The scientist always has an explanation."

"By this time you ought to know," said Ahmed, "I don't believe in the Jewish Yahweh any more than I believe in Christ or Allah."

"That is blasphemy, Effendi! I was educated at the great English Cambridge. While I was there, I heard much discussion of God and Providence, pro and con. I myself discussed theology and philosophy and the rights of man. A student of archaeology once said that the Egyptians invented the gods because they made the life of their slaves so miserable that the slaves would have revolted had they not been promised something better in the next world. I was impressed with that theory, Effendi. I am always impressed with the words of the sages, but then I come out here to my desert, where a man lives under the stars and there is peace and quiet and you can think. Yes, you can think, Effendi. And always I think if there is no hereafter, if there is no Allah and no hope, what is the reason for it all? Why does one continue to live?"

Ahmed lashed back at the sheik. "A man can live for hate."

"Can he?" asked the sheik quietly. "Is it enough to sustain life? Is a diet of gall and wormwood good for a man's stomach?"

The Druse traveled leisurely along the winding Jordan and in two days' travel from Jericho, Ahmed Fosse gazed upon the Dead Sea. The salt content was so heavy in the sulphuric-saline waters that a body could not sink in it.

There were Bedouins combing the ruins of the Qumran community a short distance from the sea and there were Jordanians in uniform patrolling the area, but Yussuf decided that they would make their camp here, although it was only an hour past noon.

"The waters are said to be very salubrious, Effendi," he told Ahmed. "Your wounds are healing well, considering, but a bath in these waters might be conducive to more rapid healing."

The Druse had staked out a tent cloth to make an area of shade and Ahmed stretched out under it. The sulphuric smell of the sea was heavy in his nostrils and he found himself breathing heavily.

The temperature was at least 120 degrees.

Finally, an hour before sunset, Ahmed took off his clothes and walked down to the edge of the Dead Sea. He looked at the water a moment, then walked into the sea.

He plunged into it and found that it was true. The buoyancy kept him afloat without effort on his own part. He turned on his back and floated, while the burning sun, still strong, forced him to close his eyes.

He spent an hour in the water and when he came out, he wondered if the saline water had indeed been beneficial. One of the Druse applied the ointment to his back as he lay on his stomach under the canvas.

"It is healing nicely, Effendi," the man said. "The scabs are forming well and there is little infection."

"I'll be as good as I ever was in a week," Ahmed replied. "Thanks to your ointment . . ."

"And the waters of the sea!"

Later, the sheik said to Ahmed, "Jerusalem lies across the mountains, Effendi. Sixteen kilometers. We can be there tomorrow night. The Old City, that is, which belongs to the State of Jordan."

"I'm not going to Jerusalem," said Ahmed.

"But I thought . . . "

"The Man who called Nazareth *His* home, Sheik . . . where was He born?"

"Bethlehem, of course, but . . . "

"I would see where He was born."

Sheik Yussuf was disconcerted. Ahmed's plans had not been according to his own reasoning.

They toiled over the mountains the next day, but they kept to the western edge and worked their way along the great city of the Jewish peoples.

The Great Partition had not been decided by the Jews, or their mortal enemies, the Jordanians. Each side had had a hand in it, but outside influences were vast. The final partition was decided upon by a committee in the United Nations in New York City. Neither side had been satisfied with the decision, or the division, but if anyone had the greater cause for complaint, it was the people of the new nation, the people of Israel.

The part of Jerusalem in which their history and tradition had been established so firmly, the Old City, had been given to the Jordanians.

And so had much of the country

surrounding the city. A nearby city, for instance.

Bethlehem.

The City of David, the city of which Jesus Christ had been born. A city that was Holy to the Jews and Christians alike was in hands of the enemy of both.

The Arab kingdom of Jordan.

33

DURING the hours that they skirted the eastern boundary of Jerusalem, Sheik Yussuf remained away from Ahmed. He was busy with his own thoughts as Ahmed was with his, now that they were nearing the end of their journey.

Eight days had gone by since the day that the sheik had rescued Ahmed Fosse from the Amazon and her companions. The sheik knew as little about Ahmed as he had known eight days ago.

Late in the afternoon the sheik pointed to the west. "Across the border there is the ancient Jewish village of Ramat Rahel. It is no more than two kilometers from where we stand, but it might as well be a million. No Arab can cross this border, no Jew would be permitted to come here."

He turned to the south and pointed down the Jordanian highway, along which they were traveling. "It will be the same from the House of Meat ... Beitlehem, as the Arabs now call it . . . "

"Bethlehem," said Ahmed, "in old Hebrew, House of Bread!"

"House of Bread, House of Meat," retorted Sheik Yussuf. "The City of David, the City of Christ's nativity. It is where we part company, Effendi?"

"When we reach Rachel's Tomb, you will have fulfilled your business agreement," said Ahmed.

They reached Rachel's Tomb inside an hour, the splendid tomb that had been built upon the site of the old grave where the patriarch of the Jewish people had buried his wife.

It was time now for Ahmed to part with Sheik Yussuf and his followers.

The Druse had apparently been coached by the sheik. They lined up along the road, Ahmed at their head. Ahmed faced them, bowing to each in turn.

"May Allah be with you," he said to each man, until he came to Sheik Yussuf.

He extended his hand, but the sheik preferred the formal bow. He was all Arab now.

"May you find here what you seek, Effendi."

"I'll find it," said Ahmed, "or my bones will turn to dust in the city of the Jewish great ones."

Sheik Yussuf and his 'cousins' turned and watched Ahmed walk into Bethlehem.

Ahmed had gone a good hundred yards when the sheik said to the Arab nearest him, "Follow him, do not let him know he is followed, but keep him always in sight. When he sleeps, be near. When he is awake, be not far away." He singled out another Druse. "Go with your brother, Shar ben Kfar. That way one pair of eyes will always be open. You will report to me whenever there is anything to report . . . "

The two Druse started into the city after Ahmed.

34

IN Bethlehem, all feet turned to the Church of the Nativity. In Arab hands, much of Bethlehem was still Christian. The buildings were Christian-built; they were maintained by Christians.

The custodians of the houses that had been built to worship the Christ were priests of Christ. They remained aloof from politics, from the shifting fortunes of war and upheaval. They enjoyed immunity from the temporal rules of the city.

Ahmed Fosse, wearing Arab garb, received no especial attention from the passers-by on the streets. He encountered Jordanian police, men wearing the uniforms of the military of the State of Jordan.

He was an Arab in a city owned by Arabs. He could go where he willed. Even into the churches of the Christians.

He found himself before the sprawling Church of the Nativity. He walked up to the door and he touched it, but he did not enter. He backed away and, after a while, walked away from it.

He walked the ancient, narrow streets. He stopped in at stores and came out again. He went into hotels and restaurants and cafés.

Night fell upon the City of David and of Jesus Christ. Ahmed continued to tour the city. He seemed to be searching for someone. Not someone he knew. Someone whose character he would know upon sight. He found him sprawled in the doorway of a mean stone house, on a mean, narrow street.

He wore European clothes, shoes with great holes in them, and he had not shaved in several days, yet was not growing a beard. His breath reeked of the forbidden wine.

Ahmed crouched to his heels beside the Jordanian man. "Allah is merciful," he said in Arabic.

"Allah be damned," retorted the evil-looking one.

"You are hungry, Effendi?" Ahmed asked.

The man thrust out a filthy hand. "I

414

have not eaten in two days," he whined. "My children cry because there is no bread for them."

"There isn't any bread," said Ahmed, "because you have spent your money on wine."

The man spat at him. "Pah!"

But he sat up. His eyes were bleary and he belched.

"What would you do," asked Ahmed, "for a thousand pounds of Jordan money?"

"Would I have to kill more than one man?" cried the Jordanian derelict.

"The task is more difficult than killing a man."

"Two men, Effendi? I accept your terms."

"Not two men," said Ahmed. "And the pay is great, much greater than a thousand pounds."

"How much, Effendi?" cried the Arab hoarsely.

"Four thousand pounds . . ."

"There is not that much money in all Jordan. You are making sport of me. You know that I am a poor man, that I would do anything, yes, *anything*, for a few pounds and you tantalize me with . . ."

"Four thousand pounds," repeated Ahmed. "The risk is great, the pay is proportionate . . . "

"Show me the money, Effendi!"

"It is American money."

"Is it not good in Jordan?"

"It is good in any country on this earth."

Ahmed stood, did something with his boot heel, and produced a bill, which he straightened out.

The Arab blinked. His eyes were rife with suspicion. "*That* is worth four thousand Jordan pounds?"

"I will go to a bank and get it cashed for you. In one-pound Jordan notes if you will . . . "

"When, Effendi?"

"When you have completed the task for which I shall pay you."

"How long will that be? I must eat. My . . . my children must have bread."

"You shall have the money tomorrow. When you return."

"Return? From where . . . ?"

"Jerusalem."

"That is nothing. I can go there tonight and be back in three hours."

"Not from *New* Jerusalem."

"New Jeru — " the man cried out. "But that is impossible! I am an Arab . . . "

"That is why I am paying four thousand dollars. I am an Arab myself and I cannot go into the city. I do not dare. You are a desperate man, hungry . . . your numerous children are hungry. You said so yourself."

"It is death," said the Arab in awe. "It is worse than death." But his eyes gleamed. "Four thousand one-pound bills, Effendi?"

"Fresh from the bank!"

"If I should manage to get into the Jewish Jerusalem, Effendi, what would I have to do there? How many persons would I have to kill?"

"None. You will merely deliver a message to a person whose name I will give you. You will receive in reply a chit, which will prove to me that you actually delivered the message. Then you will return to Bethlehem and receive your reward."

The Arab's lips moved silently for a moment. Then he got to his feet.

"I will surely die, Effendi, but I will

die trying. The reward is too great not to take the chance."

"Return to this place. Stay here until I seek you again. When you give me the chit, I will give you the money."

Ahmed took a scrap of paper that he had already written in one of the hotel lobbies. He handed it to the Jordanian. "You are to hand this to a woman. Her name is Carolyn Caxton ... Repeat it until you have printed it upon your brain. Car-o-lyn Cax-ton ... "

"Car ... lin ... Cax ... ton ... "

Ahmed repeated the name slowly, carefully, and had the Jordanian repeat it several times. Satisfied, Ahmed said, "You will find her at the Hebrew University. Do not give the paper to anyone but her. Only she can give you the chit that will make you a rich man. Go with Allah!"

The man ran off furiously. He would never be able to run all the way to the Old City of Jerusalem, but he would get there. He was desperate, furtive, and in all Arab cities there are desperate, furtive creatures. They form a mutual bond, an unofficial confederation, and confound and infuriate the police and other authorities.

Ahmed had known their ilk in Egypt during the winter he had spent there before going up the Nile. He had held out from Sheik Yussuf the final thousand-dollar bill for this contingency.

He was staking everything and he would now have to wait.

He left the city of Bethlehem and on the outskirts found an olive grove where he stretched out under a tree.

The Druse had not made a midday stop this day and Ahmed had not eaten since morning. The absence of a couple of meals was of no concern to him. He could go for long periods without eating and he could endure great physical hardships, if necessary.

He had almost completed the circle, Nazareth, Bethlehem. There remained now but the tying of the knot to complete the circle. A short, very short trip, into Jerusalem.

Carolyn Caxton was in the great library of the Hebrew University when one of the librarians found her out.

"There is a man outside insists he must see you. We have tried everything to drive him away, but he will not go."

"What does he look like?" asked Carolyn quickly.

"A beggar and a Gentile beggar, if I am not mistaken. He speaks Hebrew but his speech is atrocious. He says he has lived with Arabs."

"Did he give his name?"

The librarian shook her head. "He says he brings a message from another."

Carolyn got up quickly. She went out of the library.

The Jordanian beggar was slumped in a corner, but when he saw Carolyn looking about, he came over.

"Car . . . o . . . lin Gax . . . ton?" he asked.

"That is my name," she exclaimed.

The man brought out a grimy piece of paper. Carolyn unfolded it quickly. Written on the piece of paper was:

I am in the city where He was born. Can you arrange to have me come to you?

In those few words Ahmed had presented her with a gigantic task, which she

420

understood as well as did he.

The Jordanian whined: "The chit. He said I had to have a chit from you so I could receive the money."

"Of course." Carolyn drew a notebook from her pocket, tore out a page, and with a pencil wrote, *Yes, Carolyn.*

The Jordanian grabbed the piece of paper from her hand and ran out of the corridor as if ten thousand demons were after him.

Carolyn re-read Ahmed's brief note, then she tore it into the tiniest of shreds and scattered them in the corridor where scuffling feet would distribute or powder them.

35

THE Druse, Shar ben Kfar, said to the titular sheik of his clan: " ... He went through the Mandelbaum Gate two hours after sunrise. We could not follow him, of course, but we waited in the Old City. Always we kept our eyes on the gates. He returned this evening. He is slinking about the streets of the Old City and my brother is not far behind him."

"They will return here," said the sheik in satisfaction. "You and your brother shall be rewarded."

He called together several of his retainers and talked to them. The Druse dispersed.

Night came and the lights went on in old Bethlehem.

One of the Druse came trotting to where the sheik was resting from his exertions of the day, which had consisted of receiving reports from his men and dispatching them on duties he thought up for them.

"He comes," the Druse said.

The Jordanian beggar appeared in sight a few minutes later. He was shuffling along, now and then darting furtive glances over his shoulder. He seemed to be aware that he was being followed.

But in watching his pursuer he overlooked the two Druse ahead of him. One of them caught his arms, the other put the point of a knife against his throat.

"Silence, or you become offal," said the Druse with the knife.

The Jordanian started to whine and choked it off as the sharp knife point pricked his skin.

He was hurried away and a moment or two later was thrown to his knees before Sheik Yussuf.

"Search him," the sheik ordered.

The Druse were good at their trade. They found the little piece of paper torn from Carolyn Caxton's notebook. The sheik read: "'Yes, Carolyn'"

He bobbed his head. "You spoke to the girl?" he said to the Jordanian.

"I entered the accursed city of the Jews," whined the Jordanian. "I risked life and worse. All for the sake of my children who are hungry. The Effendi promised me money . . . "

"How much money?"

"A few coppers. Money that I need to buy bread . . . "

"Yes, yes," said the sheik. He reached into the the depths of his robe, fumbled a moment, then brought out a thousand dollar bill. "Was it one of these?"

The Arab's eyes goggled. "Is it true? Is it really worth four thousand pounds of Jordan money?"

"It is." The sheik came to a decision. "Go to him. Tell him you have delivered the message and collect your pay."

"The paper," whined the Arab. "He will not pay unless I give him the paper."

The sheik hesitated, then thrust it at the beggar. "Begone!"

The man scurried off. He was promptly followed by one of the Druse.

The sheik said softly to himself, "He saved the thousand-dollar bill for the final effort. The girl is involved in it. Well, we shall see."

Ahmed Fosse strolled the streets of Bethlehem. Night had come again in the ancient city and he wandered about, an Arab apparently interested in the sights of the city and yet not too interested.

He went into the street where the Jordanian beggar was waiting for him. But Ahmed noted the two Druse before a shop window only fifty feet from where the Jordanian awaited him.

The Druse had their instructions, no doubt, and perhaps those instructions included that one of them should follow Ahmed if he made his appearance anywhere near the beggar.

Ahmed continued his strolling, but he darted up narrow streets and waited at the far ends for a Druse or other hurrying pedestrian. He entered a cathedral, remained for a few minutes, and then came out.

The church was built upon the ground on which an inn had stood in ancient times. Joseph and Mary had come to this inn and in a cave beside the inn He had been born. The cave had been used as a stable.

The entrance to the cave was near

the front of the vast prayer room in which Ahmed Fosse was seated. Pilgrims shuffled past him heading for the entrance to the cave. They would descend a flight of stairs into a chamber lighted by candles and there they would see the spot where He had been born.

Ahmed Fosse did not believe, but he knew the stories. He knew that millions and millions of people for more than nineteen hundred years had followed the star of Jesus.

Myriads had died following that star. Thousands had endured unbelievable tortures. They had been crucified, burnt to death, torn to pieces by wild beasts. They had gone blissfully to their deaths, firm in the sublime belief that He would know.

For long moments Ahmed sat in the pew. And then someone entered the pew and sat down beside him.

She said: "I knew I would find you here." She pulled the bottom of her shirt from over the top of her skirt. She reached under the shirt and then put the roll of vellum into his hand. He thrust it quickly under his burnoose and under the shirt below.

He looked at Carolyn Caxton. "How did you know?"

"You found the manuscript in the Church of Joseph in Nazareth. You walked on the Mount where He preached His sermon. You came to Bethlehem and you *had* to come here."

"Why did I have to come here? I'm not a believer."

"Aren't you?" she asked quietly.

He said angrily, "Why did *you* come? You're a Jewess."

"In the Old Testament, which Christians accept, there is a story about a woman from Moab. She said to one of *my* people: 'Whither thou goest, I will go ... Thy people shall be my people, and thy God my ...'"

"No," Ahmed said bluntly. "I've told you before there's nothing in me that's worth your while."

"That is my problem."

"You know that I've used you. I used you in Galilee and I tried to use you again here. I knew it was just about impossible to do, but I thought you might just possibly pull it off."

"I can get you into Jerusalem," she said. "But you mustn't go there. Major Rosenstock of the Nazareth police is in Jerusalem. I've been watched ever since I came to Jerusalem."

"He didn't follow you here."

She shook her head. "That's one thing an Israeli policeman can't do — go into Jordan."

"You managed it."

"I had one advantage over Major Rosenstock. I'm an archaeologist. He isn't ... You have read how David's army stormed Jerusalem and took it from the Jebusites in a single day? That's the generally accepted version. It's true, but it isn't all of the truth. The Jebusites had a cistern under the city. There was a secret entrance to it outside the wall of the city. A renegade told David of the secret entrance and David led a small band into the city under it. They came up inside Jerusalem, opened the gates, and let in the army.

"The secret entrance to the tunnel was sealed after David rebuilt the city, but the cistern was used for hundreds of years later. It was even enlarged. Certain additional tunnels were cut through living rock. These were used by some of the last survivors during the siege of Jerusalem in 70 A.D. The Romans destroyed the city, and they covered up the cistern and the tunnels, but they were uncovered in comparatively recent times by archaeologists ... One of the tunnels leads from the New City to the Old. I used it tonight."

Ahmed became alert. "We can go back the same way!"

"I can, but you mustn't."

"I've got to."

She dropped her head for a moment, then raised it again and said in a low voice: "Mr. Holterman is in Jerusalem. He's staying at the King David Hotel. I — I went to him. He's always treated me with respect and I thought he might ... might help. He was terribly angry with me ... called me names. I left and down in the lobby I ran into Jacqueline Dietrich. She — she also abused me."

"That woman's cleverer than I thought," said Ahmed. "I didn't think she'd get away with going back to Israel. Not after two murders."

"She blames you for those. She said so again. She also said that she would see you were arrested for murder and hanged if you came to Jerusalem. They're all against you, Ahmed. They're all against you."

He rose to his feet. "We'll go tonight."

She was blocking his passage to the aisle. She rose, moved out, and walked soundlessly beside him to the street.

"I've got to pay the man who took the letter to you," Ahmed said, "then we'll walk to Jerusalem."

She made no reply.

Ahmed caught Carolyn's arm and drew her into a doorway.

The beggar was in the doorway, but a Druse stood in another doorway across the street. Ahmed said, "The sheik's trying to cut himself in for a slice of the pie."

He thrust the folded thousand-dollar bill into her hand. She looked at it and exclaimed, "It's a thousand-dollar bill!"

"Give it to him. He's earned it and I have no use for money. Not after tonight . . . "

She tried to read his face, but gave it up. Suddenly she thrust her hands into her pockets and started across the street.

Two doors away, a Druse came out of the doorway.

He walked out a few yards, stopped, and watched Carolyn cross the street. She reached the beggar, leaned over, and spoke to him. The man sprang to his feet, bowed and scraped. Carolyn turned back to recross to Ahmed.

The Druse faded back to his doorway.

As Carolyn came up to him, Ahmed took her arm. Without looking back he led her to the intersection of the next street. They turned the corner and Ahmed pushed Carolyn ahead of him.

"Walk!"

She went on, away from him. Ahmed flattened against the corner. He waited.

Ten seconds. Fifteen . . .

A head was thrust around the edge of the corner building. Ahmed struck it with his fist. It was not too hard a blow, just hard enough to stun the Druse.

Ahmed caught the man and laid him out along the side of the building. He said: "You rubbed ointment into my back. Your hands were tender . . . and thus I have repaid you."

He ran after Carolyn, caught her arms as he came up, and hustled her swiftly along the street.

They darted into a narrow street, waited to see if they were still being pursued, then went into another street, doubled back, and spent the next ten minutes walking about.

Ahmed did not see another Druse in that time.

They started for Jerusalem. They avoided the exit from Rachel's Tomb, but soon they were compelled to come upon the Jordanian highway that had been built since the ancient road from Jerusalem to Bethlehem had been given to the Jews.

There was much traffic upon the road, some of it automobiles, one or two horses and a few donkeys, and much foot traffic in both directions.

A swift hour's walk brought them to the gates of Jerusalem. Carolyn sent Ahmed an anxious glance or two. He was wearing Arab garb, but she was dressed as a Westerner.

"You are my wife," said Ahmed. "A

Jordan woman walks behind her husband. She does not speak to strangers, even when addressed."

She flashed him a wan smile, but fell behind a step. They passed a patrolling policeman, who sized them up, but did not stop them.

They entered the city and Ahmed was thankful for the poor lighting of the streets.

Carolyn remained the wifely step behind, but she said to him: "Right at the next corner, then left."

Ahmed led the way. Carolyn directed him again in a few minutes, then suddenly, when they were passing a century-old building, she moved up closer.

"Inside!"

She stepped past him, stooped, and did something to a keyhole. Then she pushed open a door. A dark corridor was ahead of them. Carolyn took his hand, led him in utter blankness. She counted under her breath. "Eight . . . nine . . . ten." She stopped, groped for the wall in front of them.

There was a sharp click and a panel

swung open. Dank air assailed their nostrils. She took his hand again and they stepped over a sill into the dank tunnel. Carolyn groped behind her and Ahmed heard the click of the door as it was closed. She reached into her coat pocket then and produced a pencil flashlight. She flicked it on and a beam of light showed a flight of concrete stairs in front of them.

"The Irgun used this during the War of Independence. It leads to the cisterns I told you about."

She went down the stairs. It was a long flight of more than thirty stairs. There was a right turn then and another flight of stairs. The stairs ran out, and they continued down a steep ramp that was slippery from the slime of ages.

Suddenly, Carolyn made a left turn. Ahmed, following, stopped. The cistern was spread out before them. It was a veritable underground lake. The tiny flashlight beam flashed over the water and ended in blackness beyond.

They skirted the cistern for a hundred yards or more, then entered a tunnel and began to climb upward. First a long ramp, then two steep flights of steps. The final flight and again a blank wall. Carolyn turned to Ahmed.

"Are you . . . are you wearing any other clothing under the burnoose?" she asked.

Ahmed hesitated, then nodded.

"I think you should discard it now. It will be easier. As an Arab you may be stopped."

He unfastened the burnoose and dropped it around his body. Carolyn half turned away, looked at him and exclaimed.

Ahmed had on a shirt that had been ripped down the back. The bandage about his torso was readily visible.

"You've been hurt!" she cried.

"It's all right now," he said.

"But it hasn't been attended to. The bandage is dirty . . . filthy. Your wound is infected, I'm certain . . . "

"I said it was all right," he said harshly.

She hesitated, then turned away from him suddenly and searched the wall in front of her. She pressed tentatively, then again . . . and wooden paneling slid away before her. She turned off her flashlight. Again she took his hand.

One minute later they stepped out into cool air, into a street that was well lighted, a street of new concrete, boxlike apartments.

"Let's walk fast," Carolyn said, anxiety showing in her tone. "I live only two blocks from here. We'll go there . . . "

"No," said Ahmed. "The King David Hotel . . . "

"You can't go there, dressed like — like you are."

The truth of her words was apparent to Ahmed himself. Shaking his head, he fell in beside her. She kept a step behind him.

"We're not married in Israel," he snapped.

She said, "No, we're not . . . ," and moved up beside him.

36

A FEW minutes later they passed an apartment building that was like a dozen others on the street, whitewashed concrete, boxlike. Carolyn went around the side to the rear of the building and then turned to see if Ahmed was following.

She started up a flight of stairs. On the third-floor landing she went quickly to a door, unlocked it. She stood aside for Ahmed to go in ahead of her.

She followed and in a darkened room closed the door. "Wait," she said. She went swiftly to the windows, drew shades down to the sill.

Finally, she switched on a light.

It was a small apartment, a bedroom and a combination living room-kitchen. They were in the kitchen. Carolyn came up to Ahmed, looked at his torn shirt, at the bandages underneath.

"Will you take a bath? It's only a shower, but . . . "

He nodded and she hurried into the bathroom. She turned on the water, scurried about a moment, then came out.

He went past her into the bathroom. He closed the door and, undressing swiftly, he stepped under the water. It was almost too hot for him, but he knew that he needed hot water. Plenty of hot water.

The bandages required soaking. He spent considerable time removing them and finally had to tear away the last part of a strip. He winced and knew that he had torn open a healing scab.

Behind him, Carolyn opened the bathroom door. "I just want to get your clothes," she said, then saw his back. She screamed.

Ahmed whirled. "Don't you know how to knock?"

Her hands were over her mouth. Her eyes were stricken and she began to back away.

"Your back," she said. "It's . . . "

"I know what it's like," he snapped. "I felt it when it happened."

She went out of the bathroom.

He took a long bath, using up most of

a cake of soap. He found a pair of scissors in the medicine cabinet and was about to remove it when he noted a woman's razor on the shelf.

It was a half hour before he finally came out of the bathroom. His two weeks' beard was gone. He was clean-shaven. He was nude from the waist up. A bath towel was draped around his waist.

Carolyn was sitting in a Morris chair. Her eyes were wide, glistening with tears. There were streaks down her cheeks.

A shudder ran through her as her eyes fastened upon his nude upper body.

He said: "Look at it!" and turned his back toward her.

He heard her cry out again, then a soft hand touched his back. Fingers ran along some of the welts.

He turned to face her.

She said, "I — I'll call a doctor . . . !" Then she realized that was impossible. "I'll get some bandages . . . "

"It's all right," said Ahmed. "You saw, so I thought you should see the rest of it. Some of the scars are old ones . . . Do you want to know how I got them?"

She said, "I want to know what you

want to tell me. What you do not wish to tell me, I do not want to know."

"Carolyn," he said earnestly, "look at me! What am I? Egyptian, French . . . ?"

She did not comprehend his question. There was pain in her eyes, only pain. Not curiosity.

He said: "When we were crossing the Sea of Galilee, you said that I looked like someone . . . "

"Just an idle thought," she said quickly. "I have forgotten it."

"Think of it again!"

She stared at him, took a step backward, and suddenly her right hand flew up to her mouth.

He nodded. "I'm his brother."

She took her hand from her mouth. "How could you be? He — he didn't know you. If he was your brother . . . "

"He had not seen me in twenty-five years. His brother was an eighteen-year-old boy. An American. Ahmed Fosse was an Egyptian."

"But you are in the same profession. You're an archaeologist, an expert in ancient Semitic languages . . . "

"Do you know where I received my

degrees?" he asked harshly. "In prison, Alcatraz Prison in San Francisco Bay. The Rock, they call it. I studied there. I had a lot of time ... so much time ... twenty-three years ... "

"Oh, no!"

He went on relentlessly, "Do you want to know why I was there?"

Her hand went out, palm toward his mouth as if to stop the words.

"I was convicted of killing a girl. I raped her, they said, and then mutilated her body. 'The Crime of the Century.' The only thing that saved me from the gas chamber was that I was two weeks under my eighteenth birthday when the crime was committed."

"No," she whispered. "It isn't true ... "

"The policeman Rosenstock ... has he found out yet? Does he know who I am?"

She stared at him. "He ... he identified you, but ... but ... it was another man who did those — those horrible things. A man named ... Krag."

"*I am Billy Krag!*"

She turned away from him and walked stiffly into her bedroom. She threw herself upon the bed and sobs shook her body. Ahmed looked through the door, saw her lying on the bed. He seated himself in the chair she had vacated only moments before.

Then minutes later she came out of the bedroom. She stood before him and asked: "There is nothing else you want to tell me?"

"That's all I can tell you."

He got to his feet. "I'll leave now."

He went into the bathroom to get his clothes. She said: "You can't go on the street wearing those clothes. You'd be stopped by the first policeman."

"You can get me some clothes?"

"I'll find a store that's open. If not, I'll get them to open one. Tell me what to get and I'll get it."

He gave her his sizes. "I have no money, but I'll see that you're repaid."

"It doesn't matter," she said listlessly.

She started for the door and with her hand on the knob hesitated. "You will be here when I get back?"

"I'll be here."

She went out.

He waited long enough for her to

descend three flights of concrete stairs. Then he got up and went into the bathroom. He found his discarded trousers, the torn shirt, and the battered paratroopers' boots.

He put them on and stepped out of the bathroom.

The door of Carolyn's apartment was opened at that moment and the policeman, Rosenstock, was in the doorway. His right hand was in his pocket.

Rosenstock said: "We've had the apartment under surveillance. I had an idea you might come here . . . sometime . . . "

Ahmed exhaled heavily.

Rosenstock said: "Do you want to tell me the full story here?"

"You've got the record from Washington."

Rosenstock nodded. "The United States is not interested in you. You paid your debt to them."

"And Israel?"

"I don't think you killed either Hill or Wood," said Rosenstock. "I could make out a case. I could pile up a mountain of circumstantial evidence that you couldn't look across if you stood on your toes. I could produce your American record and

I'm sure I could convict you."

"And then?"

"That's why we're talking, Krag," said Rosenstock.

"What're we talking about?"

"The manuscript you took with you from Tel Mas. It belongs to Israel . . . "

"Even if it was written by a Man named Jesus?"

"He was a Jew," said Rosenstock simply. "He was born in Israel, He died in Israel. Whether we believe He was the Messiah is beside the point. Archaeologists have found statues of Baal and Ishtar, pagan gods. They were found in the soil of Israel and they belong to us. They must remain here."

"Suppose I gave you the manuscript," said Ahmed.

"I expect you to."

"Then?"

Rosenstock shook his head. "Ours is a new country, Krag. The people came here because they suffered in other countries. They suffered from intolerance, from racial hatred, and from persecution. I do not know every employee of the Israeli government, but I know a great many of

444

them. I do not think you can make a deal, as they might say in America, with any of them. I will say this: I do not believe you killed those men at Natzrat. I will do all in my power to find the real killer. But there is a warrant out for your arrest and I must take you into custody . . . "

"Then let's go before she returns."

Rosenstock nodded. He took his hand out of his pocket. It held a revolver.

"I could not take a chance, Krag. You understand . . . "

Krag walked toward him. Rosenstock's eyes widened. His mouth opened to exclaim. Ahmed hit him.

The revolver rocked the little room. A little hot iron seared the flesh of Ahmed's right side.

He stared at the unconscious man on the floor. Then he roused himself, stooped, and scooped up the revolver. He opened the kitchen door, stepped out swiftly, and pulled the door shut. He moved away from it, across the concrete veranda.

Feet were pounding the concrete stairs, coming up. He stood in the shadows.

The head of a man appeared. Ahmed

said: "Don't raise your gun. I'll kill you if I have to . . . "

The Israeli policeman came to a dead stop. His head remained down. Then he raised it slowly and stared up at Ahmed who had moved out of the shadows into semi-light, shed from an adjoining apartment.

Ahmed took a quick step forward. The detective moved . . . and Ahmed struck his head with Rosestock's revolver.

The detective fell forward on his face, slid down three steps, and came to a stop. Ahmed ran swiftly past him, down to the second floor. A door was pulled open. A man cried out, a woman screamed.

Ahmed continued to the street.

37

AHMED FOSSE stepped under the raised window by the fourth floor fire-escape landing of the King David Hotel.

He found himself in a corridor that ran almost the breadth of the building. He went swiftly along the corridor. There was a red light over a door at the far end of the corridor.

When he reached the light he saw the lettering in Hebrew and English: *Stairs.*

He opened the door. Concrete stairs led up and down. There was nothing else in the stairwell.

Yes, there was. A service telephone on the wall.

Ahmed entered the stairwell and picked up the telephone receiver.

A voice in his ear said in Hebrew: "Service."

"Room service waiter," Ahmed said quickly. "I have forgotten the room number of Mr. Charles Holterman."

"One moment." Then: "Six-twelve A. What is your name, waiter?"

Ahmed put the receiver back onto its prongs.

He looked up the stairwell, then began to climb.

Two flights.

He came into the sixth-floor corridor and scanned the numbers on the rooms. 612-A was on the street side.

He stood before the door a long moment, then raised his hand to knock.

He changed his mind and gripped the doorknob. The door opened.

He entered.

Charles Holterman stood by a window, looking down into the street. He turned.

A spasm crossed his face causing his facial muscles to twitch.

Ahmed closed the door behind him.

"You know me?"

Holterman nodded. "I have been expecting you. You crossed the world to get to me and I knew you would find me here."

At Tel Mas Holterman had looked older than his forty-seven years. Now, only two weeks later, he looked like a man of sixty or more. His facial muscles sagged. His eyes had deep creases under them.

Ahmed, in this final scene, looked younger than his actual forty-three years.

He was facing the brother he had sworn to kill.

For twenty-three years Ahmed had thought of his brother. He had thought of him every hour of every day. He had thought of him during hours of the night. When there had been no hope, when the days and months had stretched into endless years, hatred had kept him sane. Hatred had made it possible for him to endure the twenty-three years.

And now when he was facing his brother he asked himself:

"Is there still hatred in my heart?"

He said aloud: "I thought of the words. I thought of what I would say when this moment came."

"Say them," said Charles Holterman. "Say them and then do as you must do."

"I had you two weeks ago," said Ahmed. "I learned that your ambition was even greater than my hatred. I had it in my hands to show you the fulfilment of that ambition. I was going to let you touch it and then I was going to kill you."

"Go ahead," said Holterman. "I'm ready."

Ahmed reached under his torn shirt and took out the age-old vellum scroll. "Here it is," he said, "a piece of parchment, written by Jesus to His friend, who became the Apostle John. This is what you wanted so much."

He held it out. Charles Holterman's dull eyes focused upon the parchment in Ahmed's hands. But he made no move to take it.

"Don't you want it?" cried Ahmed. "I'm giving it to you."

The bedroom door opened. A woman came out.

Phyllis Holterman.

She said: "I denied you the last time we met."

Ahmed looked at her steadily. "And now?"

"I want to hear it from him."

Holterman cried out hoarsely: "I can't . . . "

"I want to hear it," said Phyllis Holterman.

Holterman looked at the woman who had borne him *and* his brother. He looked at his brother and then he went to a chair. He fell heavily into it and kept his eyes on the pattern of the rug on the floor.

Phyllis Holterman waited.

Ahmed said: "Tell her, Charles . . . "

Charles Holterman remained mute.

Ahmed said: "I decided to visit you that summer. They didn't want me to go and I didn't have enough money so I hitchhiked. Somewhere in Oklahoma I ran into a man with a broken-down car. He sold it to me for ten dollars. I patched it up and drove to San Francisco. You borrowed the car from me one night." He gestured to his brother. "You can take it from there, Charles."

A low groan came from the lips of Charles Holterman. He spoke finally. "I was in with a crowd like myself. We had too much money, we had tried everything. First whisky, then heroin. I picked up the girl and . . . " His face twisted. "You know what I did. You stood trial for it as Billy Krag because that was the name on the car registration. *I* did it — not Billy Krag — not *you!*"

"That isn't all, Charles," said the man who faced him.

Charles Holterman raised his eyes and looked at his mother.

"Yes," she said, "there's more."

Anguish twisted his aging features. "I got down on my knees. I begged. You — and Father — had put all of your hopes in me. Fred was wild, he was not going to amount to much. I — *I* was the brilliant one. You told me so. Dad told me." His voice failed, then came on again stronger. "He knew it and I reminded him of it. On my knees! I told him that he was still under age. Nothing serious would happen to him. Manslaughter, at the worst. I had promised him that when things died out I would tell Father everything and he could use his money and influence to get him out ... "

"You left me in prison," said Ahmed ringingly. "You never told them the truth. They thought of me as Billy Krag ... "

"I couldn't, said Charles Holterman. "I didn't have the strength ... of Billy Krag. I've been a weakling all of my

452

life." His eyes met his mother's. "He has *your* strength, Mother. *I* never had it."

She said quietly, "You're going to have it now, Charles."

He shook his head. "It's too late. I'm too tired."

Phyllis Holterman regarded her oldest son for a long moment. Then she looked at her younger son.

"I denied you two years ago. It's your turn now."

Ahmed's eyes fell upon the vellum scroll still in his hand. He held it up. "The Man who wrote this was denied three times in one night." He held it out suddenly. "Take it!"

She took a short step backward.

Frederick Holterman, who had been Billy Krag for twenty-three years and Ahmed Fosse for two, turned to his brother, who was still slumped in the chair.

"Do *you* want it?"

Holterman's mouth formed the short word once, but no sound came from his lips. His mouth moved again and the word came.

"No!"

Ahmed looked again at his mother, then he turned and went out of the room.

She watched him go, she waited until the door had been closed on him, and then she said to her eldest son: "Go after him. Get down on your knees to him again. But go after him . . . "

He stared up at her, then he raised himself to his feet. He walked to the door, hesitated a long moment, then opened the door.

The man who had called himself Ahmed Fosse pushed the pearl button by the elevators. An elevator stopped at the floor. The door opened.

Holterman came around a turn. "Wait!" he called.

Ahmed stepped into the elevator. The startled operator looked at his torn clothing.

"Down," said Ahmed.

She closed the door.

Carolyn Caxton sat in the lobby of the King David Hotel. She was watching the street doors. She did not see Ahmed

Fosse come out of the elevators. She did not see him until he had stopped by her chair.

She looked up, her eyes widening in shock. Her hands gripped the arms of the chair and propelled herself up.

"I knew you would come here. Then you've . . . seen him?"

He nodded. Her eyes were wide, questioning. He shook his head.

The greatest relief he had ever seen in a human face swept her features. Her eyes came alive, brilliant.

"Will you take me home?"

He touched her arm and they started for the door.

At the desk stood a tall man wearing an immaculate white linen suit. He turned. It was Sheik Yussuf ben Adhem. He came toward Ahmed Fosse and Carolyn Caxton. He said: "Effendi, there is a business matter I would like to discuss . . . "

An elevator door clanged open. Holterman came out.

"Wait!" he called poignantly. "Wait, Fred!"

Carolyn stopped, looked back. "It's . . . your brother."

Ahmed continued through the door. Carolyn made her decision. She followed him. The sheik shot a quick look at Charles Holterman and fell in beside him. They moved together to the door.

Across the street, behind a window on the second floor of an apartment house, Jacqueline Dietrich whipped up the rifle she had gripped in her huge hands for so long.

She leveled it through the window and pulled the trigger.

The bullet missed Ahmed Fosse by inches. It crashed the plate glass of the door behind, the door through which Charles Holterman and the sheik were coming.

Carolyn screamed in terror.

Ahmed had not yet located the rifle. A second steel-covered slug smashed out concrete chips two inches from his right boot. He saw the flash of the gun then and his quick eyes found the window.

He shoved Carolyn aside so violently that she was hurled to the pavement three feet from him. He started forward, across the street.

Jacqueline's third bullet caught him

squarely. Even then he took three more steps before he dropped to his knees.

He tried to raise himself, but could not make it.

He fell forward onto his hands.

He was still on his hands and his knees, trying desperately to raise his head, when Charles Holterman sprang in front of him. He saw the woman in the window, saw the rifle aimed down at him. He threw up his hands.

"Don't!" he cried. "Don't shoot . . . !"

Jacqueline Dietrich fired once more. The bullet went into Charles Holterman as he shielded his brother.

It was Sheik Yussuf who got to the far side of the street. It was the mercenary man of business who pounded up the stairs of the apartment building, who broke down the door of Jacqueline's apartment.

He faced her as she turned on him with the Winchester.

And then, without getting paid one single agorot for the job, it was the sheik who destroyed the murderess.

He flicked open a switch-blade knife and he cut her open from her throat down to her stomach.

He had been in the hospital three days before they would allow her to see him. She sat beside his bed then, holding his hand.

After some time, he said: "The manuscript . . . was it . . . damaged?"

She shook her head. "No. It was as clean . . . as perfect as when it was first used."

"Where is it?"

"It is at the university. They . . . they have read it." She stopped.

"They accepted it?"

She hesitated, then shook her head. "They used the Carbon-14 test on it. The parchment is old enough, but they insist that the writing is too clear . . . too fresh. It could not have been written by . . . Him."

The man who had called himself Ahmed Fosse thought of what he had been for twenty-five years. He thought of what he had become as he sat that night on the Mount near the Sea of Galilee. He thought of the things he had thought then . . . of what he had learned since he had first touched the nineteen-hundred-year-old roll of vellum parchment.

He *knew* the truth.

THE END

THE WILDERNESS WALK
Sheila Bishop

Stifling unpleasant memories of a misbegotten romance in Cleave with Lord Francis Aubrey, Lavinia goes on holiday there with her sister. The two women are thrust into a romantic intrigue involving none other than Lord Francis.

THE RELUCTANT GUEST
Rosalind Brett

Ann Calvert went to spend a month on a South African farm with Theo Borland and his sister. They both proved to be different from her first idea of them, and there was Storr Peterson — the most disturbing man she had ever met.

ONE ENCHANTED SUMMER
Anne Tedlock Brooks

A tale of mystery and romance and a girl who found both during one enchanted summer.

CLOUD OVER MALVERTON
Nancy Buckingham

Dulcie soon realises that something is seriously wrong at Malverton, and when violence strikes she is horrified to find herself under suspicion of murder.

AFTER THOUGHTS
Max Bygraves

The Cockney entertainer tells stories of his East End childhood, of his RAF days, and his post-war showbusiness successes and friendships with fellow comedians.

MOONLIGHT AND MARCH ROSES
D. Y. Cameron

Lynn's search to trace a missing girl takes her to Spain, where she meets Clive Hendon. While untangling the situation, she untangles her emotions and decides on her own future.

NURSE ALICE IN LOVE
Theresa Charles

Accepting the post of nurse to little Fernie Sherrod, Alice Everton could not guess at the romance, suspense and danger which lay ahead at the Sherrod's isolated estate.

POIROT INVESTIGATES
Agatha Christie

Two things bind these eleven stories together — the brilliance and uncanny skill of the diminutive Belgian detective, and the stupidity of his Watson-like partner, Captain Hastings.

LET LOOSE THE TIGERS
Josephine Cox

Queenie promised to find the long-lost son of the frail, elderly murderess, Hannah Jason. But her enquiries threatened to unlock the cage where crucial secrets had long been held captive.

THE TWILIGHT MAN
Frank Gruber

Jim Rand lives alone in the California desert awaiting death. Into his hermit existence comes a teenage girl who blows both his past and his brief future wide open.

DOG IN THE DARK
Gerald Hammond

Jim Cunningham breeds and trains gun dogs, and his antagonism towards the devotees of show spaniels earns him many enemies. So when one of them is found murdered, the police are on his doorstep within hours.

THE RED KNIGHT
Geoffrey Moxon

When he finds himself a pawn on the chessboard of international espionage with his family in constant danger, Guy Trent becomes embroiled in moves and countermoves which may mean life or death for Western scientists.

FATAL RING OF LIGHT
Helen Eastwood

Katy's brother was supposed to have died in 1897 but a scrawled note in his handwriting showed July 1899. What had happened to him in those two years? Katy was determined to help him.

NIGHT ACTION
Alan Evans

Captain David Brent sails at dead of night to the German occupied Normandy town of St. Jean on a mission which will stretch loyalty and ingenuity to its limits, and beyond.

A MURDER TOO MANY
Elizabeth Ferrars

Many, including the murdered man's widow, believed the wrong man had been convicted. The further murder of a key witness in the earlier case convinced Basnett that the seemingly unrelated deaths were linked.

A GREAT DELIVERANCE
Elizabeth George

Into the web of old houses and secrets of Keldale Valley comes Scotland Yard Inspector Thomas Lynley and his assistant to solve a particularly savage murder.

'E' IS FOR EVIDENCE
Sue Grafton

Kinsey Millhone was bogged down on a warehouse fire claim. It came as something of a shock when she was accused of being on the take. She'd been set up. Now she had a new client — herself.

A FAMILY OUTING IN AFRICA
Charles Hampton and Janie Hampton

A tale of a young family's journey through Central Africa by bus, train, river boat, lorry, wooden bicycle and foot.

SEASONS OF MY LIFE
Hannah Hauxwell and Barry Cockcroft

The story of Hannah Hauxwell's struggle to survive on a desolate farm in the Yorkshire Dales with little money, no electricity and no running water.

TAKING OVER
Shirley Lowe and Angela Ince

A witty insight into what happens when women take over in the boardroom and their husbands take over chores, children and chickenpox.

AFTER MIDNIGHT STORIES,
The Fourth Book Of

A collection of sixteen of the best of today's ghost stories, all different in style and approach but all combining to give the reader that special midnight shiver.

DEATH TRAIN
Robert Byrne

The tale of a freight train out of control and leaking a paralytic nerve gas that turns America's West into a scene of chemical catastrophe in which whole towns are rendered helpless.

THE ADVENTURE OF THE CHRISTMAS PUDDING
Agatha Christie

In the introduction to this short story collection the author wrote "This book of Christmas fare may be described as 'The Chef's Selection'. I am the Chef!"

RETURN TO BALANDRA
Grace Driver

Returning to her Caribbean island home, Suzanne looks forward to being with her parents again, but most of all she longs to see Wim van Branden, a coffee planter she has known all her life.

DEAD SPIT
Janet Edmonds

Government vet Linus Rintoul attempts to solve a mystery which plunges him into the esoteric world of pedigree dogs, murder and terrorism, and Crufts Dog Show proves to be far more exciting than he had bargained for . . .

A BARROW IN THE BROADWAY
Pamela Evans

Adopted by the Gordillo family, Rosie Goodson watched their business grow from a street barrow to a chain of supermarkets. But passion, bitterness and her unhappy marriage aliented her from them.

THE GOLD AND THE DROSS
Eleanor Farnes

Lorna found it hard to make ends meet for herself and her mother and then by chance she met two men — one a famous author and one a rich banker. But could she really expect to be happy with either man?

BALLET GENIUS
Gillian Freeman and Edward Thorpe

Presents twenty pen portraits of great dancers of the twentieth century and gives an insight into their daily lives, their professional careers, the ever present risk of injury and the pressure to stay on top.

TO LIVE IN PEACE
Rosemary Friedman

The final part of the author's Anglo-Jewish trilogy, which began with PROOFS OF AFFECTION and ROSE OF JERICHO, telling the story of Kitty Shelton, widowed after a happy marriage, and her three children.

NORA WAS A NURSE
Peggy Gaddis

Nurse Nora Courtney was hopelessly in love with Doctor Owen Baird and when beautiful Lillian Halstead set her cap for him, Nora realised she must make him see her as a desirable woman as well as an efficient nurse.

THE SONG OF THE PINES
Christina Green

Taken to a Greek island as substitute for David Nicholas's secretary, Annie quickly falls prey to the island's charms and to the charms of both Marcus, the Greek, and David himself.

GOODBYE DOCTOR GARLAND
Marjorie Harte

The story of a woman doctor who gave too much to her profession and almost lost her personal happiness.

DIGBY
Pamela Hill

Welcomed at courts throughout Europe, Kenelm Digby was the particular favourite of the Queen of France, who wanted him to be her lover, but the beautiful Venetia was the mainspring of his life.

SKINWALKERS
Tony Hillerman

The peace of the land between the sacred mountains is shattered by three murders. Is a 'skinwalker', one who has rejected the harmony of the Navajo way, the murderer?

A PARTICULAR PLACE
Mary Hocking

How is Michael Hoath, newly arrived vicar of St. Hilary's, to meet the demands of his flock and his strained marriage? Further complications follow when he falls hopelessly in love with a married parishioner.

A MATTER OF MISCHIEF
Evelyn Hood

A saga of the weaving folk in 18th century Scotland. Physician Gavin Knox was desperately seeking a cure for the pox that ravaged the slums of Glasgow and Paisley, but his adored wife, Margaret, stood in the way.

DEATH ON A HOT SUMMER NIGHT
Anne Infante

Micky Douglas is either accident-prone or someone is trying to kill him. He finds himself caught in a desperate race to save his ex-wife and others from a ruthless gang.

HOLD DOWN A SHADOW
Geoffrey Jenkins

Maluti Rider, with the help of four of the world's most wanted men, is determined to destroy the Katse Dam and release a killer flood.

THAT NICE MISS SMITH
Nigel Morland

A reconstruction and reassessment of the trial in 1857 of Madeleine Smith, who was acquitted by a verdict of Not Proven of poisoning her lover, Emile L'Angelier.

THE PLEASURES OF AGE
Robert Morley

The author, British stage and screen star, now eighty, is enjoying the pleasures of age. He has drawn on his experiences to write this witty, entertaining and informative book.

THE VINEGAR SEED
Maureen Peters

The first book in a trilogy which follows the exploits of two sisters who leave Ireland in 1861 to seek their fortune in England.

A VERY PAROCHIAL MURDER
John Wainwright

A mugging in the genteel seaside town turned to murder when the victim died. Then the body of a young tearaway is washed ashore and Detective Inspector Lyle is determined that a second killing will not go unpunished.